A STOLEN PAST

A STOLEN PAST

JOHN KNOWLES

A William Abrahams Book

HOLT, RINEHART AND WINSTON
NEW YORK

Library of Congress Cataloging in Publication Data
Knowles, John, 1926–
A stolen past.
I. Title.
PS3561.N68S8 1983   813'.54   82-15472
ISBN: 0-03-062209-3

FIRST EDITION

Designer: Kate Nichols
Printed in the United States of America
1 2 3 4 5 6 7 8 9 10

Grateful acknowledgment is given for use of
lyrics from "Ah! Sweet Mystery of Life"
by Rida Johnson Young and Victor Herbert.
Copyright © 1910 (renewed) by Warner Bros.
Inc. All rights reserved. Used by permission.

ISBN 0-03-062209-3

To Fritz and Lola Liebert
with love

AUTHOR'S NOTE

This novel is a roman à clef. Three of the characters are based on people I knew well, all of whom are now dead. In the book, as characters they soon departed from their originals and developed fictional lives of their own.

All the important events which take place in this book, and all the other characters, are entirely imaginary.

A STOLEN PAST

1

I have never been one to return much to my own past. I feel a very real attachment to the schools where I was educated, but a decade can go by between visits. I treasure the memory of the Maryland town where I grew up, the great trees, the drifting smell of summer mowing, the lazy, semisouthern town square, the roads wandering out from it into the low, shimmeringly green hills. But I haven't seen it in twenty years.

No more am I a faithful alumnus of Yale, "Mother" as we with all due irreverence used to call it—her. Mother Yale was a four-year adventure that was soon behind me and then lost in the past; I managed to keep in touch with one or two friends I made there, not more.

I seem to be one of those unsatisfactory people who don't keep up a correspondence, contribute only erratically to alumni funds, and in general live in the present, careless of the past. Life seemed crowded enough as it was; with specters of the past being continually evoked, it would have become intolerably cluttered.

1

Or so I believed.

And yet, here I was driving north on the old Merritt Parkway to spend several days in New Haven, at Yale. However, this was strictly business, as unsentimental as the 1980 Oldsmobile with which I efficiently clocked off the Connecticut countryside.

I had been asked to give a lecture there. One of my novels was extremely popular with students, and while Yale in its loftiness considered being asked to speak there such a distinction that the "honorarium" was minimal, still I did possess some vestigial loyalty. Perhaps I had a tincture of sentimentality after all.

It was a radiant October day: Connecticut suggested an outrageous show-off, the low hills overflowing with autumnal brilliance, eruptions of golden leaves, friezes of crimson, the pines maintaining their sober greenness amid the blaze like sentinels.

All this last glory of the growing season was nevertheless contained, neat, firmly—for centuries now—under control: this was New England.

The Merritt Parkway itself, up-to-date and innovative during my college years, had settled into a rather refined middle age; its fieldstone bridges and careful landscaping spoke of another era, of the Depression and the WPA and "beautification." Nearer Long Island Sound there now stretched something called the Connecticut Turnpike, which hurtled cars and trucks in their thousands across the state, all speed and no beautification and no nonsense.

Back here in the hinterland the dear old Merritt Parkway curved with the suaveness of its years through the hills toward New Haven.

Since I was going to be staying on the Yale campus itself,

in a suite of rooms in the Slave Quarters of Pierson, my old college there, in other words three days of total Yale immersion, I tried to feel my way back into its atmosphere, as I had known it.

Tableaux rose up in my mind, undergraduate moments, scraps of experience: drinking champagne and brandy and whatever else went into the concoction called the Green Cup in the scarred-table precincts of Mory's; walking into the cathedral splendor of the Payne Whitney Gymnasium every day for swimming practice; the wind whipping up Chapel Street, or was it Elm? as we hurried back from class for lunch; a boring teacher droning on about geology; a gifted teacher illuminating E. M. Forster's *A Passage to India*; the Yale Bowl, full and roaring for the Harvard game; drunks; fraternity dances; a self-important meeting of the Editorial Board of the *Yale Daily News* presided over by the Chairman, a campus celebrity *ex officio* and in retrospect quite a bore.

What pattern emerged from this montage?

Certainly there had been variety. There had been privilege, although I had not seen that at the time. I had even acquired some learning, a healthy body as a result of the swimming team, and also some badly needed self-assurance. It had all gone by so swiftly, then receded as swiftly into the past.

I turned off the parkway and started through the suburbs toward the campus. Reaching it, I felt a tingling sensation at the back of my head and in my stomach. Fear? Of course not, what could there possibly be to fear?

And yet something told me that it was fear. I was afraid that some valued aspect of the past might be broken, some illusion shattered by coming back here; something I valued was endangered by my venturing to return to these vistas, these towers, these people and memories.

From my sitting room in Pierson the first person I telephoned was Millicent Moncrieff, of course.

"Hello, *Allan*! So you're installed. Wonderful! Are you comfortable, do you have everything you need? Good." Her high-pitched but musical voice, cultured to a degree but unaffectedly so—she *was* cultured—flowed on in its warmth and cordiality. She was eighty years old. "Now. Lunch tomorrow, is that convenient? Good. Let's meet at the Beinicke. One o'clock. I'll have a man named Avery Sansom with me. Does the name mean anything to you? No? Well, he's held major editorial positions in New York over the years, and now he's retired and he's going to write Reeves' biography! Isn't that thrilling? After those other trashy or inaccurate or just plain dull books about him, to have a real, *accurate* biography. I know you'll enjoy meeting each other, and of course he'll want to interview you about Reeves. Till tomorrow then. One o'clock."

Interview me about Reeves Lockhart: a twinge of something stirred at the back of my head.

What could I add to what was public knowledge about him? Three Pulitzer Prizes, two for novels and one for his classic play, *Neighbors*; worldwide fame; his memorable lecture appearances that seemed to combine T. S. Eliot with Laurence Olivier and a bit of Charlie Chaplin thrown in; his erudition, his magnetism, his singularity, all were known and had been recorded. Three European governments had sent representatives to the memorial service at Battell Chapel here on his death in 1975. Thirty years ago he had been the master fifty-year-old literary figure and I had been the obscure disciple, age twenty-one. What would I have to contribute? I had been so dazzled, so overwhelmed by him that I had had no perspective.

As it happened, Mr. Sansom never felt a need to interview me.

From somewhere, obscurely, I felt that I was beginning, now that I was back here among the courtyards and turrets of Yale, to gain a perspective on my undergraduate years, and presumably that would include, at last, a perspective on Reeves Lockhart.

As I walked out of the Georgian courtyard of Pierson College and came to York Street with Gothic Branford College across the way, and further down the street other colleges rising formidably behind their moats, and beyond the expensive clothing stores, Mory's, and the massive Sterling Library, I realized that I had been happy at Yale, that those had been stimulating and various and enriching years.

The past was a treasure and a fragile one. I would no more read *The Great Gatsby* again than take up hang-gliding; what if it turned out not to be the perfect novel that I remembered? My parents used to take us children to Rehoboth Beach in Delaware in the summertime, and it had been peaceful, unspoiled, pure sea and sand. I had heard that it was crowded with high-rise buildings now. I would never see them. Louisa May Robbins had been the prettiest girl in our Maryland town, slender and radiant as a tulip. I had run into her recently at Washington National Airport and beheld a squat, round-faced matron from whom all magic had long since fled. I fled as soon as decently possible too.

Wasn't the past the only thing we truly possessed, irrevocable and unchangeable? It was there, the ballast of our lives, stabilizing us. Should it ever be disturbed, tampered with, even revisited?

Crossing the busy intersection of York and Elm streets, I mingled with the boy and girl students, dressed with elaborate casualness, and, as they flashed grins at one another, revealing uniformly perfect teeth. They hurried on their way, appearing just as self-absorbed, intent on their goals, and oblivious to irrelevant pedestrians such as myself, as we had been on these streets.

I strolled along the Cross Campus Walk, a welcome swath of expansive lawn amid the massive university buildings and the encroaching city, and continued on to a large, singular cube of white and gray marble isolated behind a dry, sunken, marble moat. Was this Merlin's Palace? No, this was the Beinicke Rare Book Library, repository of numerous literary treasures, including the manuscripts of the writings of Reeves Lockhart.

Crossing an immovable drawbridge I passed into the glowing, opulent, subdued, immensely high interior, a glass-enclosed core of old and valuable books rising through the center of the building. A smoky vestige of the brilliant outdoor sunlight filtered mysteriously through the translucent marble walls.

I waited in the lobby, examining some Ezra Pound manuscripts on display, and promptly at five minutes to one a diminutive figure in a forest green woolen suit and forest green Robin Hood hat with a dashing feather emerged from the depths of the building and bustled toward me: Millicent Moncrieff.

Although not particularly tall, I rose far above her. She reached up, threw her arms around my neck, and gave me a big kiss. I was so gratified at beholding her, seemingly still full of a Lockhart-like vitality, talking in enthusiastic bursts, as Reeves had done: "I want you to meet Avery Sansom," turning to a conservatively dressed, sixtyish man of pleasant, conventional appearance behind her, "and don't you look well!" She took a step back and eyed me rather narrowly. "So this is how you turned out! How long has it been since we've seen one another? Twenty-five years? You were so *thin* as a young man. We all wanted to hug you, and then feed you! And now you're four-square and complete. I like what's happened to your face. You look enlightened, and secure. So full of doubts your face was sometimes, years ago. I should have known all this from your books. Shall we go? The Graduate Club is just a step from here, you remember."

The club occupied a smallish white clapboard Colonial house facing the New Haven Green, and inside had that old-homestead-reluctantly-commercialized feel of other New Haven clubs. It seemed to emanate resentment at not being still occupied by some fine old New England family, and the staff and guests slipped in a rather subdued manner through the rooms, vaguely trespassers.

We were seated at a table in the little low-ceilinged dining room, cheerful from the light of a row of windows, and as we were having a preliminary drink—red wine for me, a Bloody Mary for Millicent, a Scotch and soda for Avery Sansom—I began to recede into reverie as they talked, inevitably, about the papers and correspondence of Reeves Lockhart that they had been scrutinizing in the library.

So Reeves Lockhart, that unquenchably vital man, was now a section of the archives of a library; he was a mass of manuscript pages and letters; he was seven novels, four plays, and some miscellaneous writings; he was, to at least a couple of hundred of us, a striking and vivid memory.

Millicent Moncrieff was the guardian of his work and his memory. She had been a student of his at Connecticut College for Women before his first success, and afterward she had gradually metamorphosed into the role of his housekeeper and companion. During their forty years together they had even come to resemble each other physically somewhat.

Each of them was so bright, so articulate, so energetic and constructive and alight with devotion to principle, that they simply rose above any implication of immorality in their ménage, any tincture of the illicit. It was unthinkable and so it was unthought.

Seated at lunch in the Graduate Club, I became aware that Millicent felt she and Avery Sansom were boring me, and that would never do.

So she inquired about my work and I said Yes, my novel *Crossing the Frontier* continued to be taught in schools from one end of the country to the other; no, my other books had not done as well; yes, I enjoyed lecturing at universities a few times a year; yes, my marriage had been over for years; no, there were no children. "Are you lonely?" she asked with her customary kindly candor.

After a pause I attained a similar candor and replied, "Oh yes. But then all writers are lonely. It is a lonely profession. That is its occupational hazard, that and alcoholism, which is usually an attempt to banish the loneliness. Wasn't Reeves"—he had always been Mr. Lockhart to me but time marches on—"lonely?" Then I realized the tactlessness of the question. Millicent had been his companion most of his adult life.

She did not appear offended. She reflected. "I believe he sometimes was, yes," she then said slowly. "He went away often, you know, to write by himself, to some obscure

8

village in Austria, for example, or Quebec City, or Puerto Rico. Any number of places. And although he spoke the language virtually no matter where he was, yes, I think he was lonely at times. As you say," she finished, brightening, "it's the occupational hazard."

Satisfied that she had removed any sense of my being excluded, she allowed the conversation to follow its natural flow back to the Lockhart Papers. I listened with detached interest, and then was suddenly brought up to sharp, almost stunned alertness when I heard Millicent· say, ". . . a one-act play which I liked very much, quite somber, for him. It takes place in Chicago, in 1911. It was called . . . let's see. . . ."

"*Bernice!*" exclaimed Avery Sansom. "I remember seeing the outline for it among his papers."

At the mention of the name of that play I felt the encrustations of thirty crusty years break up and fall in fragments away from me, and standing revealed was the moment then brought glowing into my consciousness: an upstairs room in this very clubhouse, a table, some chairs, and Reeves Lockhart, alive and alert, enacting his newest one-act play for me, called *Margery*, called that until three or four minutes into the play, when the dialogue between a Mr. Whitaker and Margery suddenly became a dialogue between Mr. Whitaker and "Bernice." He was reading:

MR. WHITAKER: I don't like your tone. You've been employed to work here. You can begin by answering that doorbell.
BERNICE: I don't have to—

Lockhart then looked up from his typed pages at me. "I changed her name," he said.

9

I nodded; I had noticed that. I was in a number of ways in step with his mind.

Mr. Whitaker, it developed as Lockhart's vivid, energetic rendering of the play progressed, is the owner of a livery stable in Chicago early in this century. "What do you suppose they called a livery stable in Chicago in 1911?" Reeves Lockhart suddenly demanded of me.

I shook my head in bewilderment and felt a small, momentary stab of despair: the endless *problems*, vast and minute, involved in being a writer!

He read vigorously on through his play, its colors and contours darkening as it moved without wasted motion toward the denouement.

Bernice had been hired by Mr. Whitaker to keep house for a mysterious stranger, who soon arrives. A bond of some sort, a solemn, even grim bond is sensed to exist between Bernice and the stranger. It emerges that he has come straight to this house from a prison, where he has just completed a long sentence for swindling hundreds of people out of their savings. His daughter, a young woman now, whom he has not seen since she was a child, is desperately trying to reach him, leaving letters and messages, unsure where he is, of how to get in touch with him.

And now the shadowy bond between employer and servant emerges into bleak clarity. She knows the prison he has just been released from; she too spent years there. She is a murderess. Because of this crime she has had to abandon her children. Between them, they arrive at the dire conclusion that he must abandon his daughter now.

BERNICE: We did what we did because we're that kind of person—the kind that think they're smarter, better than other people. . . . And people that think that way end up alone. We're not *company* for anybody.

So the stark play ended, in guilt, somberness, solitude.

"It's about one of the Capital Sins," Lockhart explained. "Which one is it, do you think?"

The Capital Sins, the Capital Sins. I rummaged back into my childhood instruction in religion and managed to unearth them: Pride, Covetousness, Lust, Anger, Gluttony, Envy, and Sloth.

Anger? Not really. How angry is a swindler? Envy? No-o-o.

"Pride?" I ventured at length.

He cocked a bright glance at me. "Pride," he pronounced with satisfaction. "The Capital Sins are not in themselves sins, you know. They are the states of mind which *lead* to sin. And the greatest of all, the worst of all, is Pride. These people, my characters, they will brook no interference in their wishes, they must have what they must have, no matter who suffers."

"So they wind up alone."

"So they wind up alone," he echoed in that classical actor's voice, edged with its implications of irony, destiny.

It was a shining evening, a brilliant evening for me, a glittering Broadway first night staged for me alone at the Graduate Club.

"Broadway must be glamorous," I said dreamily as we descended the old creaking stairs to the ground floor.

"It's a lot of work, for the playwright," he observed guardedly. "And of course, yes there *are* the bright lights, the bright lights. . . . What you call 'glamorous,' " and I knew that this word was inadmissible to his vocabulary, a

11

word from the movie fan magazines which no master of English, such as himself, would utter except within quotation marks.

Driving him in my car through the black, blustery November night toward his home outside New Haven, where Miss Moncrieff figuratively if not literally had a lamp burning in the window for his return, I wondered why he had presented this one-man performance of his newest play for me alone. My reaction to it could not have been very helpful or illuminating: "I think that's really strong . . . so moving . . . those characters are really interesting," and so on, honest and sincere sentiments, but of what use could they be to Reeves Lockhart?

He has no son, I suddenly reflected, no children at all.

My research in those days on anyone who really interested me was pretty thorough. I had read all his plays and novels, also his essays, commentary on his work, and even the entry about him in *Who's Who*, and I knew that he had been, as it happened, born the same year as my father.

And I had realized almost from the beginning that Lockhart was a teacher, a born teacher if there ever was one, a teacher now too rich and famous to be contained in any school, a teacher without a class. So I was, for the moment at least, that class, the sole student in a tutorial with one of the best tutors imaginable, a course with no matriculation, no tuition, and no examination, or so I thought.

Whatever other artistic gifts I possessed, I certainly possessed artistic egotism. I was is no way fazed by this situation. A world-famous writer concentrating on Allan Prieston, age twenty-one, with no visible accomplishments in writing, scholarship, or any other field this side of the Yale swimming team: that seemed perfectly appropriate to me. I interested him, my very tentativeness and inexperience appealed to both the teacher and the unfulfilled father in him.

As I stopped the car in front of his house, lost in shrubbery and evergreens on a hillside, I felt a new rush of confidence from the one-man show I had just been privileged to experience, and so I asked directly:

"Mr. Lockhart, do I have any talent?"

A brief silence, slightly taken aback, and then, "Well now, why do you think I've gone on reading your work and discussing it with you? Of course you have talent," he continued scoldingly, "you're gifted, you have many fine literary qualities."

A glow began to spread within like dawn rising over Athens.

"Your problem is," he added brusquely, hurriedly, "you're not grown up yet. Emotionally you're green. You don't really know who you are." He was out of the car, the door slammed. "Good night!" he cried on a rising, encouraging note, and all the same the inner dawn went out like a candle in the wind.

A week later, a blustery Thursday afternoon, the wind kicking up dead leaves, and the sky, steely and lowering, moving menacingly overhead, I was crossing the New Haven Green diagonally, and coming toward me, bearing down on me, I saw a Theodore Rooseveltian figure: Reeves Lockhart. He was quite close before his sharp gaze through the enlarging lenses of his glasses recognized me. "Hello there!" he called out jovially. "Good to be out on a day like this, isn't it! Stimulating!"

We southerners normally ran for cover and a bourbon on days like this, but never mind. "It sure is, sir!"

He wore a slouching fedora and an expensive gray tweed overcoat that somehow looked as though it didn't belong to him.

"Now—ah—champ," he began, "Prieston" for the moment having slipped his mind, "when I said that you were 'green' the other night, I didn't mean, you understand, that you were green *all the way through*. No indeed, you have your areas of maturity, and of incipient maturity. You just have to go on growing, go on maturing, like everybody else. And you will, you will!" he finished optimistically. A brisk happy nod and he was past me, disappearing into the gray wind.

Dawn began a tentative movement toward rising over Athens again.

"I don't see why you let this old codger influence you so much," remarked my roommate Greg Trouvenskoy offhandedly, himself a study in insouciance, stretched out full-length on the couch next to the fireplace in our living room, buffing a ski boot. "You let him make up your mind for you about everything, even about . . . especially about yourself. If he says you're okay, then you think you're William Shakespeare, Jr., if he says something negative, then you're Joe Hack, failure. What he says is just one man's opinion. He doesn't know everything."

But he *does*, I protested inwardly. I've never met anyone—heard of anyone—who knew so much, was so well informed, widely traveled, articulate.

Aloud I remarked, "Well, he *has* won three Pulitzer Prizes."

"Prizes," echoed Greg. "Can you picture the kind of jerks who award literary prizes? People like Creeping Jesus."

14

Creeping Jesus was Professor Macrell, an anthropologist who lived in bachelor quarters across the way and spied on and reported on students in surrounding rooms, we all believed.

"He's one of the most famous and prestigious writers in the world, and he reads my work and helps me with it. *Of course* I take what he says seriously."

Greg went on buffing away. Ski boots had to be and look perfect. "You'll never make a writer by imitating somebody else. Does *he* imitate anybody? Did he ever?"

"No!" I almost shouted. "And I'm not imitating him or anybody!"

"Sure? Well, anyway, how can you make a writer? You're so *green*."

Why in the world had I ever repeated that remark to him! Now I would never hear the end of it. One way Greg asserted his three-year seniority in age over me and vastly greater experience in service overseas in the war, was by means of a continuous and often rather brutal teasing, if that was the word: "baiting" was more like it, if not "tormenting." At the time I believed he strongly disliked all kinds of things about me; now I understand that this was his stubborn defense against showing affection, or love.

I was green. It was one of the qualities that attracted people to me, I see now, this vulnerable, aspiring, untested youthful inexperience. The other side of that, they eventually found to their surprise, was a determined and single-minded ambition that made the special attention paid to me by, for example, Reeves Lockhart, perfectly appropriate. Half the time I assumed I was totally negligible, and the other half that nothing was too good for me. I tested my surroundings daily to see which of these at the moment seemed to be true.

I sometimes wonder where this unconscious arrogance and presumption in me came from. Mother? No. Father? No. Out of the blue? All other sources being apparently negative, that had to have been it.

I cannot recall the mechanics of my coming to spend so much time with Reeves Lockhart. I certainly did not hang around outside his home. I can't believe he simply dropped in at my rooms in Pierson College. I must have found reasons to be continually on the telephone with him. One way or another I saw him in most of the aspects of his life, and gradually the shadows flanking the brilliance began to emerge, the abysses dropping ominously from the peaks.

In his first, hugely successful novel, which was set in the seventeenth century, *The Road to Ste. Michèle*, there is the headmistress of that rarity of the period, a school for girls. She is an extraordinarily brilliant and creative woman, centuries ahead of her time, and she chooses a young girl to train as her successor. In her haste to pass on all she knows, the headmistress overwhelms and cows the inadequate girl with her brilliance.

I had the feeling that Reeves Lockhart was continually on guard against similarly overwhelming me.

One day we were discussing the Germans over lunch in his favorite New Haven restaurant, Kaysey's. Lockhart was perhaps the most popular and respected American writer in Germany.

I knew of only one way to broach the subject with him, and that was baldly, head on.

"Mr. Lockhart, do you *like* the Germans?"

"Oh well," he replied breezily, "I'm so old now"—he was fifty—"I like everybody!"

This was one of the paradoxical statements he was periodically throwing at me. Like everybody because

16

you're old? But I thought people got narrower and crankier as they got older. "Yes," he went on, catching my puzzlement, playing to it, "soon I'll reach that great enlargement of life, the age of sixty." Enlargement? Sixty! I would never understand or catch up with this man.

He had of course whirled away from giving a direct answer to my direct question. I don't remember his ever answering directly. He answered by allusion, indirection, example. Half an hour further into our conversation, he tossed out in passing, "You must visit south Germany sometime, well, really Austria. Do you like the Baroque?"

I said that I thought I did.

"If you respond to it, there is of course Salzburg. Yes, well, Mozart, of course. Yes, yes, the Germans. Yes, I like them. But as Gertrude Stein used to say with that great yea-saying laugh, 'There's a little bit of uncooked dough in the middle of every German.' "

There was the answer; an answer of sorts, at least, to my question.

"Now the French of course," he went irrepressibly on, "will always be the most civilized people in the world. You know it, I know it, they know it. They *are* good taste, the quintessential French are. Good taste isn't everything; far from it. The French. Once I arrived in Paris without a reservation and went to hotel after hotel, coolly turned down everywhere. Millicent was with me. 'They don't want us,' I complained, 'the French don't want us.' Eventually an *hôtelier* took pity on us. Well, it was at the Crillon. If you're homeless go to the deluxe palaces. They always have space and most of them are so arrogant they can't *believe* anyone less than a millionaire would dare cross their threshold.

17

"The French are like family. You see all their faults, but they're in the last resort family.

"My French is all right. So is my Italian. And Spanish. And German. Hit or miss, I speak those languages hit or miss.

"In Germany everybody assumes I'm a professor. Every kiosk keeper calls me 'Herr Doktor.' I always play up. You must always play up. If someone assumes you have the ear of the President of the United States, play up! They want that of you. When they find out better, never mind!" He stopped, eyed the menu, and then murmured, "Tell me, when are you going to start to travel?"

It was the headmistress of *The Road to Ste. Michèle*, sparing the neophyte from inundation.

I'm sure I had been looking at him a little apprehensively as he had thrown out these random insights about Europe. He reminded me of a geyser in Yellowstone Park, erupting, then falling quiescent, for a while.

"Very soon, I hope. I've got to travel—"

"If only to define your own background better."

"Next summer, maybe. France, I think."

"Um." He was having second and third thoughts about my choice. Characteristically he did not declare them immediately, and when he did so it was only by implication.

"Aren't you Reeves Lockhart?"

A woman was leaning eagerly down toward him.

"Why—*yes*," he answered with an appearance of cordiality, but his thick salt-and-pepper eyebrows went up in a way I sensed spelled annoyance.

"Well, I just thought your writing—I've read so much— your plays too—I just had to—here in New Haven we're so proud you're here! Tell me, Mr. Lockhart, how long have you made New Haven your home?"

His fixed, false smile appeared. "Thirty-seven years now," he observed expansively. "A long time. I like it so much here, the reserve of the people . . . the . . . um . . . New England sense of . . . privacy."

"Oh yes indeed. And tell me, your next book . . ." She hesitated, colored, suddenly tittered uncontrollably; he looked up at her with a mischievous, not unkind twinkle; she burst out, "Enjoy your lunch!" and was gone.

Lockhart returned to his tuna fish salad. "When I was young," he murmured, "I certainly wish I'd taken a pen name."

This, like so many observations about the life of a writer which he made to me, was thrown out that I might consider it and make what use of it I wished. He was teaching, offering insights, sidelights, always. This one I flatly rejected out of hand. Not use my own name? But *of course* I was going to sign my writing with my own name. I might just possibly become famous, and I wanted Allan Prieston to be the name readers would recognize.

Now I suppose it is, and I wish when I was young I'd taken a pen name.

He was so far ahead of me; now that I am the age he was then, I have grown into many of his opinions and choices, but his pointing out thirty years ago where I would eventually arrive has not saved me from having to make the toilsome journey myself.

". . . no question but that *Bernice* could be very effectively staged," Mr. Sansom was saying, as I came out of the shock of memory and back to the luncheon table at the Graduate Club.

"Yes, I suppose so," said Miss Moncrieff a bit nervously.

"You don't want to release it, have it performed?" he pursued.

"Well . . . well, you see, *he* didn't. And so"—she rolled her old, still bright, light blue eyes apologetically up at him—"how can I?"

After a silence he asked rather diffidently, "You don't feel you can take . . . now . . . a slightly *independent* line? Stand back from his—the work he left unproduced, unpublished, and—"

"Please, kind sir," she interrupted, in itself very unusual for her, "may we leave this subject for now? This is *such* a delicious lunch!"

Institutional tuna fish, a Yankee attempt at corn bread, and a marginal salad lay before us. Millicent Moncrieff, with Reeves Lockhart, had dined at the finest restaurants on three continents, so she could not have believed her own words. She was changing the subject, and just to make that change irrevocable, she turned her perky face to me:

"Do you know something, Allan? Something Reeves once said about you . . . oh, a long time ago, about the time he was writing *Bernice*, as a matter of fact. It was soon after the night he read it to you here. We were having cocktails, just the two of us, in the house out in Hamden. I had read one or two of the things you'd shown him and I was curious about you, already a little impressed, even by this apprentice work. You don't mind my calling it that, do you?"

"It was apprentice work at best," I said with a laugh, recalling those sketchy, imitative and uncertain stories.

"So that evening I said to Reeves, 'Tell me about young Master Prieston,' and he said, 'Very ambitious. Talented.' Then I said, 'Oh, come off it, Reeves.' My slang showed we had just come back from a visit to England. 'Is he going to make it?' That expression showed we'd also been hanging around the Algonquin in New York. Nobody talks about anything else at the Algonquin except Is he, she, or it—the play, of course, any play—going to make it. So, let's see, where was—oh, yes. Well, Reeves sat silent for a while, gazing thoughtfully at the floor. Then he said in that, well, marvelous voice. . . ." Millicent glanced at me for a confirmation of this description and I nodded firmly. "Reeves said, 'Oh yes, he'll make it, as you say, all right. And . . . I wonder what he'll lose along the way.' " She paused and looked with genuine curiosity and also sweetness at me. "And what have you lost, Allan?"

I looked back at her across the luncheon table and slowly repeated the question to myself.

2

I was twenty-one years old, and I was still in many ways an adolescent, still partially lingering in what was called the Awkward Age. Reeves Lockhart had written somewhere that goodness had the longest awkward age, but I knew even then that I was not good, not full of virtue, secretly even perhaps a little dangerous. Was I like the characters in *Bernice*, brooking no interference with my wishes, ready to swindle . . . to kill? . . . if someone crossed me where I felt my deepest interests seemed threatened?

I didn't know then. But I know, and knew, that I was not in his definition of the word, good.

Greg Trouvenskoy opened the door and walked into my bedroom, not knocking, of course. "I'm driving to Byeville this afternoon. Going to see the folks. Want to come?"

I had planned to work the entire weekend on a history paper attempting to prove that Austria-Hungary and not the kaiser's Germany was responsible for the outbreak of the First World War, and I did not see when else I could do it and still get it in on time, but this invitation swept everything else aside.

His parents *were* the First World War, in a sense, and I was always drawn toward what was alive, not what had been recorded. Austria-Hungary, a fossil out of the past, would have to wait.

"Sure, Princie, I'd like to go."

He shot a tough glare at me. "If you call me that stupid nickname in front of my folks they'll—"

"Send me to Siberia?" I put in as guilelessly as possible.

The glare intensified.

I began to throw a few things into an overnight suitcase. Just how seriously did he take his heritage? I wondered, not for the first time. After all, he himself had never set foot in Russia, having been born in London years after both his parents' families had been murdered or driven out by the Bolsheviks.

"Tell me something, Greg, just how uh Russian is it going to be at your folks' house? I mean, seriously, I don't want to say anything wrong or make a *faux pas* or anything. For instance, do I call your mother 'Your Highness'?"

"Sure you do," he hooted. "Of course you do. And when you leave her presence you back out, bowing with every step."

"Seriously—"

"Seriously, my mother is an American citizen, a New Deal Democrat, and if you call her 'Your Highness,' she'll laugh in your face. We *lost* the revolution. We haven't got *any money*. The only things they were able to take out of Russia were some jewels, and they were almost all sold to pay for the house in Byeville. My mother's sane, right? So is Dad. Maybe"—he added a little abstractedly—"not a hundred percent reliable all the time—after what they've been through, who would be?—but sane. Because they're Americans and they live in the present and they don't spend their time polishing up the old samovar."

Polishing up the old samovar, I gathered, was for elderly White Russians who were still waiting for Nicholas and Alexandra to come out of that cellar in Siberia, miraculously alive, and lead everybody back into their palaces in St. Petersburg. Others, the Trouvenskoys of that world, didn't waste time polishing up the old samovar—whatever a samovar might be.

Greg had a used Pontiac convertible that he forced to perform feats of speed and response not in the minds of its designers. We had not been killed in it yet.

"What are you going to be if you grow up?" he asked me as we shot across western Connecticut.

"Of course I'm going to be a writer," I answered. "I already am a writer, sort of. Mr. Lockhart says I have—"

"Please knock it off about Pulitzer Prize Lockhart for the duration of the weekend. What makes *you* think you can be a writer? Hardly anybody can make a living at it, I've been told. My father sure as hell can't."

I thought about my answer. Then I said, "Well, I've always been a really voracious reader. Read everything. I never heard of a writer who wasn't like that. I've always made up stories in my mind, just for the fun of it, automatically, while mowing the lawn or something. And then, well, I like to write."

"Are you supposed to like it?"

"Beats me, but I do. And what are you going to be when you grow up?"

"You've got a lot of crust asking a twenty-four-year-old

veteran of the European Theater that question."

"Yeah, but what's the answer?"

"The thing is," he said ruefully after a pause, "I don't know. I'm the first person in the family who's had to ask himself that question in three hundred years. First generation born in exile, that's me. We had, you know, estates back in Old Russia and we just lived on them or in a palace in Petersburg and that was that. Some of us went into the army. One or two were ministers to the tsar. But none of us ever worked for a *living*. I'm the first who ever had to ask the great American question: what am I going to do in my life?" He drove on, a little more slowly now, in silence. Then he brightened.

"Guess what? Merry's coming over Saturday for dinner." Merry Carr was at Vassar College, only a few miles from the Trouvenskoy home in Byeville and Greg was kind of engaged to her, on a provisional basis. She was a glittering-looking rich California girl and the one thing that had impressed me about her was the amount of liquor she drank, gaily and prettily and you might say innocently, but still she drank it, all of it. Greg was no slouch either. As in all even vaguely southern states, Maryland had a bumper crop of party drunks and closet alcoholics and weekend blackout artists, and being around heavy drinkers always made me a little edgy. I had seen a pillar of the community fall flat on his face and a society matron unable to get up her front steps and a seventeen-year-old boy too befuddled to open the next bottle of bourbon.

Russians had a reputation for heavy drinking, everyone knew that. I wondered about Prince and Princess Alexis Trouvenskoy, whom I was very soon going to meet in their "spooky" home, as Greg had described it, Edgewater.

We arrived shortly after dark and my first impression was just that Edgewater was large, looming rather spectrally up among some big old trees, itself obviously old, an old presence beside the Hudson River.

We went up some steps, crossed a small porch, and came into a high-ceilinged hall with a stairway on the left curving gracefully upward. On the right there was a small, dimly lit dining room with a table set for four.

Continuing through the hall, Greg led me into a very large living room with a high ceiling, an elaborate Victorian chandelier scattering thin illumination, and six French windows looking out, presumably on the Hudson River, their glass panes now dully black and somber. Other rooms went off left and right. It was obviously quite a large house for the three members of the Trouvenskoy family, especially if they were as impecunious as Greg said they were. There was something clammy about it, as though a housewarming had never been held or been held but failing in its purpose. The black somber glass windows, the big unlit fireplace, the vague pattern of the whitish wallpaper on the inner walls, different kinds of old furniture scattered thinly about, all emanated a sense somehow of barrenness.

On the left a tall narrow door stood ajar. "The folks'll be in there," said Greg, heading that way. It crossed my mind that there was something faintly odd about their not coming out to us. Surely they had heard the car arrive, the front door slam, footsteps in the next room. Greg went through the doorway, I following, into a rather small chamber that struck me as singular, the ceiling invisible high in the darkness, light flickering out from a busy fire in a big fireplace, a couple of dim, shaded, old-fashioned floor lamps in corners throwing small additional illumination, and there, sunk into two low, deep armchairs flanking the fireplace, were Her Highness Princess Zinaida Petrovna of Russia, and her husband, Prince Alexis Gregorievich Trouvenskoy.

The prince rose, a tall, well-set-up man in a ruby smoking jacket, and came toward us, greeting me very cordially. "Welcome to the Frankenstein mansion," he said with a grin.

"Oh stop it, Alex," came a throaty voice from the other chair. "You'll make the young man uneasy." I went to her chair and she grasped my hand—was I supposed to kiss hers, and how was that done exactly? I looked down at a very white face dominated by large, dark eyes, with black hair parted in the middle and pulled down across her ears. She wore long gold-colored earrings, and a high-necked dress that seemed to be black. She gazed up at me politely, something reserved in her smile, from arrogance, or simply because she was just meeting me for the first time. Or was she shy? That seemed unlikely, but while her husband appeared open and uncomplicated, she clearly was anything but. I saw that I was not supposed to kiss her hand. "Have a glass of sherry with us," she said in her low-pitched voice. "Gregory, give your mother a kiss and then get two more glasses of sherry." Gregory, startling me, had just kissed his father on the mouth and now he bent down and did the same to his mother. Old Russian custom, I said to myself. "Please sit down," the princess said to me. In the dimness back from their chairs, facing the fireplace, I discerned a couch and made my way to it, a heavy, long, high, overstuffed, faintly musty couch. Greg disappeared into the blackness to the right of the fireplace and returned with two glasses of sherry.

They asked how our drive up had been and how were things at Yale and what part of the country was I from. "Maryland," said the princess, "the Eastern Shore is so pleasant and rural. And I've always been interested in Baltimore, and there is that valley outside it somewhere, horse country."

It would become clear as the visit progressed that, impecunious or not, the Trouvenskoys had managed to get acquainted with most parts of the United States.

Her English was mid-Atlantic, and without a Russian accent except for the word "Russia," which she pronounced very emphatically and gutturally, coming down hard on the *R*. Alex, as he told me to call him, had, on the other hand, a rather heavy Russian accent, although his English was very fluent. When they wanted to consult each other quickly, they lapsed into Russian.

A little later I started to ask her if she knew the Shenandoah Valley in Virginia, and had begun to say, "Mrs. Trouvenskoy" automatically, stopped myself, and was trying for the first time in my life to call someone "Princess" when she cut in. "Call me Naida. Zinaida is such a mouthful," and I saw that she had sailed right past her title, she didn't want to hear it, it was out of place here or alien or it revived bitter memories; for one or all of these reasons, or others, she did not want to hear it.

Would she, would they both, similarly avoid discussing Nicholas and Alexandra, the Anastasia mystery, Rasputin, Prince Yousoupov, all figures I longed to hear about from people who, miraculously to me, had actually been there, had known these legends. That in itself seemed as amazing to me as if they had been intimates of Marie Antoinette and Louis XVI, had sat through the Reign of Terror and were here, lounging comfortably in their armchairs, those historic figures and events alive in their memories, epic visions that were otherwise wholly dead.

The conversation did at one point veer like a sailboat in

the direction of that lost Russia. Greg remarked that "Vyrubova's snapshots have been given to Yale," and I started to ask who this obviously Russian "Vyrubova" might be, but Alex cut in suavely, firmly changing the tack. "Such a great library, the Sterling. Like an English cathedral inside. I hear they have a great collection of western American manuscripts and memorabilia. Our west is really fascinating. Naida and I drove out to Jackson Hole last year." Jackson Hole: how far could you get from St. Petersburg? And it was "our" west, and Old Russia faded into the dead past once again.

After about a half-hour we went in through the big outer room, through the hallway, and into the small dining room for a supper of cold cuts and cheese and Italian bread and salad and red wine.

Princess Zinaida sat at the end of the table next to the swinging door leading to the kitchen. In the candlelight her upright posture, the curve of her eyebrows, a certain good-humored authority in the low-pitched voice, contained fragments and hints of a destiny that had disappeared.

I was seated with my back to the outside wall of the house, facing Greg. Behind him there was a small oval-topped fireplace and above it in the dimness I was able to see indistinctly a large oil portrait, and to make out that it was of Princess Zinaida as a young woman. In it she was seated, in evening dress, wearing a small tiara. The figure had the same long neck and unforced upright posture as the middle-aged woman on my right, wearing for adornment tonight only the dangling gold-colored earrings which were just as certainly not valuable as the tiara just as certainly had been.

Greg had begun a funny and typically derisive account of my writing ambitions and the course called Daily Themes I was taking. He described how we students in the course were required to produce a three-hundred-word essay five times a week, an essay seeking to convey one emotion, such as jealousy, or love, or fear.

"Tell us about this course," said the prince with a certain special emphasis: he really wanted me to tell them—him—about this course.

I remember Greg saying to me that his father was, or was trying to be, a writer, and had been trying for some years. I recalled how his "career" had come about.

Ten years earlier, in 1940, Naida's mother, the grand duchess Anna, had died. Like all the Romanoff women, she had possessed a great deal of very valuable jewelry, and this asset alone she had succeeded in preserving from collapse and revolution when she managed to escape from Russia with her two young daughters, Zinaida and Tatiana. Her husband, Naida's father, Grand Duke Peter, had lingered behind in Petrograd hoping for a better turn of events, lingered too long, been interned by Kerensky, and then in October 1917 been put into a cell in the Peter and Paul Fortress by the victorious Bolsheviks. A year later, when it looked as though the anti-Bolsheviks might win the civil war and restore the Romanoffs, Grand Duke Peter was taken out and shot.

When the grand duchess died in 1940, she still possessed some of this jewelry. What remained was divided between the two daughters. Naida quickly sold most of what she inherited, and with the proceeds they bought Edgewater, setting Alex up there for a career in writing. He had just resigned from a deeply antipathetic job in public relations in New York—"People like me don't know how to *relate* to the *public*," he had remarked wryly at the time. "For three hundred years the Russian public had been relating to *us!*"—and sat down in Edgewater to pursue his long-dreamed-of literary career.

For practical purposes, he wrote in English. Fluent though he was, Russian, not English, was in his blood, and after that French. Writing in his third language, always on Russian themes, he was not able to achieve a success with his four books produced in ten years. He had enjoyed one book-club sale that brought in $17,000, but that had been all the appreciable money he had been able to earn. Naida by now had nearly run through what remained of her inheritance. She had been trying herself to write, write children's stories, but publishers had not been interested. What they were interested in, deeply, were her memoirs. Was her cousin Tsar Nicholas II as weak as history claimed? Was his wife Alexandra an hysteric whose dominance of him led to their destruction? Was Rasputin her lover? Princess Zinaida adamantly refused even to discuss making such revelations in print, no matter how much money publishers might offer for them, no matter how welcome such money might have been.

"The old inheritance is dwindling away," Greg had told me one day recently. "We've got one ace in the hole though. There's one diamond that mother hasn't sold yet. It even has a name: the Militsa Diamond. We figure it's worth about a hundred thousand dollars and getting a little more valuable every year, so we're holding on to it until the last minute to get the best price."

"Tell me about this writing course," Alex said again. He leaned across the old mahogany table in the candlelight toward me.

So I described how hard it was to think of five separate

vignettes each week, each one portraying a different emotion. I described how valuable this was nevertheless, because it exposed on paper how worthless promising ideas in the mind could turn out to be. "It clears out all the rubbish," I said, "exposes it to cold print. Once in a while one of them turns out to be pretty good." I added that we were reminded in the course to use the five senses— hearing, taste, touch, smell—and not just sight in our writing. I said that the key technical insight offered to us was to understand that in fiction you show, you do not tell.

His face, with its high Slavic cheekbones, olive skin, bluish eyes, intelligent and sensitive expression, frowned. "I don't entirely understand what that means." He looked, almost glared, hard at me.

I tried to explain. We sought to portray an emotion, not to label it. In one of my themes a young man, engulfed in jealousy because his girl is going for a stroll in the park with another young man, tracks them like a White Hunter in the bush. I described meticulously just which tree he hides behind, just which rock he chooses for concealment in spying on them. I never used the word "jealousy." At the end of the story when, from his hiding place in some bushes, he sees the young man merely take her hand briefly, he crushes in his own hand some dark glasses he is holding, and the blood begins to flow.

In this way, I said, we tried to transfer the experience from the page into the reader's fund of vicarious experience, so that the story in a sense *happens* to him. We did not explain it to him; we made it happen to him.

"I see," said the prince, still frowning. He saw, but could he do it, utilize this technique? It was all so different from the literature he had in his bones, so different from Tolstoy with his analyses and dissections and dissertations. I comprehended that Prince Alexis was nineteenth century, and earlier, to the marrow, and he was a semi-Asiatic Russian. How on earth could he ever sell a story to *The New Yorker*, edited as it was with the affluent middlebrow folk of Fairfield County today firmly in mind?

Alex began to talk about Chekhov in this context and I tried to follow what he was saying, but I had as much trouble understanding just what he was driving at as he had had with me.

There was a hooting sound in the distance, a whistle. Then a minute later I heard it again, closer. It was a train whistle. No one else at the table appeared to notice it. Then faintly I heard what was surely the engine of a train; it was drawing nearer. The whistle, quite close, erupted in a shriek again. The train incredibly was bearing down on us; it was thundering toward us, amazingly near; I looked wild-eyed at the others: nothing, not an eyelash batting. The stark glare of a powerful light shattered the room's dimness, flashing across the wall, the portrait; the engine roared up to us—then, it hurtled past, then the clank and rattle of freight cars. . . .

"What in the world—"

"Oh," broke in the prince with a chuckle, "we're so used to it. Don't even really hear it anymore. That was the 9:02 out of Poughkeepsie. The New York Central. The main line is just the other side of our back fence."

"To build this beautiful house," I mused aloud, "next to the railroad tracks. How peculiar."

"Oh, but they didn't," put in the princess quietly. "This house was built around 1830, long before the railroad came."

"I see. And does it ah . . . well . . . ?"

"Bother us? Not really. You get used to it." She paused, then murmured abstractly, "You get used to anything."

Losing your position, losing your country, losing your money, your father taken out and shot. Princess Zinaida had had a lot to get used to in her life.

"Wait'll the express comes through around two in the morning," put in Greg gleefully. "Your room is on that side of the house, and it'll knock you right out of bed."

"Thanks for telling me," I said.

"Would you rather be surprised?"

"Well, no."

"It isn't that bad," said Alex. "By the end of the weekend you'll hardly notice it."

I doubted that but I was obscurely thrilled at having the New York Central thundering by right next to what I guessed was considered the back of the house. The ceilings lost in darkness, the somber blind windows facing the great river, the tall brooding trees, the dispossessed royal princess in exile, all this odd and tragedy-tinged atmosphere seemed completed by a night train hurtling by through the backyard.

"Naida," murmured Alex, "I think the samovar is ready. Shall I make the tea?"

He started to get up, but she said, "No, I'll do it," and rising, she went to a small table beside the fireplace, I following her every move, all eyes. On the table there was a rather large brass or copper urn, bulbous, with handles and a spigot. This she opened and poured hot water into a teapot. After letting it steep she poured us cups of tea, then put the pot on top of the samovar to keep it warm.

So now I knew. New Deal Democrats or not, frequenters of Jackson Hole, Wyoming, or not, avoiders of royal titles or not, the Trouvenskoys kept their samovar very highly polished indeed.

3

The following morning I awoke in my high, four-poster bed to a glowing autumnal day. Caressing harvest-time sunshine shed its radiance over Edgewater and over the Hudson Valley, a reassuring golden brightness that burned off the specters and vaguely sinister emanations of the night before.

Somewhere below in the house marvelous choral music was being played and sung on a radio or phonograph, Russian choral music I was sure. I got dressed and went into the outer hall and knocked on Greg's door. He was awake and he called me to come in. His was a front corner bedroom, and there were two long windows facing the side of the property, and two other long windows looking out at the expanse of gently sloping lawn down to the broad and majestic Hudson.

The trees scattered here and there on the lawn—tall and thin locusts, maples, oak—had deepened into their final autumnal hues—burnt orange, ruby, russet, chocolate brown, old gold—on the branches and scattered over the green lawn beneath, creating a final magic before the desolateness of winter closed over the house and the valley.

"How'd you like the two A.M. special?" asked Greg as he pulled on some dungarees and an old shirt.

"Forewarned is forearmed. I only jumped two feet off the mattress. And I didn't have even one heart attack."

"We like it." He turned to a mirror on top of an old chest of drawers and began to brush his rather curly brown hair. "You know we get a lot of callers here, old reverent Russians who want to see Mother. As if she were an ikon or something. So after they've kissed her hand and cried and had a cup of tea and told us how they saw the tsar in some procession in 1913 in St. Petersburg, then they want to tell us *their* story of how they got out of Russia hiding in a peasant cart under a bale of hay. If I'm here, I hold them off until 4:03 and then ask them their life story, and at 4:04 a very long freight train comes through and we don't have to hear a word of it."

There was something cruel in this story: indeed, there was a small streak of something that might be called cruelty in Gregory. I could imagine him playing this trick on pilgrims out of a kind of rough mischievousness. I could not imagine the princess lending herself to it, nor Alex either for that matter.

"Your folks go along with that?" I put in offhandedly.

"Oh, you know. They don't. They have their duty, to be a kind of musty role to people who want to live in the past. They're nice to them. They don't like to think about the old days much, or not at all, but they're nice to them. But me, I've never seen Russia, never will. What's all that to me?"

We went downstairs to the big old-fashioned kitchen.

When it came to breakfast, Her Highness was entirely American: fresh orange juice, oatmeal, blueberry pancakes. In the morning light, without earrings or a formal black dress, wearing a simple blue housedress, she was somehow even more dramatic looking than the night before. With her very dark eyes, black hair parted in the middle and lying close along the sides of her head, her white skin, her relative tallness, and most of all the unforced uprightness of her carriage, shoulders back, head erect, and the low-pitched slightly amused voice, she was truly a princess. "Alexei has gone into Rhinebeck to have the car 'looked at,' as he put it. Poor Alexei, he hasn't a clue what's under the hood. Not that I do. Now, if it were a *horse*, he could put his finger on precisely what was wrong. With the car . . . well, once he was certain the motor had 'collapsed,' and in fact it was out of gas."

"Why didn't he let me look at it?" asked Greg, who was, in fact, very good at repairing things. "Why spend money if you don't have to?"

Naida sighed wearily. "Why indeed?" she murmured.

"Anyway," he continued, "I can fix the roof on the boathouse."

"Yes, do. The neighbors will want to store their old Hudson River sailboat there again this winter. I get a little rent from it. We can't have it leaking."

After breakfast Greg and I went to the cellar to get some tools. The cellar was a catacomblike labyrinth of dim, white-walled little rooms, mostly windowless, with low ceilings. Some of the rooms had no light at all and if they had contained a skeleton I wouldn't have been surprised.

Greg found what he was looking for, and we went up and out through the big living room, through one of the French doors to the front veranda, which extended the length of the house proper. There were six big circular white wooden pillars supporting a roof two stories above. The exterior of the house, made of a kind of fine stucco, was stained a tan-brown and it had altogether a look of quiet impressiveness, even a certain subdued grandeur.

I could understand now why they had bought it, impractical though in many ways it was. Big houses sold cheap in 1940, and this one provided an appropriate setting for a royal lady in exile. Those White Russian pilgrims coming for audiences with her need not be disappointed.

The sweep of lawn and the wide green flowing river stretched broadly below us. "What a great place this is!" I exclaimed.

"I love it," murmured Greg. "Wonder how long we'll be able to keep it, though."

"But you own it outright, no mortgage or anything."

"Yes, there is. And the upkeep . . . oh well, something will turn up. Maybe I'll marry an heiress," and he grinned at me.

But Merryfield Carr was no grinning matter; she *was* an heiress and my first impression had been that she was very interested in Gregory Alexis Trouvenskoy.

The boathouse, a small weathered wooden structure next to the river wall on the left, looked as though it needed work. Greg scrambled up to the roof, I handed him the tools, and then he said, "Go and take a walk. You don't know how to drive a nail straight. Besides, I don't think this roof'll support two of us."

I wandered around the property, which extended for hundreds of yards on both sides of the house. Next to the foundation there were big spreading juniper bushes. Scat-

tered here and there on the lawn were groves of arching
locust trees, spreading maples, dignified spruce. A vegetable garden was near the rear fence with the railroad tracks
just beyond it. Drooping willow trees lined the gravel
driveway.

The outstanding feature of the house was a very large
and beautiful octagonal library attached to its north side by
a short hallway.

I went into the house to look at it. Except for the entrance
face, the other seven sides of the octagon were broken by
French windows. The high-domed ceiling ended in a skylight, and the entire effect was of an exhilarating lightness
and grace. The walls were white plaster; there was an
antique writing table facing the river through the French
windows, a huge old Persian rug, settees, a large circular
table, shelves holding leather-bound sets of Russian,
French, and English literature. There were four oil portraits, two men and two women, which I took to be eigh-
teenth century and Russian. This beautiful room seemed to
contain what valuable articles they had been able to
preserve from the wreckage. The desk looked valuable;
maybe the portraits were too.

On one small table were prerevolutionary photographs in
silver frames: A superb, stone-pillared palace on a canal
with huge ornamental wrought-iron gates guarded by sentinels. I was sure this had been her home in St. Petersburg.
Another showed a seated lady holding an ostrich-feather
fan and wearing a high tiara and many ropes of pearls.
Grand Duchess Anna? There was also a distinguished
bearded gentleman in officer's uniform. Grand Duke Peter?
And there was a seated group of people who were as
recognizable as they were tragic: Emperor Nicholas,

Empress Alexandra, the four good-looking daughters, the delicate son. It had been signed, with an enormous flourish, *Alexandra*, and more conventionally, *Nikolai*.

Altogether, Edgewater on a day like this was as sun-filled, airy, open, and cheerful as it had been enclosed, shadowy, sinister, and glum the night before, and for the same reason: there were so many big windows everywhere, filling the rooms now with sunshine and reflected sunshine; at night they became blind and black, an empty darkness pressing against them, as though about to break in and engulf the house.

I sat down in an old armchair with a book I had found on the shelves, the memoirs of Prince Felix Yousoupov, in which he describes how he and his cohorts murdered Rasputin. It had been inscribed by the prince to Naida and Alexei. I skimmed over the early chapters describing his boyhood and was reading with repelled fascination of the botched and bungled murder when Greg came into the library.

"I'm reading about all the trouble they had killing Rasputin."

"Oh?" He dropped down onto the big shabby sofa and stretched out. "Fixing that boathouse is more work than I thought. 'Oh my aching back' as we say in the military service." He glanced appraisingly across at me. "You certainly are getting wrapped up in Old Russia."

"Well, it interests me, and the things you've got in the house, those photographs, for instance—signed by the *tsar*—they sort of put me right back in that period."

"Hm. Do they? Well, we've got something else a lot more symbolic of Old Russia."

"Yes?"

"Yes." There was a pause; he gazed at the ceiling.

"Well," I said in exasperation, "what is it?"

"Hm? Oh. Well, as a matter of fact it's in this room. By the way, where are the folks?"

"Gone on errands."

"It's right here in this room. Do you want to see it?"

"Of course I do."

"Okay, go over to those portraits and take down the second lady on the left."

I removed the portrait and was surprised to see a small combination-lock wall safe behind it.

"Don't just stand there staring at it, open it. Turn the knob right to 7."

After a certain hesitation I took hold of the knob and turned it to 7.

"Now left, back past 7 to 3."

I did that.

"Now right to 9."

I turned the knob to 9.

"Pull," he ordered.

I pulled, the little door swung open, and I saw inside a number of documents and also a small blue velvet jewel case.

"Bring the blue box over here," he said.

I brought it to him; he opened it and lifted out a stone. "Hold out your hand." I did so and he playfully dropped the stone into it. I gazed down, fascinated at a complexly cut octagonal bluish jewel. It was not a ring or part of a necklace, it was simply the jewel itself.

"What is it?" I asked quietly.

"It's the Militsa Diamond," he said, "named for one of the old grand duchesses. Pretty, isn't it?"

I stared down at the subdued flashes of its facets as I

moved my hand, at its bluish depths, no flaw anywhere, serene, cold, seemingly perfect.

"Shouldn't it be in a bank?" I asked a little nervously.

"The folks don't believe in banks. They had millions of rubles in banks in Russia and the day the Bolsheviks took power, they confiscated every deposit in every bank. Then during the Depression in this country, they lost more money in some bank when it failed. They don't trust banks."

"Aren't you afraid somebody might break in and . . . I don't know, force the safe and steal it?"

"Hardly anybody knows it's here. We don't talk about it. But when I saw you were turning into such a Russian history nut, I knew you'd want to see it."

"What a beauty. Who was the grand duchess Militsa?"

"Mother can tell you. On second thought, better not mention to the folks that you've seen it, all right? You know. . . ." He eyed me briefly.

I didn't exactly know, and I was uneasy, but I murmured, "Yes." Then I added, "You've got it insured, of course."

"We can't afford insurance."

"Oh boy."

"I think I'd better put it back."

"Yeah, do," I said with relief.

He returned it to the safe, closed the door, spun the dial, and replaced the portrait. Then he and I stood there rather aimlessly for several moments. Finally I said, "Were you able to fix the roof?"

"Uh-huh. When Mother gets back with my car, I've got to go and have my hair cut. So I'll look okay for Merry."

"You look okay now."

Gregory was a good-looking young man, square shoulders, Slavic high cheekbones, cool blue eyes, full mouth, with a forthright, engaging manner. He was popular at Yale, popular while having few close friends. He somehow seemed to signal that he did not want people to get really close to him. Myself, being years younger, too young for war experience, a "provincial" as he never ceased to remind me, from the wilds south of the Mason-Dixon Line, I was somehow different and admissible. Perhaps he thought he could do no wrong in my eyes, and he was more or less right. I stood impressed by his background, his extensive and dangerous war years, his athleticism, his whole amused and self-confident demeanor.

One thing about his life at Yale, now that I was becoming more familiar with his family's financial situation, was how his Yale expenses were met. He had, as all veterans did, the G.I. Bill of Rights, but that fell far short of covering everything. I now surmised that his parents were straining every financial resource to make up the difference.

Greg and his parents did various errands and chores for most of the rest of the day. Princess Zinaida had already taken my measure, apparently, because she showed me where all the various tsarist memoirs and histories were in the library, brought me a ham sandwich and a glass of iced tea there at noon, and left me to browse and read with fascination.

The extravagance of the Russian aristocrats and royalty, the family feuds and scandals, the superstitions, the two hundred retainers who accompanied the dowager empress Marie when she traveled in her private train to Biarritz; teen-age Prince Felix Yousoupov of the striking good looks disguising himself in women's clothes and his mother's jewels, including her tiara, to sing in a Petersburg cabaret until a family friend in the audience recognized to her dumbfoundment the tiara; Grand Duke Sergei, the ogre of the Romanoff family, being blown to bits by an anarchist's bomb in front of the Kremlin; his wife, saintly Grand Duchess Elizabeth, gathering up the pieces of his body and later forgiving and praying for his murderer; the heir to the throne, Tsarevitch Alexis, on the brink of death time after time from hemophilic bleeding, being saved by the hypnotic presence of Rasputin. . . .

Overpowering, melodramatic, lurid, and doomed, the destiny of Old Russia was crowded into the shelves of this serene room on the Hudson, opulence and lucklessness and blood and tragedy from a world that was dead, or, after all, not really dead, not yet.

Scanning a shelf, I was startled to see *The Road to Ste. Michèle* by Reeves Lockhart. I pulled it out. It was a first edition, and to my further surprise, there was this inscription:

> *To Naida and Alexei, with all affectionate best thoughts,*
> *Reeves*
>
> *Dubrovnik*
> *July 10, 1927*

The man had been everywhere and met everyone.

Greg returned at 6:30 with Merryfield Carr. I was sitting with his parents waiting in the small, dim inner living room; they received her exactly as they had received me. They waited for Greg to bring her in to them. The princess was gracious but never stirred. The prince was cordiality itself, on his own terms. There was some vestige of protocol in all this that neither Merry nor myself could be expected to understand.

I had yet to see anything faze Merry, and I did not now. With her fine features, chestnut hair falling to her shoulders, fresh skin, bright and observant green eyes, a voice that was at once confident and laughing and yet somehow vulnerable, a supple body wearing tonight a demure dark green dress with a thin gold bracelet and a small gold pin, she always seemed to fit easily and agreeably into any situation. She and Gregory were apparently developing a rapport that went deeper than flirtation and dating; they seemed to be, or to be becoming, real friends.

Both of them were very downright and unpretentious, he about his *passé* royal blood, she about her money. Those were accidents of birth, and Greg and Merry seemed determined to be evaluated for themselves and not for appurtenances they happened to possess.

"I love this *house*," she exclaimed after Greg had shown her the main downstairs rooms and taken her out on the lawn in this mild, moonlit night to see the façade. "It's so old, and dignified. We don't have much like this in California."

"I so liked Pebble Beach there," remarked Naida, "and Monterey. And Big Sur."

"We enjoyed Baja California too," added Alexei.

And so the evening proceeded pleasantly, and a shade more formally than the dinner the night before. Zinaida had prepared an excellent meat dish that, it took me some time to realize, was simply meat loaf, but the best meat loaf I'd ever tasted. Afterward we listened to some of the recorded Russian choral music in the splendid acoustics of the library, and then the prince and princess retired upstairs, and the three of us drove to a crowded nearby roadhouse where there was a jukebox and a busy bar.

Greg and Merry treated themselves liberally to Scotch. I had a couple of beers. Neither of them seemed to turn a hair from the Scotches. A rather lanky girl from Bard College and I picked each other up for a while. When she learned that I was staying at the locally famous landmark house, Edgewater, with its exotic inhabitants, she insisted on meeting Gregory, Prince Gregoire as he was listed in the *Almanach de Gotha*, and tried to bait him about the oppressiveness of the tsar and the Romanoffs. She was, she told us, a Trotskyite.

"*Are* you!" remarked Greg, grinning, eyes bright with amusement. "I'm a McKinley Republican myself. Why did we ever give the women the *vote* in this country!" You did not bait a master of baiting such as Greg.

"You idiot," put in Merry with a giggle. "We've been secretly running things forever here."

"You're from Vassar, I suppose," said my Trotskyite with distaste.

"Mm. And you're from Bard."

"That's right. On a scholarship."

"And more power to you," rejoined Merry, eyes roaming over the dancers and the drinkers at the bar.

"Do you want to dance again?" I flatly asked my partner. She eyed me. "I think I'd better go back to my crowd."

"If you're happier there," I said rather irresponsibly.

"We're all one big happy united country," said Merry pleasantly. "And it's all going to work out."

"I doubt that," she said, and left us.

"The sins of the fathers," groaned Greg, rolling his eyes jokingly to the ceiling. "All we've got left is the blame, and none of the cash."

"At least they're not going to assassinate you," said Merry lightly.

"That's true," said Greg with a slight frown.

"Oh dear, oh me," she hastened to add, "you . . . I forgot . . . your grandfather . . . I shouldn't have—"

"Oh come on. I never knew him. He . . . died years before I was born."

"Still, it was marvelously tactless of me to say that."

"Let's dance."

"You don't really know how to dance."

"Let's dance."

"Whatever you say, sir."

Later they drove back to the house to leave me there before he took Merry back to Vassar. On the way to Edgewater she rambled on, slightly disconnectedly now, about her winter vacation plans. I half listened. ". . . and Sun Valley is great at Christmas time . . . maybe the Bahamas . . . Stowe once or twice . . . a couple of plays in New York I'd like to see . . ." Rich girl, I thought to myself, a nice very attractive girl, but, or rather and, rich, so therefore making certain taken-for-granted assumptions, at least after a few drinks.

The next morning, Sunday, the music that flooded through the octagonal library was of a heightened splendor, the gorgeous and moving hymns and anthems of the Russian Orthodox church.

The weather remained unseasonably mild, and Naida and I were having after-breakfast coffee at a little table on the veranda among the pillars, the music flowing out to us through the French windows of the library. The sweep of green lawn below was strewn with the ruby and gold leaves, suggesting flat, cast-off jewels of some giantess who had swept through the valley.

"Indian summer," I remarked.

47

"I like that concept," she said promptly. "It's uniquely American. The last burst of beauty before the long coldness. Of course, here, in the Hudson Valley, people don't know what cold is, really." She was looking off toward the great river but not really seeing it. She was going, at last, to say something about Russia. I waited; for some strange reason I was almost holding my breath. "In Petersburg," she murmured, "with all the canals filled with ice, and the wind cutting across from the Gulf of Finland, *that* was cold. Like a razor. Not to be resisted. No furs were thick enough. Our coachman . . ." and she seemed to shudder almost imperceptibly. "I was too young to realize it at the time. . . ." She fell silent.

Finally I ventured to prompt her: "The coachman?"

She recollected herself, withdrew into her usual reserve, but her deeply ingrained manners forced her to answer my question.

"Oh, you know," she said quickly. "When we went to some party, a ball somewhere, the rooms would be almost too hot, there would be flowers everywhere, even palm trees. And outside, all the coachmen were waiting, for so many hours, in that coldness." There was a long silence. "I was awfully young," she finished, barely audible. Then her large, nearly black eyes looked across at me. With an effort, it seemed, the habitual amusement came back into her voice. "What a bookworm you are. You must come again. Even a reader like you can't have made a dent in our library. Come and use it," and then after a pause she added with an odd little chuckle, "while we still have it."

"I would love it. There was one book I was really surprised to find. It was Reeves Lockhart's first novel. And it was inscribed to you and Alex."

"Oh—yes, yes. Yugoslavia. In the twenties. Yes, Reeves Lockhart." She was frowning slightly. There was an uneasy pause.

"I know him very well," I pursued. "He lives right outside New Haven, when he's not traveling to Timbuktu or someplace, that is. I'm . . . well, I'm trying to write, sort of. He helps me. He's a genius, I think." I waited.

"Oh, of course, of course, so gifted," she put in unwillingly, her good manners forcing her to.

"Last week he read his new one-act play, acting out all the parts, just for me. Upstairs in the Graduate Club."

She looked at me sharply for an instant, almost suspiciously. Was there something suspect in my being close, in a certain sense, to Mr. Lockhart?

Naida started to rise, saying, "I really must go upstairs and see what's keeping my men."

There was one final scene I had to play out with her, and this might be my only opportunity. I wanted to go and jump in the Hudson instead and have it sweep me down to New York and out to sea, but I had my lines that must be spoken. Other friends of Greg's who had stayed at Edgewater had told me what to do.

"Princess Zinaida," I began, her title spontaneously popping out, "I want you to let me chip in on the expenses. All that wine! It's only fair."

Her deep and dark eyes looked at me with candor, an invincible Russian candor as I learned to recognize in the years ahead. "We're so broke," she muttered. I pressed, God forgive me, *ten dollars* into her hand. It should have been fifty. I could have afforded it.

We all had a lot to forgive ourselves for: her freezing coachman, my ten dollars . . .

4

Yale in the autumn of 1980 had a briskness about it I did not remember from my student days there. Everyone was in such a hurry. Even on the weekend all the students seemed to be in a terrible rush to have fun. Even the dead leaves scudded in bursts across the courtyards of the colleges and past the old churches on the New Haven Green. Migrating ducks pulled themselves swiftly high overhead toward the south; along the Connecticut Turnpike, near the harbor, cars and trucks hurtled along. The cloistered peace of the ivory tower? Forget it. New Haven, Yale, were in a headlong rush into the future, or perhaps all the hurry was a near-desperate attempt to keep up with the present.

Millicent Moncrieff was an island of calm amid all this flux. Her mind seemed just as feisty and energetic and muscular as Reeves's had been, but it functioned in an aura of repose, of inner certitude and self-knowledge.

Two nights after my lunch with her and Avery Sansom she invited me to go to a play at the Yale Drama School. I took her to dinner in the clubby atmosphere of Mory's and afterward we walked along York Street toward the solid brown-tan stone University Theater. The play that night was to be Eugene O'Neill's *Long Day's Journey into Night.*

It was a very chilly evening, a cutting damp wind swept through the streets warning us "This is New England! Almost November! We've got you until late March and you're not going to forget it!"

Minute Millicent Moncrieff was wearing a cloche hat and a brown woolen coat with a wide fur collar, a style I remember from the 1930s. She pulled the collar up around her cheeks. The coat itself looked new and expensive. Her royalties from Reeves's plays and novels rolled in steadily and heavily every six months. "My, isn't this bracing," she said.

"Mm."

"You don't like it. You're a southerner, if I remember correctly, aren't you?"

"Border state."

"Same thing. Now we"—"we" always meant herself and Reeves—"tend to come fully alive in this weather. *All* our forebears were New Englanders. It's in the blood. The languorous tropics were not for us. Reeves was always hiding away on top of some Alp, or else way up in Canada. He did, to be sure, retreat to the Arizona desert later in life for two years, but that was more or less doctor's orders. Occasionally we would go to Puerto Rico or the Bahamas for a winter visit, but only for a visit, only a visit! Then back to freezing, windswept New Haven and the *real world.* Not everybody's real world, but ours. Reeves always said, 'If you're not born to one of those tropical paradises you can't live there successfully. You go bad, like cream left out of the refrigerator.'"

After a short silence Millicent asked, "Do you ever see

your Trouvenskoy friend? Is the princess still alive?"

"I believe so."

"Do you ever see either of them?"

"No, no."

"What an ordeal they all had to go through."

"Yes."

"You don't want to talk about it, do you?"

"No, I really don't. Would you?"

She paused, and then said, "I suppose not." There was another pause and then she added, "I know what really happened. Reeves told me at the time. I know what you did."

"Is it all right if we don't talk about it?"

"If you wish, of course."

We reached the theater and proceeded through the hub-bub toward our seats. Millicent with her habitual courtesy and warmth responded to many greetings from a number of faculty people and even one or two students. "Oh I still see a few of them," she said cheerfully in answer to my query. "You know how Reeves *always* wanted to be in touch with young minds."

Drawing a breath, I then answered with emphasis, "I'll say I do!"

She gave Reeves's brief, barking laugh. "Of *course* you do. Well, I try to keep it up a little. I don't have the strength I used to have. But I try to keep it up at least a little."

We reached our seats, fourth row on the aisle; the house was filling up, obviously it was sold out; the lights dimmed, and the curtain began to rise slowly.

As I watched it disappearing above the proscenium, I thought of Lockhart's plays, many of which, very innova-tively at the time, dispensed with curtain and proscenium, even with sets and props. "All you need is a plank and a passion or two," he said of the theater. Tonight we were having traditional theater, and although I remembered that he had admired this play, he did not care for its traditionalism.

The taut and searing drama began: drug-addled mother, miser father, drunken-failure older son, sick and daunted younger son. All four actors soon revealed that they were going to be at least adequate in their extremely difficult parts.

Lockhart once again thrust himself into my consciousness: it had been many years since I had thought so much about him, but here in New Haven he was inescapable. My Yale friend Bradford Dillman, four years after graduation, had played the younger son in the original Broadway production of this play and I had been close to it at every stage, seen it a number of times then. I extravagantly admired everybody and everything about it. "Mmmmm, yes," Reeves had said at the Algonquin bar after we had seen the play together, he for the first time, I for the third, "well, yes, but Mrs. Tyrone, Mary Tyrone, now if you saw an actress with real femininity, with truly womanly power in the part, then you would see its greatness."

"We're not seeing that in this production?"

Since he wanted to admire, wanted to see achievement at its highest, his voice had a regretful tone as he murmured, "No."

Tonight in the University Theater the play moved inexorably on, these four people stripping away one another's self-deceptions and false façades until the raw mutual destructiveness and mutual love lay bare. Despite my absorption in seeing it once again, an event that took place in this theater, an event I had long forgotten, came into my mind's eye: Reeves and I were attending an experimental play by a student playwright called *Utter Beyond*. The "set" was simply a black dropcloth at the rear of the stage; the three characters, two men and a woman, wore dead-white robes. It was very serious. There were lines such as "In the evening of the dream lies their beginning" or it may have been "In the evening of the dream lies there, beginning," and "The wisp of cosmos, can it still the beat of time?" And so on. These characters were supposed to be trapped in an elevator, but apparently the elevator was a symbol for hell, or at least limbo, or else it was a battlefield at the end of all wars, or possibly an insane asylum. The somber Gallic influence of Sartre was everywhere.

Lockhart was giving the play his habitual fixed, hopeful attention. I knew he could not agree with this assertion of the meaninglessness and pain of life—it was the antithesis of everything he believed in and expressed in his work—but he was giving it every chance to make its points with him.

About fifteen minutes into the play, the three-quarters-full house, mostly students, became actively restive. Murmurings, shifting postures, a few people walking out began to disturb the evening. When the woman character, who was nameless, cried in anguish, "I need—oh, I don't know *what* I need!" a carrying voice from the rear of the auditorium could be heard remarking, "You need an acting coach." A light ripple of startled laughter flowed over the house. When one of the men intoned darkly, "I suspect there is no escape from here, none. We are trapped," another voice close to the stage put in sarcastically, "*You* are trapped!" and the laughter was more fulsome. Members of the audience were beginning to tell one another jokes and to laugh loudly at them.

Reeves Lockhart, tweedy and professorial with dark-rimmed glasses, was on his feet. We were close to the front of the house. "That will be enough of that," his carrying voice cut through the hubbub. "You're here to watch a serious attempt at drama." The voice carried into the remaining pockets of chatter, which fell silent. The actors stood still, gazing at him. Into the hush his voice in all its unforced authority went on, "This is a university. That word's root is 'universe.' We examine all things here. We give them their hearing. If you don't, you don't belong in a university, and I will at least ask you to leave this theater."

He sat down to silence and then a certain patter of applause. Then a hush.

The actress turned back to one of the actors. "I have scraped the walls with my hands," she began uncertainly, pantomiming that action, "and found no aperture, nor even a knob." She continued this speech, regaining confidence as the respectful silence from the audience persisted, and the play proceeded without further trouble to its conclusion.

Outside, as we walked toward my car, I asked his opinion of the play. "Oh well, we all have our lonely moment in rooms. But," he finished crisply, "we go on eating, we go on eating!" He was silent for a moment and then added, "If Sartre knew what he was spawning. But foolish play or not, I can't sit back and let an audience turn into a rabble. After all, they weren't *chained* to their seats. It is possible to creep out decently. Not terribly grown-up, Yale students, sometimes. Adolescence in this country is by far the longest in the world. It's a by-product of our wealth and prosperity. Children, children, youth, youth! That's the popular cry. I want to yell, 'Adults, adults, maturity, maturity!' But I fear few would listen."

He directed me to drive the car into downtown New

Haven, past the Green to the older part of the city where university people seldom went. "We've got to get the callow ring of undergraduate silliness out of our ears," he explained. "Only a honky-tonk will do."

On a dark side street we pulled up at the Deutscher Haus, a German-style cellar of many small rooms and alcoves, *oom-pa-pa* canned music, beer, pipe smokers, dimness, drunks, sawdust on the floor, a derelict or two. "It's a little shady, a little *louche*," he remarked cheerfully as we made our way to an alcove table after both bartenders had greeted him by name, "just what we need."

He ordered steins of beer for us and after a few healthy gulps he said, "Sartre is a very great influence in Europe these days, you know, and as tonight's play proved, he's becoming an influence here too. He is so *well-educated*! So *completely* educated. The French are nothing if not thorough when it comes to education."

Much later, four beers later, he returned to the subject. "I wish I'd waited, before publishing anything, waited until I'd completed, truly completed, my education. I never did, and now it's too late."

"You're the most learned person I've ever met."

"I am extremely widely read, in five languages. But that is not the same thing as being a fully educated man, which is what Sartre is. He can stand at the center of his mind and look down the length of the *allée* of philosophy, of science, of art, of theology. Anything. He is the arbiter of French culture." His eyes, behind their heavy lenses, glowed.

And that, I suddenly realized, is what you want to be in America. And famous and covered with honors though you are, that you can never be. Because, so you tell me, you are not completely educated.

But there is another reason, I reflected. America is so very much bigger and more variegated than tightly organized France. Nobody, however total his education, could achieve Sartre's position here.

And yet you long for it. And you can never have it.

To shake him out of the very—so I believed—uncharacteristic melancholy into which he seemed to be slipping, I mentioned my visit to the Trouvenskoys' and told of finding his inscribed book.

"Yes," he said rather suavely, "Naida and Alexei. So many losses and tragedies have been heaped on their heads. The rivalries and secrets in a dispossessed family like that! When a family drops overnight from everything to nothing, it's a cataclysm. All kinds of subsidiary dramas follow in its wake. There is at least one still happening in the family now, a terrible injustice and tragedy."

"There is?" I prompted, fascinated.

He leaned back, took a deep breath. "I think it's time for one more stein. Hans!" and I knew he would tell me no more.

Well, I'm sure it doesn't involve my friend Greg, I thought. How could it? And the kind princess and the struggling prince; I hoped it didn't involve them either.

I would of course have been positive, had anyone suggested such a thing, that it could not conceivably involve me.

5

"My but that's powerful theater—dire, but powerful," Millicent remarked after the performance of *Long Day's Journey into Night* ended and we made our way with the crowd out of the theater. "It's at once very Irish and quite New England."

We stepped out into the chill, dank night air. How inhospitable New England was to me, a semisoutherner, even after all the years I had spent here, with its penetrating winds and chills. Yet she genuinely loved it, winter winds and all. So had Reeves.

I asked her to wait in front of the theater and, walking to the corner where my car was parked, drove back and picked her up.

"Such a nice, roomy, powerful car," she observed as we drove away toward her house in Hamden. "You always, even as an undergraduate, had a nice car, I seem to remember. Reeves said American men had to have good cars because there was always the likelihood of having to or wanting to move, either westward or upward or downward or somewhere. European men have always been so settled. If your father is a postman you are likely to become a postman. Everything here on the other hand is so provisional. We currently have a peanut farmer in the White House, for example. When Reeves and I first knew you, years ago, we had an ex-haberdasher as President of the United States. And so on. Provisional. Changeable. Moving." She paused. "*Such* a nice car," she repeated, almost to herself.

"I think," she eventually went on, "that the reason Reeves felt at home in New England is that it is the least provisional part of the country, New England and I suppose the old Confederate states. We are rooted here. We have, more than most Americans, a past. The past is important, you know, powerful, even sometimes dangerous."

I was silent. I agreed with her so completely that I somehow didn't dare speak. A crucial part of my own past was rising up everywhere around me here in New Haven, and she was one of its specters.

All this was obvious. And now, as I waited for a traffic light to change, Reeves Lockhart popped again into my mind. I was beginning to feel haunted by this man five years dead. "You have a tendency, Prieston," I heard him say as he had said about a bad short story of mine thirty years before, "to skirt dangerously close to the weighty self-evident. These reflections of yours on the past just now, for instance."

Reeves Lockhart, with all his charm and kindliness and erudition, had nevertheless been a very tough literary taskmaster. He would brook nothing second-rate. Some kind of insight stirred at the bottom of my mind.

"Tell me, Millicent, why did Reeves publish so little in his later years? There he was, in what they call the prime of

life"—I'm in it now, I suddenly reflected rather uneasily—
"he was world famous, publishers and play producers
clamored for his work, and he released hardly anything."

"He was a perfectionist, you see, and as he got older and
even better read and more cultivated, he . . . well . . ."
She was finding it hard to proceed, and yet, from a sense of
doing some kind of duty, proceed she did. "He did not feel
that so much of his later work—and he did a great deal of
it—was of the highest caliber. He became, I sometimes
thought, overcritical of himself. And then," she finished,
barely audibly, "there were his depressions."

Depressions? Ebullient, feisty Reeves Lockhart de-
pressed? One more wholly unforeseen facet of the man
sprang suddenly into view.

And then I recalled dropping in one day at their Hamden
house, soon after seeing *Utter Beyond* with him. As I
mentioned, I didn't drop in unexpectedly on them, but this
was an exceptional occasion. It was about two in the afternoon, and getting into my car I had noticed some papers
under the passenger's seat and, pulling them out, found
that they were the handwritten manuscript of *Bernice*.
He must have forgotten it there after the reading. It was
clearly the only copy. Scared at my responsibility, I drove
immediately out to Hamden.

The house was a short distance up a rather steep and
winding side road. It was gray fieldstone and clapboard,
lost in trees, mostly evergreens. As I stepped inside, and
Millicent smilingly motioned me toward a long, shadowy,
low-ceilinged living room, I got a feeling of coziness and
comfort. The doorways were rather low and narrow. The
house had been built in the late 1920s with the large royalties from his first success, and must have been quite innovative then. Beige, gray, subdued browns dominated, with

bright dashes of color here and there, and numerous twen-tieth-century paintings on the walls. The living room was, in the final analysis, a conventional room. An artist, at home with his time and his place and his society, lived here. There was individuality; there was no rebellion.

The artist now came . . . well, lurched into the room. He was holding a highball glass and wearing a tweed jacket, open-necked shirt, and baggy trousers. For the first time I saw him without his glasses, which when he wore them somewhat magnified the size of his eyes and made them appear warm, humane. I saw now that they were of average size, light blue, and at the moment bright with stimulation, mental and alcoholic. They also, when listening to some comment of mine, fixed me with a look, almost a glare, of a certain impatience and an almost terrifying intelligence.

"Prieston! *Hello* there!" he called out with even more warmth than usual. "Oh you've got my *play*! Imagine that, Millicent, I *forgot* my play!"

"Well," she replied, "now it's safe and sound and—"

"Forgot it and so maybe it is, when all is said and done, forgettable, a forgettable play. I rather suspect that it is. What do you say, Prieston? Have a drink. Milly, will you—"

She nodded unobtrusively to me, I mouthed "Beer," and she went out.

He semiflung himself onto a couch, motioned me into an armchair, and leaning forward, elbows on knees, hands clasped around his drink, repeated, "I think it may be forgettable, my"—pronouncing "my" with light irony—"*Margery*."

"Uh," I began uncertainly, "you remember you changed that name. Now it's *Bernice*."

The bright eyes fixed me with piercing approval. "So I did, so I did. You see how forgettable it all is."

"I thought it was a very fine, powerful play," I ventured.

"Well, after a certain point in writing . . . " and his expressive face sought to complete the thought: I interpreted the wry grimace to mean, I've written so much, used up so much of my material, I can't tell anymore what's good and what isn't.

"Prieston," he intoned, "Allan Prieston. A slightly special name, ever so slightly eccentric. Like you!" He burst out with that barking laugh, and there was some kind of breakthrough in this candor.

Trying not to feel the least bit taken aback—although I was, in spite of myself—I murmured, "I know most people spell that first name Allen or Alan, but Allan was my mother's family name so that's why it's spelled that way. And 'Prieston,' well I've always thought one of my semiliterate forebears couldn't spell Preston right so he spelled it that way and it stuck."

His gaze roamed over the room. Millicent came in and handed me a cold beer in a long tapering glass. Lockhart contemplated his own glass; it was empty. "Milly, will you . . ."

"Of course," she said cheerfully, crossing and taking it from him. A slight schoolmarmish quality I had felt about her now vanished: tolerant, cheerful, even approving in her demeanor, she went to replenish his drink.

On a small table next to her habitual armchair there was a light-colored highball.

"My parents didn't drink," Reeves suddenly observed. "Father always knew what was best for the world and he decided early that the world shouldn't drink. Spent a good deal of his spare time trying to enforce that. You know, going up to people at, say, a political caucus or some such function and saying, 'See here, Clarence, you don't need that whiskey. It's bad for you. Think of your wife and children.' He was not a terribly popular figure, as you can imagine. I *love* to drink, and I drink a great deal. Not when I'm working, never associated it with work at all. But otherwise, you bet. I *love* to drink. A very large number of American writers are what are called today 'alcoholics.' I detest that terribly clinical word. Let's just call them plain drunks, which is what they are. Do you know whom I'm talking about? No? They're all your idols, all your generation's literary idols, that's who they are. I'm not naming any names. I am *not* an idol of your generation. No no, no protests. You respond to my work, I see that, but I am rather out of fashion with the young these days. Well, not entirely. But I am not the idol that Ernest is, or that Scott is getting to be again."

Millicent, who had returned and stopped to listen, handed him a dark highball. "Ernest," she put in, "what a pity he's become so fatuous. Talking about getting 'into the ring' with Flaubert, and knocking him out! Puerile."

"I," asserted Reeves, "am not a drunk, myself. I like drinking. I am not a drunk. It is one of life's pleasures, and must be controlled as such. But sometimes," he finished in his unconsciously dramatic voice, "sometimes you have to wonder: What am I to do with my despair? What do you do with despair?"

"Why," put in Millicent, "you live through it and it wears away and you press on with all the constructive and creative and joyous things in your life."

Reeves startled me by making a face at her, almost sticking out his tongue at her. Assuredly, this was a different Lockhart. This was a mischievous, a despairing boy. This was why he drank: to release that boy, to ventilate that despair. I sensed that he had never been so glad to see me before. The boy wanted to be seen by a perceptive disciple like me; the despair needed to be shown me, so that I, an aspiring writer, might make of it what I would, just as he had offered me so much else to use as I might.

His alarmingly penetrating blue eyes were on me; from her chair by the fireplace Millicent looked at me benevolently. I saw that in the theatrical sense I was "on." I was here; very well, now I was expected to contribute something.

"I seem to be turning into the Red Reporter on the Yalie Daily," I said. "Last night they sent me to cover some lecture by a Communist from the *New Masses*."

"Well, at least we let the poor Communists come here and speak their piece," observed Reeves, switching to instant soberness, at least for the moment. "We still have a university here. Did he say anything of interest?"

"Oh there was a lot about Wall Street exploiting the working man—"

"Oh my. Nothing deeper than that? Like an old gramophone record out of the 1930s."

"I just put in the paper what he said as accurately as I could," I went on, "and he came around this morning to get some copies of it. He seemed surprised I hadn't distorted it."

Reeves drew a contemplative breath. "Journalism is fine for a while," he said abstractly.

"You are saying?" I prompted.

"Hm? Oh. Journalism, it's fine for a writer—I'm talking about someone who wants to write literature—for a while. Precision. Accuracy. Mingling in the rough and tumble— 'rough and tumble'; what an interesting *cliché*—how many Roughs and Tumbles do I know? Well, in any case, don't tarry in journalism very long. If you need to support yourself while you're doing serious writing, then teach mathematics!" I shuddered at the mere possibility, which did not, in my case, exist. "Drive a taxi. Don't do anything that uses the word-manipulating side of your brain. There are so many tricks to writing. . . ."

"Now Reeves," said Millicent in a gently reproving tone, "you don't mean tricks. Please don't try to upset Allan here."

"Upset, upset! Of *course* I'll not upset him. You under-estimate his stability, my dear Milly." This conversation was beginning to develop as though I were not here. "His egotism stabilizes him. He's got a nice sinewy artistic self-confidence, deep down in there. In the end," he sighed acceptingly, "he may reject me, or rather, my work."

I stared at him. Never. And today, after thirty years of being able to consider and reconsider his work, the answer is still the same.

Coming back to our rooms in Pierson a little later, I found Greg waiting for me. "I see you've been with the Great Writer," he remarked.

I glanced at him.

"I can always tell," he went on. "You have a stupid grin on your face after an audience with him."

"I do not have a stupid grin on my face."

"You light up," he pressed on, "with an inner glow."

"Oh, balls."

He eyed me. "You've had a couple of drinks," he then said flatly. "In the middle of the afternoon. That's how I know."

I flopped down in a shabby armchair. "Well, you're

right. You know what? He was drunk." I could have bitten my tongue off the moment I revealed this news to Greg. I was simply handing him more ammunition to deride and ridicule my apprenticeship to Reeves Lockhart. At the time I thought he really believed my behavior somehow odd and ridiculous. At the time, it never occurred to me that his denigrating it might contain an element of jealousy.

"Drunk, was he? I'm not surprised," he observed, continuing to leaf through an issue of *Life*. "Decadent artist. Drunk in the afternoon." He tossed the magazine aside. "How about a game of squash?"

I wished I'd stopped at two instead of going on to three glasses of beer at Lockhart's. Squash? "Okay," I said offhandedly. He would beat me, of course; he always beat me. I was good at squash; he was very good.

The court was off one of the subterranean passages of Pierson. A white box with operating-room illumination, it provided a setting for more intense exercise in a shorter period of time than any I knew. We banged and slammed and stamped around our court for an hour, and then, with burnt-out muscles and running with sweat, we stumbled back to our rooms. "Don't dress in your usual rags," he said as I was drying off after a shower, "today's my birthday. I'm treating you to dinner."

"Your birthday? I didn't know that. How old *are* you now, Gramps?"

"Eighty. And ornerier than hell."

"You're telling me? Gee, I ought to have a present for you. I know. I'll get Mr. Lockhart to autograph one of his books for you."

He was turned away from me, and there was a pause; there was no derisive comeback from him. "Okay," he said shortly. Fancy that: he *wanted* an autographed copy of one of the novels.

I put on some gray flannel slacks, a brown tweed jacket, a blue broadcloth button-down shirt, a red-and-green striped tie—the number-one uniform, in other words—and with Greg, similarly dressed, we walked to his car. "I thought we'd go to that country inn," he said.

This was a restaurant in a fine old Colonial inn off the Merritt Parkway which we had come on by chance once before. It was expensive. Gregory was making this an occasion. "Well, if we're going there I ought to be paying for it, since this is *your* birthday," I remarked as we headed in the car out of New Haven.

"You haven't got any money."

"That's not true. I haven't got *a lot* of money, but I struggle through."

"Struggling through," he remarked rather grimly, "isn't good enough. You don't really live life if you have to struggle through it."

"Yes, well, that's the way most writers have to live, and that's probably the way I'll have to live . . . if I do . . . you know . . . turn out really to be a writer. Reeves Lockhart is one of the exceptions—best-selling novels, hit plays . . ."

"What does he have to say about your prospects, I mean financial prospects?" For the first time Greg was mentioning Lockhart with respect.

I looked across at his face in profile, the firm-featured face that looked as though a punch would not unduly disconcert it. I looked to sense his attitude, saw nothing revealing, and then said, "I don't know why you think Mr. Lockhart would discuss my future finances with me, but in fact he has. Well, not discussed directly. He hardly ever discusses anything directly. But once I said to him that I wondered, much as I wanted to be a writer, whether I could make a living at it, and he leaned back in his chair and said, 'One of my one-act plays, it's called *The Overnight Train to Sandusky*, has been bringing in to me ten thousand dollars a year for the last twenty years.' That's all he said. Then he changed the subject. But I knew he was giving me a piece of advice. He believes I could make an okay living being a writer."

"Well," murmured Greg, "if *he* thinks so. . . ."

Greg certainly was being uncharacteristically agreeable tonight about Reeves Lockhart. Maybe he should be the Birthday Boy more often.

As matters have turned out in the three decades since then, Reeves Lockhart was right.

The country inn, called the Red Rooster, was uncrowded on this weekday evening. We were given a table in the dim, heavy-beamed bar next to a crackling fire in a big stone fireplace. Copper pots and pans hung here and there on the unfinished wooden walls. The atmosphere was dark and rustic and Colonial and simple and expensive. A waitress in Colonial dress took the cocktail order Greg gave her: two very dry vodka martinis with lemon twists. This evening, as we said in the South, he was not going to be just whistling "Dixie."

We started talking about his parents. Alexei's latest manuscript, a fictional treatment of Peter the Great's visit to Holland, had just been turned down by his previous publisher and the prospects for it were not good. Naida had just declined an offer from the same publisher to write, with the help of a ghost writer, a description of the family life of

Nicholas and Alexandra, with special emphasis on the youngest daughter, Anastasia, to whom Naida had been especially close. She had, once again, declined to publish anything about the Romanoff family. "They just want the sensational stuff," complained Gregory. "They want the dirty linen. Mother will never show them so much as a napkin. The thing is, were they offering a deal, give us Anastasia and we'll publish Peter the Great in Holland?" His high-cheekboned face in the candlelight frowned in puzzled anger at me. "Well. You're a writer. Were they offering her a deal, a bribe?"

I frowned back at him. "How do I know? I've never even met a publisher. It certainly is quite a coincidence, though, they make the offer, she turns it down, and then the book about Peter, which they'd been considering, gets turned down. Was that the progression?"

"Yes," he answered grimly.

"It does look suspicious."

"Writing," he said disgustedly. "Now do you see why I've got no time for it and all you writers and all that? You're as bad as the Bolsheviks."

"Oh well not all *that* bad!"

"Well." He looked around, signaled the waitress. "Another round, please."

Into his second martini, Greg began to mellow. "You know," he conceded, "you're not so bad to share rooms with. I mean, you know who's boss and you know how to stay out of the way at the right time—"

"You are older and you were in the war, really in it I mean, you were 'in combat' as they say, and yes, being just too young for all that I guess I do defer to you a little." I had never been so candid with him; two martinis had a power

69

all their own. "You seem to like me, and that's important and—"

"You're all right," he cut in nonchalantly.

"—we get along very well and besides, you're basically lonely."

"I'm *what*!"

"You're basically lonely, or maybe I should say, you're basically a loner. Everybody likes you. You're popular, that stupid student concept. *You're popular*," I repeated in my Zasu Pitts voice. Then, returning to a normal tone, "But, even though everybody likes you and invites you to things and the clubs all want you as a member and everything, nobody has been close to you and now I sort of am and"—my God I was getting sloppily sentimental; martinis!—"and well," raising my glass, "happy birthday, Princie!"

He burst out in a happy laugh, and I knew I had been right: he had been lonely, and I had alleviated that.

We devoured the best roast beef I ever remembered, there by the fireplace, with a bottle of Pommard to go with it, and a rich French dessert followed by cognac. Over the cognac Gregory reached a stage where he was actually going to confide in me. I confided in him and he seemed to appreciate it; for him to deign to confide in me was a concession indeed.

"What do you . . . um . . ." he began casually, "think of Merry?"

I sensed that my opinion of her had a certain importance to him, and would have some influence on his own. "I think she's a terrific girl, she's very attractive without being, you know, exactly a knockout. She's interesting looking. I haven't spent a whole lot of time with her but I think she wouldn't get boring. There's something original about her. She thinks for herself, I guess is what I mean. She's not going to bore you."

"She never bores me," he murmured.

"More to the point," I said, "what do *you* think of her?" After a silence he said, "I think I'm falling for her."

"Good."

He eyed me. "Why 'good'?"

"I think it would be good for you to fall for someone, that's all. I can't say why. Yes I can, I think. It's the same thing. The loner falls in love. That's good for the loner."

"If," he put in dryly, "she doesn't dump me."

"She's not going to dump you. I've watched her with you. She's already fallen for you."

"You think so?" he asked guardedly.

"I do. Well listen, you're not so bad. Why shouldn't she?"

Another silence, then: "Why should she?" he asked a little grimly.

You don't recognize your good qualities, I said to myself in surprise. You don't always have a very high opinion of yourself. You find it a little hard to believe that this smart, amusing, good-looking, rich, desirable girl could be falling in love with you. Why should she? you're asking yourself.

"One more cognac," he said.

"Okay, Princie, it's your treat. Tell you what. I pay for the cognacs. I have to do that at least."

"You're on."

Into our third cognac, I, who drank the odd glass of wine or beer and let it go at that, was hazily drunk. Gregory was controlled and mellow. "I'm really falling for her," he said. "Partly it's because she's from California." I waited, not taking the trouble to be puzzled by this puzzling statement.

"What's that got to do with it?" he asked rhetorically. "It makes her seem more American than these East Coast girls. These girls around here are a little Europeanized, some of them are, and I don't like any *Europeans*. Europe destroyed us. Europe killed my grandfather. My folks are messed up—no, don't deny it—they're messed up and it was because of what happened to them in Europe. I'm an American and I'm going to marry an American, a real American, and that's that. Also, I'm falling for her. I'm just, well, falling for her. It's that simple."

And oh, so complicated, I thought with drunken sagacity.

The birthday was, it seemed, a watershed, to a certain extent in Greg's relation to me, and very much in his relation to Merryfield Carr.

As I said, he had a cautious, guarded, secretive, loner side. He had let down these defenses over our highly lubricated dinner at the Red Rooster and exhibited the reality of a bond, a link, even a certain dependence on me, and he had faced up to and voiced his desire for and fears about Merry.

Now he was prepared to act. Christmas vacation was approaching and plans had to be made. When I came out of my bedroom the next morning Greg was on the telephone in the living room, talking to her at Vassar.

"The thing is, if we want to stay at Chet's Merry-Go-Round, we've got to make reservations right now and hope it's not too late. It's the best place to stay and there are nice people there and no ski bunnies—"

He listened to some comment of hers and then said a trifle awkwardly, "It's not all that expensive and I'll talk Allan into sharing my room—"

"You will, will you?" I mouthed at him and he nodded

dictatorially back at me, "And we'll all have a good time. Are we set, then? I'll call now and make the reservations. In the meantime, don't flunk out." Pause. "Straight A's?" Was there a certain hollowness in his: "Well, that's impressive." Then, "I miss you." Pause. "I'm really looking forward to this." Pause; a murmured "me too," and he hung up.

"I can't go skiing at Christmas," I protested. "My family'd kill me. I have to be at home for Christmas."

Greg was heading out the door to his first class, which he was not cutting as often these days. "You'll have Christmas with your folks. You'll join us in Manchester, Vermont, on December twenty-seventh. Got that?"

"Uh—well—I—three's a crowd."

"Let me worry about that."

As the door slammed after him and I headed for the bathroom I thought, He only really wants me there to split the cost of the room.

And so Greg had invited me to go along and reduce his expenses. I considered. After all, Chet's Merry-Go-Round at Big Bromley near Manchester was a kind of private club, and I had always been curious about it. It would be interesting to stay there. I liked Merry. Greg was, I supposed, my best friend. I loved to ski. There would be lots of young people around. Why not?

That afternoon I had been invited to tea in the Master's House in Pierson. The side entrance to this house, a capacious red-brick Georgian town house built into the college structure, was adjacent to our rooms in the Slave Quarters. These half-dozen suites were called that because they were in a tiny cul-de-sac of white-painted stone with black iron grillwork reminiscent, I guessed, of New Orleans.

Yale University had many frills. Now, in the years following World War II, the frills which could be dispensed with, such as a maid coming in daily to make our beds, such as waitresses in the dining halls, had been. All that and much more were gone with the winds of war.

But certain frills were as solid as rock and not so easily abolished. The Slave Quarters, with its flagstone courtyard and fireplaces in the students' living rooms, was one of them. The solid Gothic flamboyance of Branford and Saybrook colleges across York Street, their curlicues and gargoyles and casements and fitted stonework, not to mention the skyward-thrusting Harkness Tower which they incorporated, showed a medieval gift for rising above mere money lost to most of us. Wolf's Head, a senior society wedged between Pierson and York Street, to which Gregory belonged, behind its forbidding fieldstone wall, looked like the costly suburban villa of some frightened Wall Street financier.

The construction at Yale during the first half of the twentieth century had been done with extravagance, and with a sense that these buildings must last practically forever. They were re-creating Oxford in America, so that what they erected must be virtually timeless, consciously monastic, and designed for the education of gentlemen, scions of wealth destined to be leaders. The fact that Yale in 1950, not to mention 1980, by no means conformed in its entirety to these projections could not change mortar and stone and brick. The architects in those days had gone to their drawing boards with visions of cathedrals and monasteries and vast English country houses dancing in their heads, and, judging from the results, they had also been presented with a blank check. They proceeded to erect soaring naves and towers, rambling moated castles, rangy brick country palaces exhibiting, in general, a fine plutocratic disregard for the workday city that surrounded them. Yale stared out from its walls and moats, an enclave of privilege and power, past the routine city of New Haven, toward destiny.

None of this occurred to me when I was a student there. At that time I simply took Yale for granted; it seemed to be what a university was supposed to be. If I had any specific sense of it at all, I assumed that it was a very well equipped laboratory where I was supposed to work out certain experiments, all involving myself, and all ultimately intended to answer the overwhelming questions of youth: who am I, what am I going to become?

In the grip of these two fundamental imperatives, so much so that I was not even aware of them, I put on the number-one uniform again and walked the short distance from the Slave Quarters to the side entrance of the Master's House.

Inside, in the long living room with pale walls, the master and his wife milled about with other faculty people, a sprinkling of students like myself, and, holding her own in the middle of the room with two professors of anthropology, Millicent Moncrieff. Presently she separated herself from them with her usual courtesy and came over to me.

"My, wasn't Reeves in high spirits yesterday!" she began, eyes brightly turned up to me.

"Yes, yes he was."

"And alternately down in the dumps. They go together you know, euphoria and despair, in many people."

"Do they? No, I guess I never knew that. And uh I, well, I always thought Mr. Lockhart was so—I guess you would say creative, and also optimistic and constructive and positive and, I don't know, *happy*."

She balanced the back edge of her high-heeled left pump

speculatively on the floor and surveyed the room. "Well, he *is*," she asserted, "he is. But no one with Reeves' brilliance and perceptiveness and sensitivity can be forever *gleeful*. It just isn't in the human condition. There are moments of . . . well . . . despair. But he fights against them, he fights against them! And when they overcome him, as they have been doing these last few days, it ends with his taking a long nap"—she eyed me very briefly to see if I would accept this word, causing me to find its more down-to-earth substitute: passes out—"and when he awakes from this nap he looks quite refreshed and he says, 'Time to go, time to go!' and I pack his bag, and he's off. Within the hour!"

"So he—he's left, has he?"

"Yes, around ten this morning."

"Where to?"

"West."

"West?"

"Yes. West. He takes that splendid Lincoln convertible the Hollywood producer gave him for stepping in and saving that script a couple of years ago, and he's *on the road*. I pretend I haven't the least idea where he's going, he likes it that way, he just says, 'I'm going out west, Milly!' and he's off! But I've noticed in his conversation a reference or two to Banff, to Lake Louise, and I'm rather sure that's where he'll end up, and the people there, the people in that beautiful hotel I've seen pictures of, overlooking the lake, one day they'll discover in their midst that marvelous man you know and described just now—positive, creative, *happy* Reeves Lockhart!"

Whew, I breathed to myself.

Do I *really* want to be a writer?

There was a pause in my thoughts, and then came the answer: yes.

6

There was an innocence on the surface of these collegiate weekends and holidays. The memories of Chet's Merry-Go-Round Lodge at Big Bromley, Christmastime 1950, radiate a healthy exuberance and a casual ease in friendship and romance that seem now a postcard, Grandma Moses rendering of youth and snow and New England.

This was the surface impression of what was happening there. Our circumstances, our training, our expectations, even perhaps in the last analysis what we hoped for did not include raw sexual completion, not here, not quite yet. Greg was actually a rather hard-bitten sensualist on one side of his character; Merryfield was a young woman ready for love; I myself was only too open for a sensual adventure. But a strain of idealism, even I think in Greg, held most of this group of young college people back from forcing the issue to completion. Were we wrong, inhibited, frustrated, acting unnaturally? I think now that the answer to all four of these propositions is probably yes, and yet I am left with the glowing reflection of a happy—for everyone else—

sojourn in the white-blanketed Christmasy mountains of Vermont, of radiant health and uncomplicated fun for them, with the deeper issues of life and the future put to one side. They were embracing nature in her external, active, and perhaps superficial side; her depths, her mysteries, her ecstasies, her anguishes, they found ways to evade and postpone.

Greg and Merry were maneuvering toward an unforced and supple intimacy where they seemed to anticipate each other's words, even moods. I noticed them sunk in a deep couch before the great fireplace one late afternoon after an exhilarating, exhausting day on the mountain, cradling drinks—I remember that they were bourbon old-fashioneds. The firelight brought out a reddish-blond sheen in her brown hair and made his windbeaten face glow with health. Their heads were close together as they casually, intimately passed occasional remarks back and forth. Greg and Merry were happy, they were tired and content and at peace. They were made for each other, it seemed; they appeared to be finding their completion in each other, and one of these months, or next year, or whenever, I might find myself best man at a wedding. Thank God he had chosen someone whom I was as fond of as I was of Merry. My close friendship with him could continue, if their romance was indeed headed for marriage, and that was important to me and it was conceivably even more important, for reasons I sensed rather than knew, to him.

I by no means spent the holiday watching this proliferation in their lives. The mountain was there with its challenge; the wind-whipped snow everywhere dominated it and us and the lodge and the paths and the roofs and the moonlight.

Actually, I noticed Greg and Merry only peripherally: I had met a friend of Merry's from Vassar named Noelle. She was French, with long blond hair, green eyes, precocious sophistication, and a devastating ability, at age twenty or so, to ensnare, subjugate, humiliate, and reject, all in the course of one winter's holiday. Never mind the rest of her illustrious name; I'm sure she is still plowing her destructive way through the highest social levels of Paris, Deauville, and St.-Jean-de-Luz.

Noelle had been evacuated as a child from France to the United States in 1940 as the German army crashed toward Paris, and had remained in this country to complete her education. She was all too bright, only too witty, devastatingly candid, trilingual, internationally connected on the highest level, illegally seductive when she wanted to be, and I now think, quite mad. I believe the word for her particular type of incomprehensible destructiveness is "psychopathic." Every five years or so I encounter someone through whom she has cut her swath. All agree. There was a popular novel and movie about this time called *Leave Her to Heaven*. That was Noelle.

A number of years after this holiday, I ran into her in St.-Jean-de-Luz, in the lobby of a small hotel. She remained amazingly magnetic to look at, with one flaw now visible: her upper lip appeared set in a fixed curl; one day it would be a snarl. At a loss, stunned to see her, I blurted, "Noelle!" She stared at me coldly. "You remember, Noelle, Big Bromley, 1950, Christmastime."

"Mm . . . yes, mm . . . vaguely," she finished with distaste, and floated out. Had she delayed only a little longer, I might have strangled her.

Noelle preempted my thoughts and actions during this

vacation in Vermont; since, thanks to a beneficent God, she then disappeared from my life, what was said and done does not matter now.

The relationship of Greg and Merry mattered. That they both felt this was obvious. From treating me with casual friendliness Merry now began to cultivate me seriously. I was important to her now: I was the best friend. I must like her. I already liked her but she was apparently not sure of this.

The three of us were having hot chocolate in the hut at the top of the mountain. Greg and I were wearing the correct André black ski pants and similar blue parkas, knitted caps, and goggles. Merry was laid away in a form-fitting dark blue ensemble.

"It's a good thing you know something about skiing," said Greg to her. "Otherwise in that getup I'd think you came to have your picture taken by *Vogue*, not go out on the slopes."

She just smiled at him. "Listen," she then said, "I'm going down this time with Allan here. You can show off by yourself."

"He's not as good as I am," Greg warned with a grin.

"Of course not," she said with an exaggerated shrug. "Who *is*? Ready, Allan?"

So she and I trooped out, put on our skis, adjusted goggles, and with Merry in the lead, slid swiftly down the wood-lined, twisting trail, over hard-packed snow, on a day of clear sunshine, washed blue sky, and a dry, razory, breathtakingly cold wind. Past the evergreens and the white birches Merry plummeted with confident grace. I had accepted Greg as a better skier than I was, but must I accept the same superiority in her? It was touch and go as almost in tandem we schussed and checked, took short leaps and long curving runs downward.

At the bottom she sailed right into the liftline and, although the area was full of skiers for the holidays, the lines had been shortened by the remarkable coldness of this particular day. She and I were soon being carried upward on a double chair.

"It really is brisk out today, isn't it?" she remarked cheerfully in her slightly musical, somehow breakable-sounding voice.

"I'll say."

"I don't really mind it."

"I do."

"Gregory doesn't, not at all. But of course he's got those Siberian genes. I understand Russia is really the world's coldest country."

I tried to pull my knitted cap further down over my ears. "I wouldn't doubt it," I agreed. "He does seem impervious to certain things."

"Maybe that's what makes him so alive in most other ways. Some things don't seem to touch him. For instance . . . well . . . just," she laughed offhandedly, "what he's going to do after college. . . ."

"I think he's considering business in general, some phase of business as a career," I put in, the hope being father to the truth. The truth was I'd never heard him discuss the subject at any length. Of course that might be just his secretive side. "He wants to ski and to be!" I heard myself add irresponsibly. What did I mean by *that*!

"To ski and to be," she repeated gaily. "It rhymes."

"He's very competent in so many ways," I then hastened to add responsibly, and to mean it. He was competent, whether in repairing a roof or planning a trip or making quite sure he passed all his courses at Yale satisfactorily and without unnecessary work. I felt sure he would bring the same competence to his future, whatever that future might be.

"Is he?" she asked with unsuccessfully masked eagerness. "You really know him so much better than I do. You live with him. I date—ugh, 'date him,' what a tacky phrase. What I mean is, you know what he's like first thing in the morning, and not just a few mornings at a special place like Chet's Merry-Go-Round, but every morning, day in and day out, month in and month out. You know." There was a pause.

"Greg in the morning?" I said with a slight nervous chuckle, picking up my cue. "He's in a pretty good mood usually, if that's what you mean. But there's all the difference in the world between sharing some rooms at Yale and being married. I mean," I hurried on, "he'll be in a *better* mood, then, if you—"

She was trying to turn and stare at me, or at least at my goggles. "Who said anything about 'married'?" she demanded with spirit, but also with an undercurrent of amusement. "Did I mention marriage?"

It was too cold for coyness, and anyhow she wasn't really the type for it. "That's what you're talking about really, isn't it?"

"That's what *you're* talking about," she retorted a shade nervously.

"Oh come on, Merry."

She was silent, and then said, "It's too cold to beat around the bush, I guess, isn't it. Yes, we are what I guess you would call 'informally' engaged. He's given me a marvelous old Russian ring, it weighs about a ton, I can't wear it on my hand but I'm going to get a really fine gold chain and wear it around my neck. Out of sight, for now."

We soon arrived at the top, where Greg, who had shot down a steeper slope and returned ahead of us to the top, was waiting for her.

He came out of the hut on seeing us and began to put his skis back on. "So," I called out a shade derisively at him, "you gave Merry a ring that weighs a ton."

He had not yet lowered his goggles over his eyes, and he gave me a glare that in earlier generations must have preceded the banishment of offending Russians to the salt mines.

I was unmoved. "She can't wear it on her hand. Too uh bulky."

"You rat!" she snapped half angrily at me.

"Can't have any secrets from roommates," I called out airily. "I'm putting the news in the Yalie Daily and the Vassar Voice or whatever it is and in all the gossip columns and all the places news is printed everywhere. Bye!" And I hurriedly slid off before Greg could get to me.

It was a lot of fun. Even baleful Noelle had not succeeded in completely crushing all the fun for me that Christmastime. I was twenty-one years old, a junior in good standing at Yale, Reeves Lockhart had told me I had talent, and implied that I could even make a good living as a writer. So all was well for me, and now all was also well for my best friend, Greg Trouvenskoy, with his devoted, charming and rich fiancée, Merryfield.

7

Toward the end of bleakest January, a ball in honor of Merry was to be held in her uncle's house in Philadelphia. Greg was, of course, to escort her, and I too was invited.

We left New Haven Friday noon aboard a dirty old New York, New Haven, and Hartford day coach and rattled down to New York City.

There, however, the tone of the trip was transformed. Merry and her father's first wife's sister, who now called herself Connie Smith, met us at Grand Central Station, and we were within minutes installed in a long, midnight blue limousine. Connie and Merry sat on the wide, dove gray backseat, Greg and I were on the jump seats, and in front, behind glass, a chauffeur in dark blue uniform maneuvered the superb car toward the Holland Tunnel and the New Jersey Turnpike.

"It's dear of Bobby to include me," said Connie in a confident, throaty voice. "After all, I'm not really part of the Carr family at all, and never really was." She was a tall, lean, blond woman, enveloped in mink.

84

"Bobby" was Merry's uncle, R. (for Robert) Curtiss Carr, who ran the family's East Coast shipping operations.

"I insisted because"—began Merry, then broke off, giggled ruefully, and plunged—"because you and I are such friends in spite of not being really related, and, anyway he knows you and likes you. Everybody does."

"Well, it's dear of him. Now that I'm divorced again I grasp at every opportunity to get out and circulate. And this party is special, your party. I would have hated to miss this."

Chauffeured limousines seem to rise above or slither through traffic in ways unavailable to other vehicles, and in a surprisingly short time the car was speeding along on the elevated turnpike above and seemingly impervious to the industrial clutter of northern New Jersey.

"Are you two boys"—Connie began—"how dumb, you two men seeing Bobby's house for the first time?"

We said that we were.

"It's quite something. Are you interested in art?"

"Yes," I answered.

"Mm," hummed Greg.

"Allan's going to be a writer," put in Merry.

"Good," said Connie. "And you—ah—Greg?"

"God knows," he replied cheerfully. "I'll be anything I can turn out to be any good at."

"A *lot* of things," said Merry firmly. "He's meeting Daddy at this party for the first time. I've got a feeling Gregory could be very good in the shipping business."

"I don't know," said Greg guardedly. "Maybe. It certainly interests me."

"It's fascinating," said Connie. "And it's just now coming into its biggest burst of prosperity."

"Really?" said Greg, looking at her.

"Yes. Enormous expansion is going on. And the Carrs, as I understand it, are not going to let all those Greeks monopolize it, not by a long shot."

We were out of urban New Jersey now, and the car shot with smooth quietness along the dry turnpike southward between snow-covered fields in the sunshine.

There was a hamper of food on the seat next to the chauffeur, and we now procured it: cold chicken, ham, French bread, white wine. We had a picnic there in the capacious backseat, to the accompaniment of the music of Tchaikovsky, which Merry found on the radio. "Russian!" she exclaimed. "Beautiful!" She took a gulp of white wine. "I'm happy!"

Greg reached back and squeezed her hand. "Me too," he murmured.

"I hope you like Daddy," she said a little worriedly.

Greg gave his forthright laugh. "I hope Daddy likes *me!*"

"Oh he will," she said hurriedly, "I know he will."

"Jeff's what I think is called a man's man," observed Connie. She looked at Greg with frank appraisal. "I believe he'll like you."

We met Merry's father at cocktail time in the front living room of Mr. R. Curtiss Carr's Philadelphia town house.

The house was perhaps the most notable private residence remaining in central Philadelphia. Set on a corner of dignified Washington Square, it was of dark red brick, four stories high, built around 1870 and intended to last.

The high-ceilinged living room was furnished in Louis XVI with light blue walls, all of it overwhelmed and obliterated by three very large paintings in ornate gilt frames on one wall: a rosy-fleshed Renoir bathers scene;

dancers in Toulouse-Lautrec's Moulin Rouge; and an extra-ordinary van Gogh landscape of mysterious gray-green rain hurtling slantingly down upon a Provençal countryside.

A dozen Carrs and Carr connections made themselves comfortable in this remarkable room. Merry's father, Jeffrey Carr, was a big, broad-shouldered, white-haired man, older than I had expected; but then she was the daughter of his second marriage. In a carefully tailored, very dark blue suit he surprised me by being quiet-spoken, almost self-effacing, so successful that he wanted to talk about us, not himself.

"Did either one of you boys serve in the navy?" he asked as we stood holding cocktails beneath Lautrec's evocation of the Moulin Rouge.

"Nooo," we answered regretfully more or less in unison.

"I wish I had," Greg said. "The travel aspect of it, for one thing. Seeing the world. I'd have liked that."

"Yes, well, the shipping business is like that too. You're Russian, Merryfield tells me. That's interesting. I did some negotiating in Leningrad in the thirties. Beautiful city—canals and rivers everywhere. You're a Romanoff, aren't you?"

"On my mother's side."

"What amazing palaces your people lived in. Makes Bobby's place here look like a rabbit hutch. And you, son," turning to me, "Merry says you're going to be a writer."

That Jeffrey Carr would have taken the trouble to learn about his daughter's serious boyfriend was understandable; that he would extend this interest to include me suggested just why he was so successful. "That's right, sir," I answered. "I hope to. I don't know though. It's a very difficult profession."

"They all are," he observed, sipping his very weak

Scotch. "But that's one where you can work for yourself, isn't it? Those are the best professions. They're the only ones, by the way, where you can grow rich." Greg's slightly Asiatic eyes were fixed with special intensity on Jeffrey Carr, who was looking at me.

Then we all went into dinner and, fairly early, to bed, so as to be sufficiently ready for tomorrow night's ball.

Bobby Carr's wife, Hope, came from an old Philadelphia family, and both the house and the paintings had been inherited by her. It was for that reason that he chose Philadelphia as his East Coast headquarters. "It's a containable city," he said, sitting next to me at breakfast, served English style from a sideboard. We happened to be alone at the long mahogany table, looking out through a multipaned glass wall to an inner courtyard of statues and urns. Behind us, over the fireplace, a Matisse still life brightened the wall.

Bobby Carr was a younger, leaner version of his brother Jeffrey. He too seemed more interested in a totally unimportant twenty-one-year-old Yalie than in himself.

"Have you been to Philadelphia before?" he asked.

"Years ago, with my family. I remember the Liberty Bell, and that's about all. I want to see as much more as I can this time."

"I doubt that you will. Hope has got the schedule of events organized like the Olympics, that is, if the Olympics were all social and no sports."

She came into the ivory-colored room now, a composed woman in a rose-colored dress. "How did you sleep up there at the top of the house?" she asked me.

"Really well."

"Good. Philadelphians don't normally stay at parties until dawn, but you never know. So, with a good night's sleep, you're prepared."

Merry came in, her father soon after; Greg, who shared the Edwardian bedroom at the top of the house with me, came down, and the day of the Olympic social engagements began on schedule.

The climax, a dinner dance for two hundred, was to begin at seven. The Carr house abutted another four-story town house, this one a light gray stone, and although it was not evident from the outside, they were now one residence. When the gray stone house had become available two years earlier, the Carrs bought it, kicked through, figuratively speaking, the intervening wall, gutted the first two floors, and created a ballroom, with Corinthian pillars, marble floors, wide chandeliers.

Hope Carr showed it to me just before the guests began to arrive. "It's the kind of thing an Irish millionaire would have done in 1910," she said with a certain rueful cheerfulness, "but we wanted it, and now we have it." This party was to introduce their niece Merryfield to Philadelphia, and also to inaugurate the ballroom.

There were about thirty circular tables filling the room now, laid with pink tablecloths, crystal, silver candlesticks, bursts of flowers everywhere so that over the glittering room hung a gardenialike fragrance. Waiters darted here and there, making final preparations.

Philadelphians, it seemed, were prompt: they had been invited for seven, and by 7:20 they all seemed to have arrived, circulating festively beneath Renoir and Lautrec and van Gogh, or in the larger living room beneath David and Sisley. In the subdued golden lighting amid the rich colors of the rooms, the black tuxedos of the men, the silver-blue and pink and white and gold of the women's gowns, the party sprang alive and yet remained easy; these lively people knew each other so well, often from childhood; the Carrs were part of a very old society here and tonight was a kind of extended family gathering, the West Coast niece being welcomed to the East.

Merry, wearing a shining blue dress and a golden necklace, looked prettier and a good deal more sophisticated than I had ever seen her. Gregory, square-shouldered and the picture of athletic health beside her, had never looked more in his element. I heard his spontaneous laugh ring out now and then.

The evening flowed gracefully on, through a rich dinner in the ballroom where everyone seemed to have something funny and cheerful and agreeable to say to everyone else, where toasts were drunk to the lovely niece and the other guests from elsewhere—this was preeminently a Philadelphia night—back to the living rooms briefly while the tables were whisked away and a fourteen-piece dance band whisked into place, then again to the ballroom, the great chandeliers dimmed to a subdued, glamorous light, the band rousing the room with the kind of upbeat, we're-all-rich-here dance music appropriate to such parties, Merry gliding by in Greg's arms; her mother, delayed in her flight east until almost party time, dancing with me, seemed to be the kind of pretty, outgoing matron Merry would become; Philadelphia society, good-looking and dressy, was having itself a ball all around us.

"You dance better than your roommate Gregory," Mrs. Carr said with a laugh in my ear, "and my daughter loves to dance."

"He'll learn," I replied, meaning it: if Merry wanted him to be a good dancer, he would be a good dancer.

"He seems such a fine young man," she went on. "I'll bet he's popular at Yale."

"Oh I'll say he is."

"There are a lot of sides to Merry," she added candidly and unexpectedly. "I wonder if he can handle her."

I didn't know what to reply to that, but I was obscurely elated by the assumption that Merry would be his in the future to handle.

Later I was dancing with Merry herself. She was giggly and a little tipsy and radiating joy. "I'm so glad you're here with us!" she cried excitedly.

"Wouldn't have missed it for anything."

"Do you like my dress?"

"Beautiful."

"It's Dior. My first. There's a sort of built-in corset. That's why I have Scarlett O'Hara's eighteen-inch waist tonight, and why the dress flares below."

"It's terrific."

"Doesn't Gregory look handsome! My family adore him already. I knew they would."

"He looks great, and he's having a terrific time. I can see that."

"We're *meant* for each other," she said with mock rapture.

You sure are, I reflected inwardly. At least I think you are, I hope you are.

The champagne and the music and the January night flowed on, frigid outside, all warmth and radiance within, and then finally the Carrs and their houseguests trailed upward in the old house to bed, until downstairs only the watchman with his gun sat vigil as usual over the masterpieces of art; another gala English breakfast late the next morning in the beautiful dining room until the midnight blue limousine with the perfect chauffeur came to hurtle us almost noiselessly north again along the New Jersey Turnpike to New York and Grand Central, and finally Greg and

I, tired and somewhat deflated in a motheaten day coach rattling back to New Haven.

"Well, what did you think of it all?" I emerged from a kind of apathy to ask him somewhere around Bridgeport.

Gregory was looking fixedly in front of him, face set. "Solid as rocks, her family. Solid as rocks."

No reasonable person wants to spend the month of February in New Haven, Connecticut. Whatever charm the first flurries of snow bring with them sometime in November, whatever Dickensian wintry beauty a blanket of whiteness lends to the college courtyards in December, however endurable the gusts and thaws of January may be, in February there is a universal revulsion against everything that a New England winter brings with it. Vermont can be frigid but snug then. Massachusetts can possess a durable Colonial traditionalism. But Connecticut, especially that strip of it alongside Long Island Sound, is simply a wasteland, a drudge, the glum tag ends of a too-long season, the dregs of Old Man Winter, and a dirty old man he is, by the time February grinds its dreary way into the precincts of fed-up Yale University, in New Haven.

Even Reeves Lockhart and Millicent Moncrieff had prudently removed themselves to a beautiful old Spanish-style monastery converted into a luxury hotel in San Juan, Puerto Rico. Only we imprisoned students and our resentful faculty endured behind the moats and walls of the university.

"This place," observed Greg bluntly as we sloshed back along the walk toward our rooms after lunch, "ought to be given back to the Indians. Got to get out of here. Merry's studying for midterm exams; she can't get away anywhere.

You and I had better go up to Edgewater for a long weekend at least. It can't be *this* bad up there."

"Merry can anyway get out for a meal or two."

"Yeah. And the folks are giving a party for the local gentry, and the local zanies. Their annual bring-your-own-bottle-bash. It's also a get-over-the-hump-of-winter-by-getting-good-and-drunk-party. An annual affair," he added, glancing significantly at me with mock seriousness.

"Well, I wouldn't want to miss this annual affair for anything."

Preparations for the party were not elaborate. It was to be a group effort on every level. Naida prepared enough of her famous meat loaf to feed all thirty people expected, and others were to bring the *fondue*, the pumpernickel bread, the lasagna, the cold ham, the mulled wine, the fresh fruit, the pumpkin and mince pies, the candy and nuts, and a great deal of different kinds of liquor.

The Trouvenskoy cache of this last was at the bottom of their freezer in the pantry, concealed beneath boxes of string beans. Small glasses were also chilling there. "We've already put some bitters in the vodka," Greg explained. "Gives it a little extra bite. And it's got to be as cold as possible, the vodka and the glasses. That's the Russian way."

"Listen, I've been meaning to ask you for the last two months. What exactly is an ikon?"

He looked at me in semidisgust. "Those pictures in the hall, the holy pictures, with—"

"With the gold and silver overlay kind of stuck to them?"

"Yeah. It's fake. Tin, or something. Those are ikons, stupid."

"I was never entirely sure. In America we don't paint a

picture of the Madonna and Child and then cover most of it over with tin. Only mad Russians do that, apparently."

I did not get the swift, kidding retort from Greg that I expected. He was silent, looking grim for an instant.

From the pantry we heard the door on the railroad tracks side of the house burst open, the first guests arriving. Others soon hurried in out of the gray, frigid, gloomy dusk of a late February afternoon. All the chandeliers and lamps of Edgewater were lighted, fires blazed and crackled in all the fireplaces, New York show tunes poured from the phonograph; and the thirty or so "gentry and zanies" of the Hudson River Valley settled down for serious celebrating.

I had already been taken through the front rooms by Greg to be introduced to them, and after that he led me rather surreptitiously back to the pantry. Making sure we were alone and unlikely to be interrupted by any of the guests, he then fished out one of the bottles of vodka.

"Real Russian vodka, eh?" I said, examining the yellowish fluid. "Where'd you get it?"

"From a bootlegger or smuggler or something like that in New York. A guy Dad knows from the days of prohibition. You can't buy this stuff in America." Spacing his words significantly, he then added, "It . . . is . . . strong. Wait." He went out and in a couple of minutes returned with the prince and princess.

Zinaida today was wearing a long, narrow black lace dress, her long, gold-colored earrings, and a long rope of doubtless imitation pearls. She looked every inch a royal princess. "They're all here and the mulled wine is just *evaporating!*" she cried gaily. "Now let's the four of us have a real Russian toast." Gregory filled the four glasses, we held them up, Naida said something in Russian, Greg and Alexei repeated it, and then, with an aside to me from Gregory, "Gulp the whole damn thing," I tossed the icy vodka down my throat. A numb absence of feeling ensued.

"Another," he ordered. So we did it again, then a third time.

"This is where I leave you," said the princess with playful formality, and she and Alexei went back to the party.

Gradually the chilled vodka was thawing within me, and a glowing, swelling euphoric state of joyous removal was taking possession of me. I was here, a floating, carefree presence, and I was also not here at all. "How's that, sport?" asked Greg, observing me with amusement.

"Mmmyyy Gggoddd!" I was blinking my eyes rapidly. "What hit me?"

"Old Russia," he said out of the side of his mouth. "Now go out and charm some of the guests. We'll rendezvous back here later. There are four bottles of that stuff in there."

I stared at him. "Four bottles? For four people!"

"That's it," he said shortly. "Get going."

I drifted out through the swinging door into the small dining room where the table was laden with so-far untouched hors d'oeuvres, and through the entrance hall to the main living room.

The guests were standing around the room, and also sitting on the furniture and the floor, chatting and laughing. They were of all ages, sixteen to eighty or more, with the emphasis at the older end of the scale. Greg had told me much about them. I knew a few of them were famous, a few rich, one or two just this side of certifiably insane. The Hudson Valley, this stretch of it anyway, was decadent, an enclave of leftover out-of-date aristocrats, plutocrats, and fringe artists. The clothes worn by many of the women were best described with one word: original. Shawls, dangling earrings, "slave" bracelets, and gypsy skirts, or else, among the aristocrats, veiled straw hats, Queen Alexandra "dog collars," costly and expensive suits. Everyone seemed to be getting along very well with everyone else. The men wore for the most part tweedy country clothes. It was apparent that the opportunities for socializing and friendship around these parts were limited, especially in the wintertime, and these thirty people were utterly determined 1) to have a very good time, and 2) to be friendly and cordial to one another no matter what.

Through the glass doors I noticed the broad, now winter-gray, somber river as seen at dusk, looking at it past the skeletal trees across the snow-covered lawn. I'll bet the Neva River in Petersburg-Leningrad looks a lot like that right now, I reflected in my glowing, vodka-slowed state. And I wouldn't be surprised if a lot of Russians just as drunk as I am on just the same stuff are staring at it just as stupidly right this minute, no matter what time it is there.

"Hello there!" hooted a tall, bony woman with tightly curled middle-aged hair, glasses, and lots of unfocused enthusiasm. "Come, let's you and I sit down on that one unoccupied settee. I want you to tell me all about Yale today. *All* my male relatives are Yale."

I had never known how to carry on this conversation on that subject with the many women who were in this way surrogate Yale people, and I didn't know now. "Well it's um pretty much the same . . . but it's changing!" I began lamely as she steered me to the settee. "I mean, not that it's losing anything important or traditional, but it's not getting left behind either . . . " Was I saying what she wanted to hear? Was I avoiding disappointing her? Her bright, glassy eyes and fixed smile were unreadable. "I like it," I finished slightly out of breath. "Have you lived here long?" I asked, hitting the ball into her court.

"Three centuries," she answered demurely.

I tittered, looked at her: she was serious.

"We're the original Dutch. I don't think you perhaps caught my name, you're meeting so many new people . . . new to you. It's van Rensaaver. We used to have eighty square miles around here and north of here. We've still got Renshaw. That's the house. Huge and old and collapsing."

"Three centuries is a long time," I remarked. Brilliant. Oh come on, I grumbled inwardly, stop criticizing yourself. It's a miracle I'm able to sit upright and speak any English at all, after what the Trouvenskoys have poured down me. They've got *genes* for this stuff; I haven't.

After that I experienced a period of confusion, a certain blur. Later I recall sitting on the floor in the nighttime mysterious spaciousness of the octagonal library talking to Charles Cummings, who was one of the famous people present. He wrote up-to-the-minute political commentary, called "Letter from Washington," for a national magazine without, so it appeared to most people, ever venturing out of the Hudson Valley. What type of second sight, spy system, ghost writers, or creative imagination he used in achieving this was unknown. Cummings was very highly regarded nationally; his letters were always dense with insights. Friends and neighbors here in the Hudson Valley marveled and wondered, and no one ever asked him for the explanation.

"How do you write so much about Washington," I asked, "when you spend all your time up here?"

He gazed at me owlishly over his horn-rimmed glasses. "Now why do you ask that?" he eventually said evenly. Answering a question with another question, I observed to myself. These journalists.

"Because that's what everybody around here wants to know." Russian vodka had its uses.

He was very deliberately refilling his pipe. All pundit-journalists smoked pipes. "Well, the explanation is very simple. You see—" and there followed a convoluted discussion bristling with qualifications and digressions, with abstruse citations and seemingly irrelevant disquisitions, so that I knew nothing more about his habits, travels, or methods at the end than at the beginning.

"That was absolutely brilliant," I remarked, not admiringly, when he had at last finished.

"No, it really wasn't."

Charles Cummings was also famous, at least locally, for, in a friendly fashion, never agreeing with anyone about anything.

"Well," I said, getting to my feet, "if I'd understood what you were talking about, *that* would have been brilliant, on my part."

He looked very dubious about that too, pulling questingly on his pipe.

"Excuse me," I pressed on, "but I've got to see a mad Russian."

His thick eyebrows rose with doubtful inquiry about even this. I marched, or tried to march, out of the room, almost colliding with Mary Maury in the little passage connecting the library with the main living room. She was one of the bangles-and-shawls group. Her husband was a book editor, always just failing to procure a contract for

Prince Alexei. No one concerned dared allow that to interfere with their friendship up here on the Hudson.

Mary herself wrote for the theater. The theater had
shown no gratitude: no play of hers had ever been produced
anywhere. This in no way dimmed her self-presentation as
The Playwright, and the people here appeared to accept her
as such.

"I think you've had a drop too much," she began with an
ironic little smile, eyes roving over my face. She was showing herself to be mistress of the bitchy-flirt mode.

"Not nearly enough," I shot back.

She dropped her gaze, then "impulsively" seized my
hand. "Come dance with me. I adore this song." It was the
old movie tune "Cheek to Cheek" and I sensed that Mary
visualized herself and me rivaling Astaire and Rogers there
on the expanse of the octagonal-library floor in front of a
dozen soon-to-be-marveling onlookers; there was more than
one route into show business.

"I can't dance," I lied.

"But you can! I saw you one night at our local roadhouse,
dancing with the one of the Bard girls."

"Oh," I said, deflated. Gregory, Gregory, where are you
and the vodka, now that I need you?

Princess Zinaida materialized at my side. She was smiling her calm, radiant smile. "Mary dear, may I steal Allan
away? I need a strong young man to help me with something in the kitchen."

An instant's hard glance at Naida, a false smile at me,
and she replied sweetly, "I want a raincheck, and it has to
be 'Cheek to Cheek.' "

As Naida pulled me gently out of the passage she muttered from the side of her mouth— so that's where Gregory

got that habit—"That woman could curdle mothers' milk."

We made our way past convivial groups across the living room toward the kitchen. "I thought everybody up here liked everybody else," I remarked.

"I do like her. We all have no choice: we have to like one another. Especially in the winter. I *love* them all in the winter. But that doesn't mean I don't have my . . . reservations about some of them."

"She's so damn flirtatious and hostile, at one and the same time."

"Frustration. She is an artist, at least she thinks she is, and she can't get to first base. Even Bard won't do a student production of any of her plays, and her husband," Naida finished with an incredulous laugh, "is on the board of governors!"

"Gosh."

"Yes, it rankles." We went through the kitchen to the pantry. "Yes," said Naida with satisfaction, "I need a strong young man to help me with something. And what that something is, is, will you lift one of the bottles out of the freezer for me, and two frosted glasses?"

"I sure will."

"That's so southern: 'I sure will.' I love the regionalism in America. Heaven knows we have it up here. I noticed you talking to Harriet van Rensaaver. Talk about roots. Peter the Great was tsar when her ancestors settled here."

Someone had been at the vodka. The first bottle was almost completely empty. I started on a second bottle, filling our two glasses. "What was the Russian toast you did before?" I asked.

"No, you make a toast, an American one."

"Okay," I raised my glass. "Here's mud in your eye!" I blurted out unguardedly.

Her mouth fell open for an instant and then she threw back her head and hooted with laughter. Her eyes began to tear.

"Here's mud in your eye?" she repeated with wondering amusement. "I never heard *that* one before. I love it."

We each had one more *mud in the eye* glass of icy vodka and then we moved back to the party, I seemingly floating, Zinaida with just a touch more formality in her walk.

Subsequently I recall a blur of conversations; later all of us trailed into the dining room for a buffet supper; I remember Alexei sitting on a stool before the fire strumming a balalaika and singing sad, nostalgic Russian songs in a fine baritone voice; there was Mary Maury, onstage at last, doing the tarantella in the library; Gregory on the telephone to Merry, chained to her desk at Vassar by impending exams; guests at last leaving, someone asleep on a couch; carrying plates and glasses into the kitchen; mounting the curving staircase; tottering into my room; bed; sleep; the train roaring past in a blur or dream half-sleep; then, at last, awakening to midmorning sunshine.

The special quality of silence reigning over Edgewater told me that all the Trouvenskoys were fast asleep, and all the guests, even those who had dozed off in corners at some point late in the evening, had awakened and gone home.

I was the only conscious person in the house. What to do?

I felt very well. Far from giving me a hangover, the extraordinary icy vodka seemed to have cleared my head. What if I went downstairs and at least made a stab at preparing breakfast for everyone?

That seemed like a good idea. I put on bedroom slippers and a blue flannel bathrobe, a gift from a relative bearing, alas, the seal of Yale, which Greg found the silliest touch imaginable. "What if I wore the Romanoff double eagle," he scoffed, "on my ski parka? And the Trouvenskoy crest on my jockey shorts? Classy?" "I didn't buy this thing," I countered defensively, "and it's sewn in. I can't get it off without tearing up the robe." "These perennial college boys," he grumbled, "you'll be croaking out 'For God, for Country, and for Yale' when you're eighty." "I expect to be for God and Country when I'm eighty," I said. "I don't know about Yale."

Stealing out of my room in this robe, I crossed the upstairs hall silently and made my way down the stairs, through the dining room to the kitchen.

Brilliant late-winter sunshine brought a magical sheen to the snow-covered ground all around, and transformed the icicles into dazzling jewels. I could easily visualize how aglow with elegant brilliance the library with its skylight and French windows would be on such a morning.

The circular table there would be just the place for a gala morning-after breakfast. I gathered up place mats and silver, and headed there to set the table.

At the threshold I paused, gazing into the splendid room: golden light poured down from the circular panes at the apex of the ceiling; framed in the seven long glass doors were classic winterscapes—fir trees laced with gleaming snow, stripped arching maples outlined with whiteness, the smooth white lawn sweeping down to the half-frozen river, all sparkling richly in the clarity of winter's sunshine.

The room itself seemed to expand its dimension in the glow of direct and reflected sunlight, to acquire a heightened significance as though some crucial act, the signing of a treaty of peace, the climax of a great love affair, were about to transpire here.

102

I stepped into the room, which had been meticulously put back in order by Zinaida and the rest of us before going to bed.

Something was wrong with it. It was one of the portraits on the far wall. How strange. It was hanging upside down. We must really have been drunk. I put down the mats and silver on the circular table and went over to the painting, took it from its hook, and was about to rehang it properly when I noticed the safe behind: it had been pried open, hammered at. I touched the door; it drifted open. The papers I had seen there were still in place. The small blue velvet jewel case was there. With an odd chill climbing the side of my head, I opened it. It was empty.

Oh no. No. The Trouvenskoys, virtually penniless, couldn't have been robbed. No, not that.

But they had been.

Pride, they say, is the cause of more evil, suffering, sin, destructiveness, than any other state of mind open to man. They say that it leads to more deprivation, misunderstanding, cruelty, injustice than anything else.

In the years since that Sunday morning when I found that almost the last valuable resource of these Russian refugees was gone, I have thought that another couple, some American couple, for instance, would have reacted differently, more practically, more realistically.

But of course the Militsa Diamond was not merely a financial safety net worth approximately a hundred thousand dollars. It was, even more, a symbol: it stood for the glorious Peterhof Palace on the Gulf of Finland where Naida had played as a child among the magical fountains there; it represented her mother's memory, which she treasured; it stood for the whole Romanoff family, the last tangible link she possessed with them, a link peculiarly precious and delicate because so many, beginning with her father, had been murdered; it harkened back to troika rides at Tsarskoe Selo, to brilliant evenings in the imperial box at the Mariinsky Theater watching Pavlova whirl through a ballet, to stables full of thoroughbred horses and ballrooms alive with a thousand rivaling jewels; it reflected the white palaces of the Crimea, balmy in January, and cruises on the emperor's great yacht, *Standart*, with cousins Olga, Tatiana, Marie, Anastasia, and little Alexis. All were summed up and imprismed within its gleaming depths. And the Militsa Diamond had represented security for her in all its facets.

Now, standing aghast in my bedroom slippers in the octagonal library, it was I who was placed in the position of having to tell her and Alexei and Gregory that it had been stolen, in all probability by a "friend" who hid himself, or herself, until the four of us had gone to bed, falling, all of us, into, it had to be admitted, drunken stupid sleep, whereupon this "friend" could break into the little safe at leisure, pretty sure none of us would hear anything. I sank into a chair, suddenly exhausted by what I had stumbled upon. I felt light-headed. What in God's name was I supposed to do? My first impulse was to wait for them to awake, come down, and see the shocking fact for themselves. Then my outraged brain began to reassert control of itself and to attempt to think logically. A crime had been committed; the sooner action was taken the better. Not that I was going to call the police myself, but at least I had to wake them up and inform them immediately of what had happened.

And I had thought offering Naida money during my earlier visit had been an ordeal! I had not known the meaning of the word, until now.

Very slowly, almost painfully, I made my way out of the library, across the main living room, through the hall, painfully up the curving staircase, and across to Gregory's door. I could just bear to face him; I could not face them at all. I knocked softly; no response; then a little more loudly; a blurred grunt. I eased open the door and saw Greg gazing blearily at me from a jumble of blankets and pillows. "Let me sleep," he mumbled.

"I'm sorry. I have to wake you up. Something's happened."

He shifted his position, trying to get comfortable again, turned away from me. "It can wait, whatever it is."

"But it can't wait. It's serious, it's terribly serious."

"The house on fire?"

"Almost."

He reared up on his fists and confronted me. "What the hell are you talking about?"

"Well . . . there's no way to tell you but to tell you. I was just down in the library. The safe's been . . . it was—somebody got into the safe. The, well, the uh *diamond*, it's gone."

He just stared at me. "How do you—what're you talking about?"

"I can't explain it any better. Maybe you'd better go downstairs and see for yourself."

Greg got out of bed, and barefoot, dispensing with such effete details as bedroom slippers and robe, went down with me, and moving almost stealthily, as though braced for attack, entered the library and saw for himself.

"I don't believe it," he said, and, examining the door and

the interior of the safe without touching them, said it again. "I just don't believe it."

"Ought you to tell your parents now?"

He looked at me blankly. "The folks? How do I tell them this?"

"The only way there is. You just have to tell them."

"I can't!" he protested, his voice not under full control.

"But," I said quietly, "you've got to."

He kept looking at me. I just looked unhappily back at him.

"You're right of course," he muttered at length. "Let's go up and . . . well . . . somehow tell them."

"I'm not going," I murmured, "of course not. It's a family situation."

"You're coming," he ordered flatly.

"But why should—"

He grabbed me at the elbow. "If ever I needed moral support. . . " he said through clenched teeth.

"All right," I finally agreed, with deep reluctance. He kept my elbow in a strong grip just to make certain.

We went up the stairs to their door, a large Honduran mahogany carved door. It looks almost out of one of the tsar's palaces, I thought erratically.

Gregory knocked, so softly that even I could barely hear it. He waited for some time, too much time, before he finally knocked again, a little more loudly.

After a pause Alexei's voice answered, slightly annoyed, "Yes?"

"May I come in?" mumbled Greg.

"What? Who is it?"

"It's me," he said more clearly. "May I come in? Allan's here too. We—we've got something to tell you."

"Just a minute." They could be heard bestirring them-selves, and then Alexei, in a long, Chinese-looking robe, opened the door. Zinaida, her black hair loose, falling to her shoulders as I had never seen it, and wearing a pink robe, sat on the side of the high, old-fashioned bed. The room had a high ceiling, white walls, long windows giving on the Hudson, and an air, despite its size, of snugness. Alexei was looking at us in puzzlement, and Naida, pale, motionless, stared. How privileged they somehow looked here, and yet at the same time how vulnerable. These people who had suffered so many blows before they had even become adults were about to be dealt another one. I could hardly bear to see this. Why hadn't I insisted on staying downstairs!

Something about the way we looked appeared to disturb Zinaida. "I thought at least," she began with an uncertain giggle, "you'd have Bloody Marys if you're waking us up at the crack of dawn." Her eyes were serious, puzzled.

"We—well I," Gregory began with great difficulty, "you see, there's, there's something Allan found out, in the library. Well . . . it's the safe. Somebody broke into it." There was a silence; nobody moved.

"The diamond?" Prince Alexei finally asked flatly.

"The diamond is, well, the diamond is missing."

Zinaida rose jerkily from the bed and moved sharply to a window, her back to us, gazing down on the glittering white lawn and the icy river, looking out at the bleak elegance of this great northern river.

"It can't be!" said Alexei hoarsely. "What do you mean, 'found out'? 'Allan found out something'?" He turned his glare on me. "What did you find? How did you find some-thing out? And what exactly is it?"

"I"—my voice quavered—"I went down to the library—"

"When! At what time exactly?"

"I guess about five minutes ago, and—"

"And you saw something! What makes you think the Militsa Diamond isn't—"

"Alexei," began Naida in a calming voice turning toward us from the window, and then she added something in Russian. He seemed with difficulty to be getting better control of himself.

"We'll all go downstairs," he ordered. And we did, obediently, single file, silent, and we formed a kind of semicircle before the opened safe, staring at it. Alexei then proceeded very deliberately to give it the same examination Greg and I had.

"Fingerprints," Greg murmured. "Should we all be touching it?"

The prince, pale, past anger, somewhere in some emotional country unknown to me, turned his unreadable green-blue eyes toward him. "Fingerprints! Clues! Police! There's not going to be any help for this," he finished in an almost wheedling and contemptuous voice. "You don't think we're going to get it back, do you? Don't be absurd. It's gone, with everything else—"

Naida put a hand on his arm, tried to encircle his neck with her other arm. She murmured something to him in Russian.

"I'm the *writer*," he almost rasped. "I'll support you, with my pen, my mighty pen. This boy here"—me—"knows more about writing than I'll ever know! Your investment in me, all you had, useless! And now—the diamond—"

She stood, erect and pale, black hair framing her face, her hands trying to comfort him. "It's God's will," she murmured, "you have done everything you could." Then she finished simply, "I love you."

They seemed to be standing alone in this room, the two of them, isolated from us, the past stolen from them, one final time.

8

"What are these mats and knives and forks doing here?" asked Naida abstractedly, turning slowly away from the wreckage that the rifled safe represented.

I explained that I had started to set a breakfast table here in the library when I had noticed the upside-down portrait.

"The portrait was upside down?" she inquired quizzically.

"Yes."

"How bizarre." She became lost for a few moments in thought, and the rest of us, as though waiting for her, for some reason, to give us the signal for action, just stood there. Then, coming out of her reverie, she said decisively, "What a good idea. Breakfast in here. It's so beautiful here this morning in the winter sunshine. Gregory, make up a batch of Bloody Marys and—"

"Bloody *Marys?*" he echoed in mystification.

"Yes," she went on energetically, "and I'll make some of those sort of crepe pancakes, and I'm almost sure there are some frozen sausages—"

"Naida, darling," began Alexei gently.

"Yes, yes," she said hurriedly, "I know, I know what you're going to say. And I say," she went on, and for the first time I saw an edge of imperiousness in her voice and manner, "we will deal with all that later, and now we will have breakfast." She paused, and looked steadily at Greg. "Bloody Marys," she repeated. He returned her look for a moment, shrugged, and left the room.

"Finish setting the table, will you, Allan? Thank you. Alexei, some music on the gramophone. Something gay."

And so a kind of farrago of a gala breakfast began to take form.

This is insane, I thought to myself as I carried some frayed damask napkins and some stemware glasses from the pantry to the octagonal library. We should be telephoning the police, and right now.

But why? an answering voice inquired. The diamond didn't run away by itself, to be overtaken on the road if we acted quickly enough. It had been stolen. It was now hidden somewhere. Speed was not of the essence. Clear thinking, mental composure, were. And these Zinaida evidently sought to invoke with Bloody Marys well laced with the last of the authentically Russian vodka, parchment-thin pancakes, tiny hot sausages, coffee so strong it seemed unnecessary to use a cup to hold it, and Nelson Eddy and Jeanette MacDonald on the phonograph soaring into "The Indian Love Call."

By now, eating our second helping of pancakes, Naida was apparently genuinely beginning to enjoy herself. She doesn't need for everything to be perfect to enjoy herself, does she? I reflected. But of course had she not had that capacity, her life would have been pure misery from 1917 on.

"Now listen," she was saying, leaning forward, with a kind of eagerness, "just which one of them could have robbed us? Who knows about the stone being here? And who's capable of stealing it?"

All three of them then volunteered a number of names, among them Charles Cummings—"He is," observed Alexei with a shrewd gleam in his eye, "eaten up with envy. And now he's too successful to envy anyone professionally, least of all us. But there is our—well—background and he might be able to envy that." A little later, and to me most incongruously, Harriet van Rensaaver was paraded out: "Poor as a church mouse," observed Naida, "and with that enormous house and all that old-family tradition to maintain. I feel like an upstart beside her. Maybe *she* filched it." And finally the Maurys, Mary and Mervyn: "They're both," asserted Greg forthrightly, "as mad as hatters, if you ask me. Nutty as two fruitcakes. They could do anything."

A reflective silence followed this assertion, and we all turned pensively to munching once again.

And then, terribly unexpectedly and like an electric shock, an overwhelming thought sprang into the silence: these three could suspect me.

If Cummings and van Rensaaver and the Maurys, why not Prieston?

How well did they know me, really? How much did they know about me? I was a "Yale man," as they say, but what did *that* mean? I and my family were far from rich, I was about to set out into one of the financially most precarious of all professions, I had had a better opportunity than any other guest at the party to rifle the safe. Greg, at least, knew that I had seen its contents. Had he mentioned it to his parents? Were the three of them asking themselves if I had robbed them during the night?

As guardedly as possible, I looked from one to the other. Naida, tranquilly chewing a piece of sausage, was staring through the glass doors toward the river once again, heavy-lidded eyes, white face, black hair falling to her shoulders, an exotic if there ever was one. Alexei was fooling with his food. With his long, slicked-back gray-black hair and aquiline features, he looked what he was: a highbred man of great foreignness. And Greg: high cheekbones, very faintly slanting Asiatic eyes, the almost overdone Americanism of his personality eclipsed because he wasn't speaking or smiling, he too was from a far country and embodied unknowable traits.

Paranoia was Russian. If American was practicality, Russian was suspicion. Zinaida's ancestor, Peter the Great, had beaten and tortured his own son and heir to death on the mere suspicion that he might be in some way disloyal. In the present regime—and tsar and Communist were one in so many other ways—Stalin had put uncountable hordes of people to death, out of suspicion. They were today and always had been a paranoid people, that much I knew from my reading. There was absolutely nothing to prevent these three Russians from believing I had stolen the Militsa Diamond.

"How well did you sleep?" Greg asked me kind of lazily.

I could feel myself flushing crimson. "Just fine," I mumbled, "fine."

"Why do you look so flustered?" he followed up, squinting at me.

"Well I, uh, if I hadn't slept so well, my room is closest to the stairs, I might have heard something."

"Mm. True."

"*I* hear something!" cut in Zinaida. The outside door on the railroad side of the house had opened and closed; quick footsteps on that side of the house. A liberating thought hit me: Somebody's bringing it back! The nightmare's going to end!

Footsteps could be heard coming through the main living room, into the passage, and then Merryfield Carr strode brightly into the library. "Here you are! I didn't know you had breakfast in here. What a good idea."

Greg and Alex, momentarily immobilized by the unexpectedness of her arrival, were now getting to their feet. Greg helped her off with her coat made of some brownish expensive fur.

"Well this is a surprise—" he began.

"We're glad to see you," said Alex.

"How nice," murmured Naida.

"What's that funny little door in the wall?" she asked airily, brushing back her hair from her face. "It looks a little like a safe."

"Sit there next to Gregory," said Zinaida, "and I'll get you something from the kitchen."

"I'll help," I said, springing up. I felt reprieved, for the moment. A distraction had arrived. Their suspicions of me, a lurking Asiatic paranoia I was now sure they possessed, would have to wait.

"I just couldn't stand those textbooks a moment longer," Merry was saying, "and I thought, well if I couldn't be at the party I can at least drop in on the day-after postmortem. How was it? The blast you expected?"

After the briefest silence Alexei said easily, "It was, indeed it was."

Zinaida and I went out and across to the kitchen. She moved here and there efficiently, reheating food and coffee. "Do you suppose she wants a Bloody Mary?" she muttered.

"Yes, I think she does."

She was lighting with a match the flame of the old-fashioned stove under the coffeepot. "Likes her drinks, does she? You've seen so much more of her than I have."

"She . . . well . . . you know . . . Doesn't everybody?"

"Apparently," she said dryly, then with a chortle, "God knows I do. Life would be *unendurable* sometimes . . ." her voice trailing off.

A glimpse of her anguish opened before me. I felt I had to say something, and it would be genuine and it had to be important. "I—Zinaida, I'm so really *sorry* about what's happened. I wish there was something I could do, something better than just stupidly saying I'm sorry."

She was beginning to fry some more sausages. "You're good company for Gregory. He needs a good friend. That's one thing you can do."

What she said was true, as far as it went, and her calm way of saying it revealed nothing about her possible suspicions of me.

I felt there was a steadiness about her, a clear-sightedness that would, in the end, exonerate me in her eyes. At least, so I felt, standing there in the big shabby kitchen holding a plate for Merry. Princess Zinaida had a sense of realism about her, and surely that would assert itself. She would grasp the impossibility of someone like me getting up in the dead of night in that guest room, creeping down those stairs, stealing through the big darkened rooms, hammering and prying at the safe, and stealing their life savings.

"You saw the stone once then, didn't you?" she asked conversationally.

"Yes."

"Beautiful, wasn't it."

"Yes."

She put several sausages and pancakes on the plate, picked up a cup of coffee, and together we went back into the library. "I see they've already given you a Bloody Mary," said Naida cheerfully. "Now try some of this."

Merry, seated next to Greg, wearing a blue woolen dress and a thin leather belt, looked up at her wonderingly, mouth a little ajar. "But the—they've just told me—"

"Yes. Well. They have, have they?" She sat down in her place next to Alex. "Enjoy your life," she finished quietly.

"*Ah sweet mystery of life at last I've found you,*" Jeanette MacDonald had been trilling on the phonograph. "*Ah at last I know the secret of it all. . . .*"

9

Seeing an effective performance of *Long Day's Journey into Night* with Millicent was very interesting, but I had a lecture to prepare and deliver. So I sat down in the guest quarters in Pierson the next afternoon to organize it.

I was going to speak in the auditorium of the Yale Law School. This room had been used for undergraduate courses when I was a student here, including a course I had taken in political science. It was a wide, rather shallow, lightly pitched auditorium, ideal for speaking to a couple of hundred people.

At Notre Dame University I had packed a much larger auditorium than that and been given an ovation; they had loved me at Texas Christian. But here at Yale, Mother Yale, if the past was any guide, a *blasé* few dozen students would show up to follow what I said through half-closed lids, and compare it, almost certainly unfavorably, with what the current winner of the Nobel Prize for Literature had said when they heard him here last week.

Not that the lecture would fail. None of my lectures was a failure. And the person responsible for that was Zinaida.

It had been later on that stunned morning when we had awakened to the rifled safe. We were once again in the kitchen, she washing and I drying the dishes. I remarked to her that I had to give a talk in the Daily Themes class, speaking on some literary subject.

"*Any* literary subject?" she asked.

"Yes, anything at all. As long as it has to do with writing or literature."

"What are you going to talk about?"

"I'm not sure yet, but I was thinking I might discuss how T. S. Eliot's *The Waste Land* influenced Evelyn Waugh's *A Handful of Dust*."

"Huh?" she grunted, turning to look with pretended stupidity at me.

"'I—you—don't think much of the subject."

"What's it supposed to mean?"

Feeling unavoidably superior, I began, "Well, Eliot—the poet? Born in America, but—"

"I still think *Prufrock* remains his best work," she said, slicing with subdued ruthlessness through that.

"Oh." Taken slightly aback, I tried again. "You see, Waugh's title comes from Eliot's line, 'I'll—"

". . . 'show you fear in a handful of dust.' Of course. Well?"

Now in full retreat I ventured, "Well, obviously they're linked, and I thought—"

"Yes, 'obviously.' " She echoed my "obviously" the way Mr. Lockhart had echoed my "glamorous." Down off your high horse, friend, she was saying. "But why," she continued, "do you want to talk about Eliot and Waugh at all?"

"Well, because—"

118

"Why don't you talk about yourself?"

"Well I—hm?"

"Tell them about yourself. They get Eliot and Waugh every day from their professors. You're not a professor. You're a writer, an artist"—I am?—". . . and they want *that* from you, if they're going to listen to you at all. Why do you, *you*, Allan Prieston of Somewhere, Maryland, want to be a writer? How do you sit down, literally, and write? That's what I would want to hear, in their place. I don't want your theories on writers whom all kinds of experts have already examined. That's not what you've got to contribute. What you've got to contribute is you, you. That's what writing, your kind of writing, is." There was a silence, an almost tense silence. "That's what, well, Alex cannot find it in himself to do. Peter the Great. Good heavens, what has Alex to tell anyone about Peter the Great that they don't already know? And besides, it isn't even history, biography. It's a *fictional* treatment of an over-poweringly famous man. But"—she began scrubbing hard at the bottom of the frying pan—"he can't find his own subject, his own *center*, and write from that. If we could have stayed in Russia. If he could have written in Russian, hearing Russian around him every day. Then, it might have been different. No, don't bother to dry the frying pan. Stains the dishcloth. Tell them about yourself." She took off the apron. "How do you start writing something? How do you conceive it? That's what will interest them, at least, that's what would interest me, and I've always thought of myself as the average person who's interested in most things."

She had been right that day, of course, and for many years I had followed this advice effectively. I could feel audiences surprised into suspenseful silence as I began to lay before them the sources of my work. They hadn't expected that. Other lecturers didn't do it; other lecturers talked about their field; I plowed the field, turned the soil over, exposing the roots, and the horse manure as well.

Perhaps my lecture interested an audience because, in the first place, it interested me. I could only give a lecture about three times before I grew tired of it. Whether new audiences would like it or not I didn't know. I was tired of it, and so it had to be discarded. I would then put together a new one, retaining perhaps fragments of the old.

So I sat down that afternoon in the pleasant study of the guest quarters, next to the sash window with a view of the Pierson court, ragged grass, a few bare trees, the glass doors at the far end, and the red-brick tower of the college library against a foreboding, gray autumnal sky.

Whatever this lecture was to include, it was expected that I would describe how *Crossing the Frontier* came to be written because that was the one novel by me they were sure to have read—it was virtually impossible to pass through the educational system of this country and avoid it—and describe it I would. There was, however, something a little unsettling about presenting myself before these young men and women of 1980, myself middle-aged and unremarkable-looking, and they—many of them— enamored of the vision of youth I had created in that book, looking quizzically up at me ("Did *he* write *that!*"). I have sometimes thought it would have been better to retreat behind a stockade somewhere, and leave that book and its consequences and the readers' expectations and suscep- tibilities on their own. But I was simply too gregarious for that kind of literary monasticism, too desirous of meeting new people, young people, different people, too curious, too restless.

I was like Reeves Lockhart in that.

He had lectured once in the same Law School auditorium where I was going to speak. I had attended that lecture, of course, and I recall how brilliant it had been. Lockhart was among other things a performer, and that afternoon he turned the podium into a stage, striding back and forth, stage-whispering asides to the audience behind his hand, compelling our attention with suspenseful pauses, the voice soaring and growling, reprimanding, confiding, establishing an immediacy and a rapport with us which were irresistible.

This was all for a reason: he wanted us to learn something and he was willing, more than willing, delighted, to entertain us in the bargain. He was pouring sugar all over the sticky pill, a bitter pill perhaps, which he wanted us to swallow. It would strengthen us.

I recall one sentence from that lecture, one I have in fact lived by: "Destiny aids and helps along those who recognize her," he growled significantly at us, eyebrows up, eyes alive with the importance of what he was saying; a taut pause; then, in a deeper, more portentous voice: "the blind . . . she drags."

That day, sitting fourth row on the left in the packed auditorium, surrounded by other students who were in spite of themselves slipping under his spell, beginning unwillingly to hang on this compelling and famous man's words, I simply knew that those words were important. I put them in the back of my mind and have remembered them ever since. Only gradually, as the years passed, has their application emerged in life: my athletic friend from schooldays who was born to be a hockey and football coach but tried all his futile life to be a politician; the girl who

121

married and produced five children—that was what proper girls did, even girls like herself with no talent for nor patience with motherhood—with the resultant string of mental hospitals and other institutions for the children; a writer like Alexis Trouvenskoy, persisting in writing in spite of the wrong language and the wrong country. *Give up!* I wanted to yell at them. Failure isn't the disgrace; stupidity is.

They trail through anyone's life, those who flatly and bluntly and rigidly refuse to recognize destiny. They call their dire lives dedicated; they refer to this brute plodding as never-say-die; they remember that it's always darkest before the dawn; they pride themselves on their courage, their endurance. And they fail, and destiny drags them through life, face down, behind her inexorable chariot.

And there is the teacher who is so inspiring because she was born to teach and has recognized it, the business tycoon who started as an apprentice in a bicycle shop, the doctor and the lawyer and the farmer who love every disappointment and accolade of their full professional lives.

"That is the thing you said which sticks in my mind," I remarked to Reeves Lockhart at the podium after the insistent applause had finally faded away and the auditorium was emptying. " 'Destiny aids and'—how do you say it, exactly?"

"Let's see." He was gathering up notebooks and shoving them hurriedly into a battered satchel. " 'Destiny aids and helps along those who recognize her' "—he was giving it an only slightly muted version of the first dramatic rendering—" 'the blind she drags.' It's not original with me. Rousseau said that, I think. I borrow, I'm always borrowing, in my lectures, in my work, always borrowing, Rousseau, Dante, Joyce, on and on. But I only do my shopping, borrowing, shoplifting, call it what you will, in the *best* emporiums! Never forget that."

There was an exhibition at the Sterling Library which he had helped organize and wanted to see, some of Gertrude Stein's manuscripts. We walked along peering down through the glass tops of the softly lighted display cases in the nave of the massive building. There was a subdued cathedral hush here, an almost prayerful reverence for books and literature. "Under glass," he murmured, gazing at some of his old friend's pages, "how mummifying it is. And she was so alive, you know, radiating understanding and intelligence."

It was clear whenever Mr. Lockhart mentioned Gertrude Stein that he felt the deepest affection for her.

"She must have been such a remarkable woman," I said carefully. "I've tried to read some of her work and it I guess is just beyond me." She can't write, I wanted to say, but of course would never have dared.

He gave me the briefest of sidelong glances and then murmured, meditating over her papers, "Gertrude wrote on eight levels," he said in a ripe undertone, "I only penetrated three of them myself."

And he left it at that. To this day I do not know what to make of that remark. I had a certain suspicion that with his habitual indirection what he was truly saying to me was: "A brilliant woman, a remarkable woman, an amazing woman, invaluable. But . . . she can't write." I shall never know.

It was dinnertime and I asked him to let me take him to the Old Heidelberg, a ramshackle bar and restaurant next to Pierson that I was sure he approved of. He did, and we had some beef and beer there and then proceeded across the street to the college, where he went with me to my rooms so that I could give him another of my manuscripts to read.

"I can't tell you how I appreciate your doing this," I said as we walked through the darkened court. "After all, even you can't have read all the important books there are, and still you take the time to read my little—"

"Student work, promising work, I'm used to it coming in, it's one of the things I like to do when I can."

We stepped into the Slave Quarters, crossed its tiny court, and mounted the outside steps one flight to my and Greg's rooms.

As I opened the door, we saw, sprawled in his sweaty squash shorts on the sofa, grasping the neck of a bottle of beer as though he were strangling it, Prince Gregoire.

"Hi, sport. You—" And then his startled eyes lit on the formidable shape of Reeves Lockhart coming through the doorway. "Oh!" he exclaimed, swinging his feet hurriedly to the floor and starting to get up. "I didn't know you had—"

"This is Mr. Lockhart. Gregory Trouvenskoy."

"Hello, hello," said Lockhart cheerily, crossing to shake his hand. "And how are you? You've been playing ah—oh yes, I see the racquet in the corner. Squash, isn't it? So much exertion in a short time. And now you're having a good bottle of beer! It never tastes better than after some exercise, eh?"

"Don't we have some cognac?" I asked Greg.

"Yeah."

I found the bottle and Lockhart accepted a small amount in a toothbrush glass. I took a little, and we all sat down.

The external elegance of the Slave Quarters was not reflected in the interior of our living room. Two shabby armchairs and a shabby sofa, a couple of tables and lamps, an old rug: nondescript, functional, featureless, the room looked what it was, a temporary hangout for two people on their way elsewhere.

"You're Alexei and Zinaida's boy. Prieston here has been telling me about visiting up there. I used to know them years ago. Such charming people, and so courageous! What was it you mentioned at dinner?" he asked, turning genially to me. "Some problem that developed while you were staying with them recently? You said," a quick chortle, "it would ruin your dinner to discuss it just then. Dinner's over. Is this an appropriate moment?" he finished, clearly assuming the "problem" to be something amusing. But immediately he sensed something tense entering the atmosphere. "Oh I see, I've brought up something *really* disagreeable. Well," turning to a poor reproduction of a van Gogh café scene on the wall, "I see you're interested in *that* period. Gauguin, too, is—"

"Mr. Lockhart," I put in as Greg gazed at me steadily, "I would like to tell you about it now. If . . . well, you don't mind?" I said to Greg. He shook his head soberly, even though he was not entirely sober.

"For heaven's sake don't tell me any family secrets!" exclaimed Lockhart. "I'm already burdened with so many, mine and other people's."

"This is no secret," said Greg dryly. "The local press up there gave it rather a large play."

So I briefly told him of the theft of the Militsa Diamond, and of the party which preceded it. Mr. Lockhart was a brilliant man with much sympathy for the dilemmas of others, much understanding of human predicaments, and I thought it a good idea to explain the situation in detail, Greg appearing to have no objection: their financial security had disappeared with the uninsured diamond; Alexei's writing career was going nowhere; Zinaida apparently could earn nothing.

A silence followed, and somehow the energy in the room, the mental energy became centered on Gregory. I didn't know how or why this was happening, but it was as though a movie camera were now focused squarely on him. He was sitting on the couch, wearing only shorts and sneakers, clutching another bottle of beer and staring at the floor. He glanced up. Both of us were staring at him.

Shrugging his shoulders he remarked with a sour grin, "I guess it's up to me, isn't it?"

"Well now," began Lockhart in his rounded, warm, authoritative voice, "that's a tall order for a young man to be suddenly handed."

"Not so young. I'm twenty-five. The war."

"Even so. You graduate in June, do you? Yes, well, two parents to support. . . ." Lockhart's voice trailed off.

"Yeah," said Greg energetically, springing up, "I'm sure I can work it out. They're going to be all right." His slurred words told me the beers were on top of several stronger drinks taken earlier, and not that much earlier. "And they're going to stay in Edgewater! I'm seeing to that. My mother is not winding up in some fleabag. Not after where she grew up and what she was used to as a girl."

"But," put in Lockhart, frowning up at him, "are you sure the diamond can't be recovered? The list of people who might have taken it is very limited. It seems more than likely that one of your guests took it. Mustn't it have been an aberration on someone's part, someone perhaps who had too much to drink and knew all of you had had too much and were in deepest sleep? Someone *young*," he said with sudden decisiveness. "No older person, not of the type you had at your party, would succumb to such an erratic impulse. It was someone young," he said flatly. "Now what young people were among your guests?"

There was a pause, and that curious focus of energy in this room, this room of three ill-assorted people, was turning, I sensed, not on Gregory again but on me.

I was sitting in one of the deep old armchairs sniffing the last of my cognac. I took a really deep inhale of it now as I felt them looking at me, and I said, "I don't know, let's see. There was the Maurys' daughter—"

"She left early," put in Greg.

"And . . . well, not very many."

"There was Allan here," burst out Greg suddenly with a hard laugh. "He's young."

Lockhart gave that barking laugh of his and looked not at me but at Greg. Then in the ensuing silence he asked quietly, "Do you suspect him?"

"Of course not!" cried Greg. "He's too naïve."

"Naïve," echoed Lockhart. "That never prevented a crime. Quite the contrary." He looked more closely at Gregory, who was moving somewhat restlessly around the room, having found and pulled on a T-shirt. "Quite a burden you seem to be taking on yourself."

"Oh listen, I can work it all out. It'll all work out. I'm not worried."

"I still," pursued Lockhart quietly, "would have someone question the other guests, if that hasn't already been done. It seems to me that jewel might well be recovered. I can't believe that a seasoned professional jewel thief stole into your house late that night, knew just where it was kept, somehow broke into the *safe*," and here his voice acquired a querulous, questioning tone, "made off with it and disposed of it with a fence, I believe they're called, before sundown. It doesn't ring true. This is local crime, a neighborhood theft, domestic drama. Look around you. I think," he concluded, getting up, "you may well recover it."

"I don't think so," mumbled Greg. "I've given up on that. So have the folks. Two weeks have gone by. Too late." He drew a deep breath. "It's up to me to take care of them, and I'm going to do it."

Lockhart was moving toward the door. "I haven't given you the manuscript!" I cried, springing up. "It's in my bedroom."

"Don't go just yet, sir. Do you have another couple of minutes?" There was an undercurrent of urgency in Gregory's voice. "I don't meet many people who knew my parents long ago, and I want—"

I came into the room, clutching the pages of a short story.

"Well just a moment longer," he conceded, sitting down again. I gave him and myself a drop more cognac.

"You see," Greg resumed, seating himself on the couch, "they've had such a peculiar life, my parents, that I kind of don't entirely understand them . . . I love them but I just don't always *get* them, if you know what I mean." Lockhart was looking at him with that air of intelligent and fixed attention he accorded out of respect to anything that interested him or, as in the case of *Utter Beyond*, was at least attempting to interest him. I was not sure into which of these two categories Gregory fell. "For instance, they were the guests of Paul in Yugoslavia when you met them, weren't they?"

"Yes."

Paul, I knew, was Prince Paul, sometime regent of Yugoslavia, and still another cousin of Zinaida's.

"And before that mother was living in a 'grace and favor' house given my grandmother by King George. And after Yugoslavia, well, they come to America, don't they, and Dad goes to work and he isn't very good at it, and then he tries to write and he isn't successful—"

"Not financially," put in Lockhart. "So few writers are. I have been exceptionally lucky. He sent me his first two books and I read them with great interest. He has a fluency, and he has subject matter. He just, well, it's hard to establish a 'voice,' as Gertrude Stein would say. All good writers have a voice you can hear in their prose—and poetry. Your father can't find his voice. How could he? In his third language. . . ."

"Yeah, well if you knew how hard he tries! Locks himself in the library at home all day long . . . weeks on end . . . reams of pages . . . and then sometimes no pages at all and then he *really* goes crazy."

"Mm. I must have a talk with him sometime, sometime soon. You see, another thing Gertrude said which is of the first importance in imaginative writing is this: there must be an element of play in all good writing. That frees the imagination instead of the will to do the work. If you harness your *will*, and your will only, well then the writing is willful, isn't it." It was not a question. "And good writing does not spring from that, it springs from the freed imagination and *that* springs from what she—and I—can only find the word 'playfulness' to describe. It's hard to imagine Shakespeare feeling playful while writing *King Lear*, but on a certain level he must have been."

Whew, I breathed to myself. How playful do I feel when I'm writing?

"You see," said Greg, frowning urgently, "you ought to tell him that. He needs to hear things like that. He's

129

isolated. So is my mother. I think they've always been isolated. Royalty is always isolated," he said, then added bitterly, "and so is poverty, and they've got both. But not for long. I'm going to see to that. It isn't fair for them. They're not prepared for it. I'll make it up to them."

"But," Lockhart said gently, "now listen here, Trouvenskoy. You mustn't take too much on yourself. It isn't healthy. As for 'making it up to them,' you didn't take it away from them, did you." Greg took a long gulp from the bottle of beer, finishing it. "You must not feel any guilt, and I see that you do. You do, don't you?" he finished kindly.

Gazing at the floor, Greg then looked up and muttered, "Yeah, yes sir, I do."

"Now that's very very bad. You must pull your feet out of that quagmire, free yourself, and then do what you can for these parents you love."

"They try so hard," he muttered. "Mother on her knees scrubbing the kitchen floor. All right? Paul of Yugoslavia, George of England. She's on her knees with the pail of dirty water. All right? Well, it ain't all right."

Gregory was going into his self-pitying and truculent mood. Gregory had lots of moods. Gregory was a Slav. Some days I was almost afraid to speak to him, knowing he was ready to bite my head off.

"One thing, I must say," said Lockhart quietly, "that I repeat and I think you ought to do is *question the guests*. Perhaps not you, perhaps a detective, the police, I don't know. But *someone*. I wouldn't be a bit surprised if you unearthed the gem. Some frightened person would go out in the backyard and *dig it up for you*. That young person even now may be just praying to have this burden lifted. Too frightened to come forward."

Gregory was prowling around the room again. "Wait," he said. "I want to show you something." He went into the bedroom and came out with the small framed photograph of his mother he kept on his desk. She was about twelve years old when it was taken, wearing the gorgeous, strange, encrusted court dress of St. Petersburg, which included a kind of jeweled cardinal's hat on her head.

Lockhart, standing in the middle of our rather glum room, studied it. "What a sweet little girl, all tricked out in the paraphernalia of tsardom. She looks weighted down by it. But she emerged from it successfully, didn't she," he continued with characteristic optimism. "She and your father were able to shake the trappings of the old regime off—that's what staying with Paul and in one of King George's, well, charity houses was, clinging to the trappings of something that was dead and gone, Old Russia. They were too young and too realistic for that. They came here. They started over. They forgot about their titles. That was the empty past. Give them my love." He was moving toward the door. Then, in one of his inimitable asides, behind his hand, eyes bright, he confided, "Question everybody. Find the jewel. Then relax." A pause. "You're not guilty," he finished, looking at Greg fixedly for a moment. Then he was gone.

"I'm going out and get *really* drunk," muttered Gregory, looking around for his street clothes.

"Don't do that."

"Well, I'm going to."

"Why?"

"I'm going to," he repeated, more or less to himself.

10

Swimming practice with the varsity team at Yale resembled a kind of slavery in which the slaves could escape at any time—drop off the squad—but rarely did. Perhaps we suffered from a kind of mass hypnosis imposed on us by our coach, the remorseless Bob Kiphuth ("Don't just stand there, do push-ups!"). He did inflict on us a kind of bondage, swimming endless laps with our ankles tied together, for example, and we accepted it.

Late in the afternoon five days a week we practiced in the echoing, chlorine-and-humidity-laden air of the Exhibition Pool in the Payne Whitney Gymnasium. The crystalline bluish water of the pool itself, the gleaming whiteness of the tile deck under the bright lights, the gun-metal-green seats rising steeply on all sides, this rather spectacular setting lent a heightened significance to what was after all just a group of young men practicing. Of course we were members of not just any swimming team, we were the Yale Swimming Team, arguably the best, year in and year out, in the country.

On this squad, I fell somewhere in the middle area between the great stars who were destined to win Olympic titles and the drones who would rarely if ever get into a meet. I was a journeyman varsity swimmer, very good, and well below the best.

Looking back, I don't really know why I imposed this tough discipline on myself. I had been a swimmer and a good one in school; so, without thinking about it, I continued competitive swimming at Yale. Gregory, who had made and then dropped off the Yale hockey team, could not understand it, or pretended not to be able to do so. "Your face buried in chlorine two hours a day," he remarked derisively, "just swimming up and down, up and down, not *getting* anywhere!" But, like my relationship with Mr. Lockhart, I suspected he secretly rather admired my doing it, my persistence and discipline, and my modest level of achievement. He himself just couldn't stick to the grueling hockey schedule of practice and games. "I'm twenty-five years old," he argued, not unreasonably, "I'm past school-boy sports."

But I was not yet twenty-two and not past them; I think it was as simple as that. I actually enjoyed pulling myself up and down that pool thousands of times, many thousands of times. It felt good to be in the best physical shape possible for me.

Sometimes I reflected on the oddness of Gregory and me being such good friends. We seemed to have so little in common. I was a varsity athlete; he scorned that. I was an aspiring writer; he never read a book except under duress. I was a southern country boy; he sprang from international royalty.

I accepted the slavery of swimming practice as just one of those things, and I liked winning—not Yale winning so much as myself, Allan Prieston, winning. I was even then very much a self-centered individual, autonomous, "inner-directed," as all writers are and have to be; we are all, in the end, from Missouri.

After practice one afternoon in the Exhibition Pool, I lingered in the water. Kiphuth and his assistant and the other swimmers left; someone turned out the overhead lights, but the underwater lights remained on, shooting a smoky mysterious illumination through the water, which acquired a magical, phosphorescent glow; it seemed to be bearing me up, giving me greater buoyancy as I slid easily through it, turned over on my back, gazing up into the darkness. The pool was mine for those few minutes, and the gym, and the school. I felt so much at home in the water and in this pool, and a sense permeated my lulled mind that I was very much at home in this school, and would be one day in the world beyond it, too.

In our rooms one evening a week later I said to Greg, "Mr. Lockhart's right. If nobody's thoroughly questioned the guests at that party, let's you and me do it."

"Waste of time." He was getting dressed in his dark suit, shoes, tie, to go to the weekly meeting of his senior society.

"Why leave that stone unturned? It just might supply a lead at least, a clue. You tell me the word from your parents is that the police weren't doing a damn thing."

"You're right about that."

"Well then . . .?"

"We'll see about it." He pulled on a duffle coat and started for the door.

"Off to your Spook Night," I jibed. "Is it true you guys

get together in that mausoleum and wrestle each other naked?"

He gave me the tsarist take-him-to-the-salt-mines glare, and was gone.

I turned to my homework, background reading on the origins of the First World War. I was trying to disentangle the nexus of exchanges during the summer of 1914 among officials in Berlin, Vienna, Paris, London, Belgrade, and St. Petersburg, with guilt slithering somewhere amid them. Somewhere was the Death's-Head, the cabal of war lovers who pitched the old order headfirst into catastrophe, scattering the dead in their millions from the obscene mud of northern France to the dusty deserts of Mesopotamia to the endless steppes of Mother Russia, sweeping Hohenzollern and Habsburg and Romanoff from their ancient thrones, scattering the old aristocrats and the old manners and the old culture like so much rubbish into the gutter.

The telephone in the living room rang. It was Alex. I explained where Gregory was and he exclaimed, "Oh yes, his secret society. I forgot. Imagine one of us in a secret society! In Russia they existed exclusively to bring us down. What do you suppose their driving purpose is at Yale?"

"To separate the wheat from the chaff."

"Which are you?"

"We won't know until Tap Day, in May. Unless Greg forces Wolf's Head to take me, I'm pretty sure I'm chaff. Too literary. And after all, What Have I Done for Yale?"

He ruminated, and then suggested, "You swim for Yale."

"Not good enough."

"Do you care?"

After a reflective silence I said, "I don't really think so. Every club and society I've ever wanted to join and then joined, I've wondered two weeks later why it seemed important. I'm fairly sure that would be true again."

"I don't think writers belong in exclusive enclaves, do you?"

"The last place for them—us."

I mentioned Lockhart's suggestion that the guests at the party be questioned, and at the appearance of this subject Alexei's voice altered, lost its urbane, bantering tone and became older. "Yes," he agreed wearily, "why not try it? The police certainly won't. They suggested we get a German police dog and a shotgun, and then they forgot about the case as far as I can see. Question the guests. Something might turn up, I suppose." He did not sound hopeful, not about questioning the guests, and not about life.

"Tell Greg we would like to see him up here this weekend. You come too. Naida misses you"—his voice began to grow younger again—"in the kitchen. She says you're a marvel at drying the pots and pans."

I laughed at that, but then in some recess of my brain the laugh echoed hollowly. Perhaps Princess Zinaida and Prince Alexis did not really want me there for my kitchen efficiency. Perhaps they thought I just might be that drunk and impulsive young person postulated by Reeves Lockhart who had stolen the Militsa Diamond, which had been their past, and their future.

Calling on the neighbors by Gregory and me, or "questioning the suspects" as we preferred to think of it, was entertaining, sometimes hilarious, and led nowhere. It was impossible to think of any of these flighty, eccentric, or preoccupied people as safecrackers. I could imagine Harriet van Rensaaver impulsively dropping a silver saltcellar into her pocketbook and being horrified to find it there the next day. But hammer open a safe in the middle of the night? Mary and Mervyn Maury were perhaps borderline psychotics, but for that very reason too deranged to carry off this caper. Their daughter, Maureen, was, as Greg put it succinctly, "on the moon" and not a possibility. Charles Cummings was dismissed out of hand—"too conceited" was Greg's verdict—and the other guests all appeared for various reasons equally impossible.

So we sat, the three Trouvenskoys and I, that evening in the small living room where I had first encountered them, Naida and Alex in their habitual chairs, Greg and I on the sofa. We had sherry again. I could not help but think of *The Cherry Orchard*, doomed aristocrats graciously acting out their last days on the old estate before losing it forever.

What was to become of these people? There seemed to be no relative to turn to for assistance. Alexei's career would never work out. Naida would never sell her memories. Gregory was a beginner in the life of commerce.

It was a lugubrious evening, although Greg manfully tried to be cheerful, telling us about a dinner with Merry's father, in New York. I read the subtext of this monologue: I will marry Merry, her father will take me into the shipping firm, and I will then hold your life here at Edgewater together. I was sure Alex and Naida were reading this subtext too. They did not appear very stirred by it, or hopeful about it. Perhaps they were contemplating the Russian equivalent of what I was contemplating in English: there's many a slip twixt the cup and the lip.

The two of them seemed, now more than ever, stoic people, and fatalistic people. They were charming, gentle and charming, and it seemed that a baleful destiny was going to pursue them to the end.

The following morning, the house and the river still

wrapped in the immobilization of winter, the phone rang and surprisingly it was for me, and even more surprisingly it was Reeves Lockhart calling to say he had been a guest lecturer at, of all places, West Point, for the past week, and, the roads being clear, might he drop by for tea that afternoon?

"How did you know I was here?" I asked in passing.

"Oh, I know these things."

The Trouvenskoys enthusiastically agreed to his coming, Alex taking the telephone from me to urge him on. Both he and Zinaida seemed infused for the first time that weekend with vitality by his call, and even a kind of optimism came into the air.

"Haven't seen him in *years*," she remarked. "He's so brilliant that he used to make me uneasy in the old days. But now, I hope I've grown past that. He is," she added a shade abstractedly and not quite so cheerfully, "so penetrating and perceptive. I used to think sometimes he was seeing *through* me."

"He's always so full of energy and plans," put in Alex. "And he's surely the only writer *West Point* would have invited for a visit!"

"What d'you suppose he wants to see you about?" wondered Gregory aloud. "He can't be coming to see Allan, he gets pestered enough by him in New Haven."

"Old times," suggested Zinaida.

We were having breakfast at a table in the pantry. "He hasn't forgotten his old friends. Allan, I'm so glad you reminded him about us, and where we are."

"He's very interested in the missing diamond," I put in unguardedly, and then wished like hell I hadn't. It was as though I'd thrown cold water over all of them. In some way

Zinaida and Alexei felt that their being robbed had been improper, not a fit subject for conversation, something you lived with, like a demented aunt, but did not allude to unnecessarily.

Reeves arrived in his Lincoln convertible about four that afternoon. Tea was made short shrift of: "It's not too early for a drink," said Alex expansively, making Lockhart comfortable by the fire in the big living room.

"Certainly not," he agreed. "I'm staying the night with the Astors—you know the Astors"—Alex nodded—"very nearby, so I don't care *what* I drink!"

Zinaida, who had been upstairs when he arrived, now came into the room. She had for the afternoon banished from her ambience the frying pans and the unpaid bills. She had been a Princess of Imperial Russia and this afternoon she looked it, wearing a long russet gown and a golden chain around her neck hanging almost to her waist. At the bottom of the chain was a medallion with some sort of crest. With her black hair pulled close along the sides of her head and her easy erect carriage, she radiated a sense of simplicity and of distinction.

She and Lockhart greeted each other with the greatest warmth, European-style cheek kisses. Hand-kissing was for others; Reeves, it was recognized by Zinaida, Alexis, and Reeves, belonged to a kind of final extension of the family where cheeks and not hands were kissed.

As they motioned Lockhart back into his chair by the fire I noticed that Alexei, in his ruby velvet smoking jacket and some kind of embroidered black slippers, had also reacquired that air of distinction he and his wife had possessed the evening I first met them. They had slipped back into it easily and unobtrusively, as into a pair of fine but well-worn gloves.

Reeves was wearing a somewhat rumpled tweed suit; Greg and I had on gray flannel trousers and sweaters. All five of us, in other words, had rather unconsciously but instinctively donned the uniforms suitable to our stations in life. Looking at our group in this lofty room around the toiling fire, in this fine old mansion with the pristine snow immaculately surrounding it beside the great icy river, we all would have appeared appropriate to our callings in every way and with nothing amiss. As she sat comfortably upright in her armchair, you could never have imagined Naida scrubbing the kitchen; wearing a tiara in procession with her family through the dazzling reception rooms of the Winter Palace, yes, the pots and pans, no. Alexei, lounging with a tiny cigar opposite her, was the quintessential Russian aristocrat. The desperate aging failure in an old gray bathrobe in the library racking his brains for a new book idea seemed nonexistent. Reeves, articulate, forthright, in comfortable country clothes, embodied his scholarly side perfectly. Nowhere visible was the world celebrity with all the money. Gregory looked like an Ivy Leaguer: the rather hard-bitten veteran of the European Theater of Operations had vanished. And I supposed that I looked the complete Yalie too, no vestige of the unformed provincial from the Border now detectable. We wore our uniforms very successfully, everything contradictory or extraneous eliminated from the design, covered over, concealed.

And yet, did we not have aspects of ourselves to conceal that were crucial, not merely pots and accents and royalties?

Reeves and Alexei and Zinaida began talking about the

coast of Yugoslavia in the 1920s, when they had last spent considerable time together, and also of the south of France. Vodka, that dangerous Russian vodka, combined this time with tonic, began to flow again. I surmised that strong drink would be the very last luxury—if they thought of it as a luxury at all—that the Trouvenskoys were prepared to surrender.

"The young are climbing all over the south of France these days," Reeves was saying with his usual cheerful intensity. "And during the summer French workers from the north and their families arrive *en masse*. Paid-by-the-government vacations. I was talking to the Aga Khan about it just a few months ago. He's disgusted. 'Well but,' I said, 'don't you think *French* workers have the right to use *French* Mediterranean beaches?' 'No,' he growled, 'they don't. *I* do.' I rather admired the crusty forthrightness of it, indefensible though his position was."

"Everybody still gambling wildly?" asked Alex nostalgically, relishing these recollections. "We haven't been back to Europe since long before the war."

"It was another age," observed Zinaida without apparent regret. "I remember Kschessinska used to be at the tables in Monte Carlo every night in the twenties."

"Kschessinska," said Lockhart expansively, "is teaching dancing in Paris and I don't think can afford to lose any money gambling anymore. I saw her there last fall. She and Andrei were telling me about that woman, that Mrs. Anderson, the supposed Anastasia."

There was a thoughtful or uneasy silence. Then I asked, "Who's Mrs. Anderson?" I vaguely knew the answer, but wanted to hear it all.

"Oh you know—"

"She's that woman—"

Alexei and Zinaida had both started precipitously to answer the question. Naida continued, "She's a woman who's supposed to be my cousin Anastasia, the tsar's youngest daughter."

"Didn't she come here to this country," Reeves inquired in the urbane, careless manner he used when he was really after something, "around 1930 or so?"

"Yes, still another of my cousins, Xenia, invited her over." There was a pause, and then she finished quietly, "We met her."

"Yes," added Alexis noncommittally.

There was another silence and then Lockhart leaned out of his chair in my direction, as though he had instructions especially for me. "It's been a long and bewildering case," he said confidingly. Then, turning to the others, he threw in one of his asides: "Prieston here is a bottomless pit of curiosity. We'll make a writer of him yet!" Did Alexei stiffen ever so slightly at this? "Do you mind if I fill him in on the case?"

Both Naida and Alex consented readily.

"You see," he began, settling back in his chair, vodka and tonic in hand, launching into a complex human story, personal dilemma, historical mystery, and thoroughly happy at the prospect; it suited his mentality, his imagination, the curiosity that had made *him* a writer, "in 1920 the German police fished a young woman out of a canal in Berlin. She had apparently attempted to drown herself. She refused to answer any questions, identify herself, speak at all. Not knowing what else to do, they locked her up in a mental hospital, although none of the doctors, then or later, thought her insane. For two years she simply lay in bed, speechless. Later she explained that throughout this period she had been terrified, frightened that her identity would be discovered and she would be sent back to Russia, where the Bolsheviks would surely kill her, as—" He suddenly looked disconcerted.

"—as they had killed the others," Naida finished quietly for him.

A swift, penetrating glance at her, and then Reeves went on, "At last another patient, who had been in St. Petersburg in the old days, approached her and said, 'I know who you are! I saw you in Petersburg. You're one of the tsar's daughters!' and the young woman glared at her in terror and cried, 'Be quiet, be quiet!' " There was a suspended silence, and then Lockhart continued, "But the word was out. She said that she was indeed the tsar's youngest daughter, Anastasia, that she had been imprisoned with the rest of her family by the Bolsheviks in Siberia, but on the night of their murder a guard had helped her escape during the terrible confusion of the massacre—she does have some bad scars, she must have been injured somewhere—and eventually made her way to Germany. There is a certain amount of reliable collaborative evidence. The Swedish—"

"Not much," put in Alexei clearly.

After a silence, Lockhart resumed. "The Swedish consul general, traveling through that part of Siberia at the time, had his train stopped, and searched, for 'the tsar's daughter,' as the searchers told him."

"If only she . . . " Zinaida said almost inaudibly.

"Hm?" prompted Lockhart with masked eagerness.

"Nothing." A piercing silence. "If only . . . " she said in a rambling, very low tone, "a ring . . . an embroidered handkerchief . . . "

"The official investigation by the Whites," said Alexei firmly, "gave no support at all to the woman's story. The

143

eyewitness testimony was that all four daughters very tragically died in that cellar. I think that's more important than a rumor heard by a Swede on a train."

Lockhart and Naida gazed at him, Lockhart understandingly and analytically, Naida with that very dark impenetrable expression in her eyes.

After this brief interval when eyes tried to read minds, eyes tried to telegraph messages, Lockhart turned once again, in a diversionary movement, toward me. "And since then, Allan," he never called me "Allan" but had forgotten that in the pressure of this performance, "for almost thirty years now, the woman has wandered here and there, mostly in Europe, been questioned, examined, photographed, measured, weighed, 'recognized,' denounced, invited to stay in this castle, thrown out of that palace, put in hospitals for any number of ailments, tried to flee it all like some kind of royal—or imposter—Garbo, and the more she flees the more the popular press pursues her—there is a play about her running in Paris this very minute with great success—and the end is nowhere in sight!" He gave me a look of stage amazement. Just what game was he playing, and who was going to win, and what was the prize?

I should have guessed, knowing Lockhart.

"Actually," put in Alexis with cool urbanity, "the end of this drama came many years ago, in 1928, to be exact. The old empress, the tsar's mother, died that year in exile, back in her native Denmark. Virtually the entire Romanoff family gathered for her funeral. They issued—Naida's mother included—a statement that this woman had nothing in common with the grand duchess Anastasia, that she was an imposter. And that was—or should have been," he added in a way only describable as "bitchily"—"that."

Once again the big old room was engulfed in a concentrated silence. Then from Lockhart there came a soothing, carrying, "Yes. Yes, indeed, that statement was issued. And signed I believe by every member of the family present. But only one of them, Olga, had actually interviewed the woman. And yes Olga did . . . finally . . . after some hesitation . . . announce that the woman was not . . . after all . . . her niece Anastasia. And then later," he went on, "a couple of years later, the woman came to America, didn't she?"

"Yes," said Alexei, "she did. And do you know what? She couldn't speak Russian!"

"No," murmured Naida, "she wouldn't speak Russian."

"How did she look?" I put in, fascinated by the tale. "Did she look like—"

Alexei said: "It had been so long."

Zinaida, blinking, added, "We couldn't tell. It was so long ago, and all so strange. It was the people around her who were claiming it for her."

She was looking at me and did not see the glance Reeves gave her: so piercing, so X ray, that I understood how she had been uneasy about this trait of his when she was a young woman.

He leaned forward now from his chair, confidingly. The fire crackled; outside the light was fading for the day; a sheen of shroudlike grayness was settling over the snowy lawn and icy river. I knew Lockhart's moves by now; he was going to resume control of this story, to drive it to some conclusion he had decided it must reach, for reasons of artistic completeness, for reasons of truth, for the good, I sensed confusedly, of Alexis and Zinaida.

"When I had lunch in Paris at Fouquet's," he began in his

friendliest manner, "with Kschessinska and Andrei—oh yes"—turning to me—"I've got to keep our writer here filled in. Kschessinska was the greatest ballet dancer of tsarist Russia, greater, at least more renowned, than Pavlova even. Andrei is her husband. He is the grand duke Andrei Vladimirovich."

"My cousin," said Naida automatically, like a post office clerk stamping an envelope.

"Well now," resumed Lockhart energetically, "they were very much caught up in this whole case. They too had spent time with Mrs. Anderson, and they, I will have to say, firmly believe in her authenticity." There was a silence.

"I know," whispered Zinaida.

"They felt," he went on, "that no imposter could know the tiny details of life at Tsarskoe Selo and at Livadia as she did. But it wasn't really that so much as her whole manner, her demeanor, her *assumptions*, you might say, that convinced them of her genuineness."

Naida was looking at her hands folded in her lap.

"We need some refreshing of these drinks!" exclaimed Alex, jumping up. He began to gather the glasses.

I got up too. "I know why I'm invited up here," I remarked jokingly, feeling any joke, however anemic, could be useful at this moment.

Alex and I went across the big room into the small sitting room and the alcove beyond containing their little bar. Fumbling with his hand in the ice bucket, he said more or less to himself, "We should get off this subject . . . upsets her, always upsets her . . . finished, over and finished . . . it's dead and they're dead and it's all dead. . . ."

I said, "Mr Lockhart has a lot of curiosity about things."

146

"All writers have great curiosity about things," he grumbled. "That's why they're writers." He had said "they're" and not "we're," I noticed. A pang of sympathy for this gallant, struggling man struck me: he wasn't a writer, not really, and he never would be, and he knew it. We went back into the main living room where someone had turned on the lamps. With our glasses refilled Alexei moved to take over the conversation, a move that I sensed was doomed, not because Lockhart would resist it—he would, but only up to a point, a civilized point beyond which he would not go—but because Zinaida would resist it.

". . . and I have enjoyed *all* your books so much," Alex was saying to Lockhart, "including especially your latest, *Not to Praise Him*. The way you interweave diary entries and letters to bring classic Rome alive for us! It reminded me, I just mean technically, of *The Road to Ste. Michèle* . . ." and on in this vein, intelligently and I was sure sincerely praising his work. Nor was Lockhart indifferent to such praise; he liked for people to respond to and praise his work—"Why shouldn't I?" he once remarked to me, a little annoyed, "I didn't write it for the birds, you know!" And now the famous author was gracious and made all the right responses, and I knew that his mind was elsewhere. Gregory was studying his drink, and Zinaida gazed into the fire.

When Alexei's compliments came to a pause, and Lockhart, having made the right responses, said nothing, there was a silence. "Where is Mrs. Anderson now?" Naida asked into this silence. "In Paris?"

"She's in Germany. The Black Forest. Living in a kind of hut, I believe. One of the minor German princes provided it for her."

Zinaida looked opaque. ". . . a hut . . ." she echoed.

"But there's one thing," I put in, "I read in one of the books in your library. The tsar left ten million pounds or dollars or rubles in the Bank of England. If this Mrs. Anderson turned out to be legitimate, she would get the money, is that right?"

"No, it is *not* right," said Alex emphatically. "There is no money. *There is no money.* Who knows who would get it? Who cares, because there isn't any."

"No," murmured Zinaida.

"Never is," put in Greg sharply. "How about you and me getting more wood for the fire, sport?"

I got up and followed him outside to the woodpile near the railroad tracks. "Anastasia!" he grumbled, piling logs into my arms. "Grand dukes! The tsar's vanishing ten million rubles! Ever hear anything so futile?"

"But I think it's fascinating."

"It may be fascinating to *you.* To you it's like going to a movie. But they've had to live it, the folks have. Well, I'm not going to live it, because you *can't*, it's *dead.* It's like the ten million rubles, it doesn't exist anymore. Come on. We'd better go back. Can't let the fire go out. It's the only thing alive in there today." We trudged back through the snow toward the door. "I'd rather talk about *writing* than this."

In the living room Zinaida was saying, ". . . and in 1930 we moved—in 1930, of all years—to America. We hadn't really heard about the Depression, the Slump as they were calling it then. We didn't take it in."

"*We'd* been in a Slump since 1917, you see," put in Alex dryly.

"We hadn't taken it in," Naida repeated, pursuing her own thoughts. "Alexei and I, well, practicality wasn't our strongest suit, it had to be admitted." She took another sip of her drink. "But we had to come—"

"Yes," said Alex, in a mellower tone, "after living in Russia, under the tsar, whatever one might think of his policies or of the whole regime, that made living in any other monarchy impossible . . . England, well . . ."

"It just wasn't possible," added Zinaida with a certain intensity. "It would be like changing religions, somehow. We couldn't begin to feel the same loyalty, same meaning." Greg stirred restively, unnoticed by everyone but me. "We simply couldn't. So we came here, to a republic."

"And hooray for Franklin Roosevelt!" burst out Alex.

Lockhart reared back in his chair, pulled an ample, round gold watch out of the watch pocket in his trousers, and exclaimed, "Look what time it's gotten to be! I must be off!"

As Alex was helping him on with his overcoat at the door on the driveway-and-railroad side of the house, Naida said to him, "What you know about the Mrs. Anderson case is remarkable." She laughed a little hoarsely. "Maybe *you'll* solve it, and remove a family skeleton." She kissed him on both cheeks. "I'm only joking. And do come again, and not in twenty years!"

Greg and I escorted him to Hollywood's gift to Reeves Lockhart, the dashing Lincoln Continental convertible. He got in, and the car refused to start. He had inadvertently left the parking lights on, not for the first time. Gregory's cables were not in the trunk of his car, he was surprised to find, so he volunteered to drive Lockhart to the Astors' place, leaving his car to be dealt with in the morning. I went along with them.

The roads had been scraped and sanded, so we mounted without difficulty the steep hill rising behind Edgewater.

At the top we turned into River Road, which ran along with the bluff parallel to the river. As we approached the roadhouse where Greg, Merry, and I had gone that first weekend, its neon lights and general tackiness appeared to strike a chord in Reeves Lockhart. "Look at that cozy little dump," he remarked interestedly.

"That's one of the local hangouts," said Greg. "Allan here danced the night away there once with a Trotskyite."

"Did you!" said Lockhart, amused. "You must tell me about that sometime . . . a real country gin mill, from the look of it." There was a pause.

"Would you," ventured Greg, sensing something, "like to stop in and have, well, one for the road, sort of?"

"You know, I really think I would. Just one. At the outside limit, two. The Astors are such fine, constructive people. And, ah well, *formal*."

It was too early in the evening for the place to be crowded. We took a wooden booth next to the empty dance floor and ordered vodka and tonics.

"I didn't want to mention it at your house," said Reeves to Gregory, "because I know how distressing it must be for your parents. But less so to you I hope, Gregory."

I was "Prieston" to Lockhart, except for his slip of the tongue at Edgewater, because I fell into the category of his apprentice, to be held at a certain distance and instilled with certain skills. Greg, on the other hand, was the son of old friends, and therefore "Gregory."

"What I'm talking about, of course," Lockhart continued, "is the diamond. Did you ever talk to your guests, especially the young ones?"

"Yes, sir, we tried to and got nowhere. It's just vanished, like the tsar's ten million rubles. The money vanishes,

that's an old Russian custom. Now the jewel vanishes." He
was in carefree high spirits today, Gregory was, I noticed,
partly vodka-induced and partly natural. He seemed close
to breaking out of control and doing I couldn't imagine
what. "One day you've got your palace in Petersburg and
your estates in the country and your villa in the Crimea,
and the next day, poof! Vanished! I don't even think about
it, the Militsa"—he almost hissed the word—"Diamond!
What are diamonds to us, and what are we to diamonds!
Tell you what. I'm going to *recoup* the family fortune.
You know that? It's all run out, run dry, *kaput*. You know
what the French call people like me?" His cool blue eyes
looked from one to the other of us.

"I think I may," put in Lockhart finally in a quiet tone.
"You tell us."

"*Fin de race*, that's what. Is that what you were thinking I'd say . . . sir?"

"Mm," began Lockhart thoughtfully, "yes. That's what I
thought *you* thought about yourself. It ain't necessarily so,
you know."

Fin de race: the end of the family line. Greg didn't
strike me as an exemplar of the end of anything, with his
exuberance and vitality and temperament.

But his saying it brought something about him into focus
for me: a kind of desperation, a tremendous restlessness
about his family's past and all the empty grandeur that
came trailing in its wake, the flotsam of Imperial Russia,
like the spars and life jackets and deck chairs found floating
above an ocean liner's sinking, worthless bits and snippets
of greatness that has itself slipped forever beneath the eter-
nal seas. Old émigrés making their pilgrimage to Edgewater still talked about the great palace in Petersburg—it

151

was now a Soviet ministry—the Crimean villa, now a rest home, the estates, now collectivized. And there was the Militsa Diamond, now stolen.

It drove him to distraction, at moments like this, the heritage he never ceased to hear about, to hear invoked all around him, and to be, in practical terms, worthless.

"Oh yeah, I'm going to relaunch the family fortune," he went on merrily, his face slightly flushed, full of vodka's good humor and his own. "There's just me to do it and I'm going to do it. And that diamond, after all, what good was it really? So *maybe* they could get a hundred thousand for it. And after that's gone? Then where would they be? They both come from families that live to be ninety"—then he laughed harshly—"unless the Bolsheviks take one of them out in front of a firing squad, that is. So they'll live to be ninety too. Not ninety-two; I meant ninety . . . too. Did you get it?"

"We got it," I said.

"That hundred thousand would be gone and they'd sell Edgewater and then *that* money would be gone and I'm earning not-very-many thousand dollars a year as a sub-junior-assistant with a wife and three children in some brokerage house or advertising firm or something like that where I wouldn't fit in any more than Dad did—we aren't built for it—" He glanced with a certain confused humor at me. "How does Dad put it? You never forget anything."

"He says," I answered, imitating Alex's Russian accent, "*I* don't know how to relate to the *public*. For three centuries the *public* related to us!"

Gregory threw back his head and hooted with laughter. "That's it!" he cried, when he could speak. He waved his hand in a gesture of banishment over the table. "So all that's out, that plan, they retiring on the Militsa Diamond and I on Wall Street or Madison Avenue or someplace. You want to know what I think about the diamond getting stolen, Mr. Lockhart? I don't think it makes a damn bit of difference in the long run. It just means all of us three surviving Trouvenskoys have got to face reality sooner, head on. I don't even think about that diamond." He fell silent, and then we ordered our second round of vodka and tonics.

"Don't you resent, though," inquired Lockhart quietly, "the *idea* of one of your friends and neighbors stealing from your parents while they're guests in your house?"

Greg's flushed face turned toward him. "Oh—golly I—I do and—I don't know—I don't. Do you think one of them did it?" he asked me.

"Who *else* could have?"

"Well," Gregory burst out, "how about *you!*" And he gave that harsh laugh again. "You had the opportunity, sport!"

In vino veritas and many a true word is spoken in jest: these two aphorisms drummed in my head and I asked myself, despairingly, Does this family I have come to care for so much believe me guilty? Do they go on seeing me in hopes of finding proof, or of shaming me into a confession?

"Gregory," I began in a kind of desperate undertone, "do you really think I'm capable of that? And do your folks think so?"

I waited, stunned, for his answer.

"Oh listen, sport," he began with a kind of forced humorousness, "we royal Ruskies have been shot up and robbed and chased out so much, we'll believe *anything*! Maybe you did! Maybe *I* did. The only person around here I'm reasonably sure didn't is Mr. Lockhart."

"Yes, well, see here, Trouvenskoy," Reeves cut in, "you

say that Allan"—Allan—"had an opportunity to steal the diamond. That is certainly true. But the second part of any case such as this involves motive. Do you see him having a motive?"

Gregory made that banishing motion with his hand over the table again. "Everybody's greedy, everybody's capable of something like that. Don't you think so?" he asked Lockhart with directness. "Who would have thought the Germany of Goethe could permit the Holocaust? Who would have thought *we* could incinerate Hiroshima? Who would have thought the Bolsheviks could have killed millions of people? Who would have thought anything? I can believe anybody's capable of anything."

Lockhart studied him attentively. "That comes from, of course, your own interpretation of yourself, doesn't it?" he said almost kindly. "You project on the world around you what you yourself believe yourself to be."

Gregory, his face empty of expression, looked at him.

"Well!" exclaimed Lockhart, beginning to slide energetically from the booth and dropping some bills on the table. "I'm sure that's enough cash to take care of the drinks, and we must be off! Mustn't keep Mrs. Astor waiting!"

We delivered him to the baronial Astor estate above the river, and drove home, surprisingly slowly, through the rural countryside, the car's headlights cutting a swath of wintry glitter in our path through the blackness.

Gregory hardly spoke at all during the drive to Edgewater. As we were approaching the house he said in a monotone, "Your friend, the Pulitzer Prize–winner, gives me the creeps."

His speaking allowed me to break my own tense silence. "Gregory, do you or do your parents think I had anything to do with the disappearance of the diamond?"

He turned to glance at what he could see of my face from the dashboard lights. "Well . . . did you?"

"Oh . . . oh boy, Gregory—"

"No," he muttered, "we don't think so."

Don't *think* so!

11

Back in New Haven the following week, the phone rang in the living room early one afternoon. It was Reeves Lockhart. "It's a very promising pre-spring day outside, have you noticed?" In fact, I had sensed that faint hint of softness drifting along the rigorous New England wind, and a certain tautness coming into the branches of trees and shrubbery as they responded to the first intimations of renewal.

"I don't know," Lockhart went on, "whether your generation takes walks. Mine did, by the mile, and still does, when the lumbago hasn't taken over. Why don't you join me for a tramp?"

I agreed, of course, and to my surprise he suggested we meet at the gate leading to the Yale Bowl on the outskirts of town. "One of the few places in the area where you can stretch your legs," he explained.

I put on some sturdy walking shoes, a corduroy jacket and cap, and drove to the appointed place. There was a washed, glowing northern sky overhead, and brave, radiant sunshine spread across the still-frozen earth, except when fast-moving, high clouds blocked it.

At the slender columns of the Walter Camp Gate, I waited until Lockhart in his incongruous, deluxe convertible arrived. He was wearing a brown duffle coat, woolen scarf, and a slouched, sort of green Tyrolean hat.

"Now then," he said, slamming the door of his car and walking briskly toward me, "first we'll just circle the bowl and then we'll strike off across those playing fields and give ourselves a good lungful of the right kind of air."

The Yale Bowl resembled a large, military defensive emplacement, rather like the Maginot Line, I imagined, or what the Confederates erected at Vicksburg: a great earthen mound with the formidable concrete siding of the stadium rising above it. Stretching away to the west was a wide expanse of playing fields, which would soon be busy with soccer and lacrosse. At the moment I could see even at that distance a few figures tossing around a football, and on the track around the bowl a couple of runners. Like Lockhart, these private athletes sensed something promising on the wind and had to get out in it. A stiff wind was indeed blowing, making it quite chilly when, from time to time, the sun passed behind the hurrying clouds.

We set off, Lockhart establishing a brisk pace. "I'm a great walker, *great* walker," he confided energetically. "In 1930 Gene Tunney and I took a walk through the Alps, and the press couldn't get over it. He was the heavyweight boxing champion, or just had been, or was just about to be, I can't remember which, so that was all right, but *I* was a rather rarefied writer with two slender and elegant novels to my credit so far, and what was *I* doing tramping up and down the Alps with a boxer! I should have been taking tea with Lady Cunard, they felt, or absinthe with Jean Cocteau. Not plodding along with Tunney.

"I enjoyed it, I enjoyed it. Can't sit around talking about Kafka all the time, can we? Tunney was a very earnest student of literature. Used to have *King Lear* in a kind of bracket next to his shaving mirror and he'd read passages while shaving. I modeled the father on him, a little, in my play *The Nick of Time*. No pun—I hate puns—that is, unless you're a genius at them, as Joyce was—no pun intended."

"How was West Point?" I asked, just beginning to become a little winded.

"Full of Gene Tunneys. A few thousand of them, all in one place . . . well meaning . . . I was pleased to see the Trouvenskoys again after all these years. Alexei is a touching figure, isn't he? Speaking of well meaning, he means so well and yet his life has been so star-crossed and I fear, well, destiny aids and helps along those who recognize her, the blind—you know the rest."

"Never should have set himself up as a writer?"

"No," replied Lockhart in a low, regretful tone, "no." We tramped on, drawing near the bowl, which was now assuming its natural massiveness. "But Zinaida is the one who is a remarkable person. I'm not talking about her royal lineage, which is simply an irrelevance where it is not a handicap to her. She has a complex and original mind, and she can find no way to employ it, employ it externally I mean, outside of her home and marriage. I think she is, within them, as happy as most. But a lot of her is being wasted. She knows it. She drinks a good deal? Of course she does.

"Women, of course, certain women, are a writer's best friend. They understand more, sympathize more, empathize more. They will be closest to you, place themselves at your service, understand you and what you're trying to do, care about it and you, sustain you."

Really? They would? I was certainly attracted to women, but to me, especially with my education, they were distinct and apart: there had not been a woman student, or teacher, in sight at the Devon School, and they were scarcely more in evidence at Yale. I looked at them with special and perforce distant interest and admiration. Very occasionally I found an intimacy, and that could turn out, as with Noelle, disastrously.

That day, striding past the great amphitheater, I could not imagine that Reeves Lockhart would be right about this. You've been hypnotized by Gertrude Stein, I thought, and that's why you say that. And now, thirty years later, I find that in this, as in so much else, he was right and I have grown into the relationships he foresaw for me.

Perhaps the first of them was, after all, Zinaida. The few brief and fragmentary confidences that had passed between us, beginning with my offering her the ineffable ten dollars, had thrown the first frail connections across from her to me. Her sorrow about Alexei's professional blind alley, her insight into how I should talk about my writing, my witnessing the latest family loss, all were at least tentative links. And Gregory was a bond between her and me: we both cared about, in different ways to be sure, the same person, and that creates, always, a certain tie.

"You must not write too much," Lockhart said suddenly, his mind veering to another track. "Don't write, or rather I mean, don't publish, too much. You're not Shakespeare,

I'm not Shakespeare. We only have so much valid, valuable imaginative work that we're capable of, that we possess. *Wait until you have something to say.*"

We were circling the bowl, passing now into the shady side, where it was definitely cold.

"And how is Gregory Trouvenskoy?" he asked casually.

"Fine. He's in New York overnight, being interviewed about some job, I think. In fact, he's hopping down there quite a few times lately. Looking around for the right opportunity, I take it."

"Mm. I think he's quite right about himself."

"Is he? In what way?"

"Do you have on warm enough clothes? That wind can be really cutting when you're out of the sun."

"I'm fine. In what way, do you think?"

"They're such a curious and different people, the Russians. Speaking of cold—I don't suppose you've ever been to Russia? No. Well, I have. In the late twenties, a kind of abortive cultural exchange. I, like Napoleon, tarried too long and caught the leading edge of their winter! Great Scott, but what bone-freezing, mind-stopping, *breathless* cold. Like a disease, and an incurable one. It makes them suspicious and it makes them resentful and it makes them paranoid. They can be the warmest, kindest, most hospitable and most *sincere* people in the world, if they're your friends. But as Russians look out at the world, the world in general, these other qualities dominate their minds and their characters.

"Gregory is a Russian. I don't suppose he's ever been there either. It doesn't matter. He is different and he is special and he will not fit in, in the ordinary sense, in America."

I caught sight of, as it swiftly passed, this answer to my question. Gregory was right about himself because he sensed this: that he would not fit into American life.

"It all has to do with that fearful climate they have there," he went on, "the annual, endless atrocity of their winters. They are ground down by it—and this is as true of Stalin and of the tsars as it is of the lowliest peasant—that in compensation they are capable of great explosions of temper, of passions of all kinds, of truly epic recklessness. And this certainly exists in him. You heard him: anyone is capable of anything."

I thought of his headlong skiing, of his hair-raising driving, of—from time to time—his drinking.

We emerged from the chilling shade of the bowl, and the welcoming sunshine hit us lightly in the face, like holy water from a priest.

We set off across the wide flat sweep of playing fields where both the sun and the wind could get at us unobstructedly. Several students were passing footballs back and forth. Two were practicing with lacrosse sticks.

"Mr. Lockhart," I began with difficulty, "my problem with Greg, well, with the Trouvenskoys in general, is different. You see, I think—it's possible that they suspect that somehow *I'm* involved in the theft of the diamond. After all, I had a better opportunity to take it than anyone else."

"I see," he said.

"And what's more, well, this is sort of hard to explain, but once in a while I think it's just possible that I *did* take it!"

He stopped in his tracks and frankly gaped at me. I could not interpret that expression on his face; I'd never seen it before. Then he turned and resumed his brisk pace. "Go on," he said evenly. "What makes you think that?"

I took an extra breath and then plunged in. "I don't drink much, the few times I've had drinks with you or Greg were, after all, breaking training, swimming training, and I don't like to do that, so I never do except on what you might call special occasions. So, when I do drink, it really hits me. At that party at Edgewater they had some real, honest-to-God Russian vodka and it knocked me for a loop. I drew a blank. There is a void. A dream. Could I have come back downstairs in a kind of trance and opened the safe and taken the diamond and put it somewhere? The terrible thing is: *I remember the combination.* I actually opened it once when I was there, when Gregory asked me to. I could tell you what it was now."

Lockhart had broken stride once or twice during this recital, as though about to stop, interrupt me, interfere in some way, but he had apparently thought better of it each time, and was now walking resolutely on.

"The safe was forced, not unlocked, I understand," he said quietly.

"Yes, well, that's true," I commented, half assured. "Of course, I could have forced it open as well as anyone else."

"Now look here, Prieston," he began gruffly, "I'm going to be very stern with you now. I think someone needs to be, and nobody else seems to be here to do it, so I'm going to. I want to explain something to you.

"You are letting yourself slide into primal guilt again. That's what's wrong with you. You sense that there's something fundamental that's somehow wrong with you, don't you. And, I may say, with your writing."

Numbly, I had to murmur agreement.

"Now I'm going to tell you what it is. I wasn't going to, I was going to let you grow into this knowledge. But this is an emergency. Surgery is necessary."

He stopped walking, took both my forearms in his gloved hands. "You're not guilty," he said flatly. "You are not guilty. There's something you must learn. We are all born feeling guilty. In Christianity it's called Original Sin. Freud calls it the Oedipus Complex. And so on. If parents are divorced, the young children are *sure* they're responsible. If only I'd been a good boy, this wouldn't have happened. I'm being punished. We are predisposed from birth to assume ourselves guilty. In the course of maturing we have to free ourselves from that. Once again, your immaturity, in your relationship to this theft and this family you love, it's showing. It's the same immaturity which is holding you back in your writing. *You are not guilty. You didn't do it*, and when I say 'it' I don't just mean this theft, which you are incapable of, I mean all the fugitive guilts which have been plaguing you."

"But," I murmured, fumbling in confusion among my jumbled thoughts, "do the Trouvenskoys understand me the way you do?"

Lockhart responded almost rudely: "You are thinking about yourself, yourself, yourself. That is immature. That is what's wrong with your writing. The Trouvenskoys aren't thinking about you at all. They are thinking about themselves and their predicament. So. Do you want to understand what's happening? Fine. Stop thinking about yourself. Start thinking about them."

I continued walking, feeling stunned by what he had said. I knew it was true. It was sadly, abjectly, indubitably true.

I felt horrible, especially having to hear this truth from him to my face. Here was this brilliant artist who had been taking so much trouble over the inane scribblings and immature personality of me, myself, and I.

Then, abruptly, I felt better, better in a special, new sense. I wasn't guilty; I didn't do it, whether it was stealing the Militsa Diamond, or any other imaginary crime or failing of mine.

An hour later I was back in our rooms in the Slave Quarters. Gregory was out. I took up the manuscript of the short story I was working on, "Weekend on the Hudson." The muddled self-absorption of the narrator stuck out a clumsy mile, distorting the material he was trying to deal with. I had just cut paragraphs three through eleven when the telephone rang.

"Is that you, Gregory?" a voice that sounded somewhat but not entirely like Alexei's demanded.

"No, it's Allan. Is that Alexei?"

"Yes," he replied rather testily. "When do you expect Gregory?"

"I don't really know." Should I say that he had gone to New York the afternoon before and not yet returned? Why not? But some impulse made me withhold from Alexei this information about his son.

"I have something important to tell him. Well it's important and it isn't important." He sounded rather disgusted. "It doesn't change anything. Nothing ever does, apparently."

"Can I help at all, tell him anything, or—"

"You—well why shouldn't I tell you? Charles Cummings, you remember him, our nationally known journal-

164

ist? He has never been satisfied with the police investigation about the diamond. Who was? It was a bad joke. And then, you know, when you and Gregory called on him and in a way questioned him, I'm afraid he got rather offended. He, I might say, is one of the most easily offended people in the country. Was he a suspect, he wanted to know. Of course he wasn't really, but in any case he was rather offended. But he was also involved, and so he called upon some acquaintance of his in New York City, a Mr. Clanders, Jerry Clanders. He's a private investigator and expert on safes, and so on. He came here, he's examined the safe, and he's in the other room now with Naida and Charles. He said"—Alex's voice was becoming a little constricted— "that the safe wasn't forced open. You would need a stick of dynamite to do that, apparently. It was simply opened," he went on in a kind of wondering tone, as though recounting a fairy tale, "in the normal way, using the combination. Then whoever did it hammered around and pried at it with a crowbar or something like that to make it appear it had been broken into." There was a silence, and then he inquired, "What do you think of that?"

I sat there holding the telephone as potential shock waves flowed and reflowed and passed me by. Thank God for Reeves Lockhart and the authority he had in my life. *You are not guilty.* Without that emphatic absolution from him at the Yale Bowl I would be sitting here convinced I had removed the diamond during my vodka-induced blackout.

"I don't know what to think," I murmured dully.

"What's that?" he asked sharply.

"I said, I don't know what to think. How many people knew the combination?"

"That's what Naida and I have been trying to decide. Just family as—wait a moment." There was a silence as he apparently turned away to talk to someone, his hand over the mouthpiece of the telephone.

It was a measure of Lockhart's authority that my imagination did not capitulate to guilt at this moment. *He is not talking about me to this Mr. Clanders.* Nobody is thinking about me, or accusing me or even suspecting me. They are all thinking about themselves and their problems. *Stop being so self-absorbed.* That's what's wrong with you, why you can't really write, or live.

"Allan, I have to ring off—hang up now, I mean. I'm going with Mr. Clanders and Charles to the police with this information. Not that that will do any good, but, as they say, for the record. Tell Gregory to call here when he comes in."

I hung up. In addition to the new bewilderment this news caused me, there was an undercurrent of concern I felt about Alexei. He had not sounded really like himself. He was unsettled; his nerves seemed strung out. It wasn't as though there had been some new theft, some additional shock. The evidence had changed, that was all. Why had he sounded so shaken? But what could this new evidence conceivably mean?

Was Reeves right, or *was I guilty* went like a sudden buzz saw through my mind.

Rapid, firm footsteps on the outside stairway, unmistakably Greg's, and then he swung open the door and breezed in. He was carrying an overnight case and a briefcase, wearing a brimmed businessman's hat, three-piece gray suit with patterned maroon tie, and overcoat, his going-to-New-York-to-look-for-lucrative-employment outfit. He must have walked some distance; his face and eyes were bright from the brisk wind. He looked pleased. "Hi, sport. So, anything happening in dreary New Haven, or is it as dull as your face says it is?"

I looked at him, squinted at him, his eyes bright, his manner cheerful to exuberant, just back from a successful or at least promising foray into the big city.

Then it rocked me with the wrenching shock of recognition.

You stole the diamond.

He put down the two cases, tossed the overcoat and jacket on a chair, loosened his tie; and flopped down on the couch. "Any beer around here?"

"Yeah," I replied, my voice sounding unfamiliar to me, "I think there's one in the cooler. Don't get up," I went on. "I'll get it for you."

He sank back on the couch. "What service. Waiting on me. What's gotten into you?"

"Oh nothing. You just look"—I was reaching into the cooler in the corner—"kind of tired from the big city." Actually, he had never looked more fit.

I handed him the beer. "By the way, your father called. An expert has just been at Edgewater and it turns out that the safe wasn't broken into. It was opened by the combination." I felt like an inexperienced actor while making this short speech: suddenly I was very self-conscious. Where are my breath pauses? How should I inflect it? Do I look at him or not? What do I do with my hands?

He was staring down at the bottle of beer and he kept on staring down at it. Eventually he looked up at me. "Wasn't broken into? How can they prove that?"

I didn't say they had proved it, I responded inwardly,

you did. Aloud, I answered, "He's some expert, from New York. Charles Cummings imported him. He knows how to—prove things like that, I guess."

"The combination . . ." he murmured. "What does it mean?"

It means, I yelled inwardly, that either I took it or one of you three Trouvenskoys took it. And I didn't take it.

12

Late that night I lay in bed, caught in the toils of this recognition, this overwhelming sense that hit me with total unexpectedness, that Greg had robbed his parents.

I knew it.

The primitive fish at the core of us, the subconscious, had quite simply and unanswerably thrown up that fact to me. The suspicion must have been lurking around in the depths ever since the morning I discovered the loss and his odd insistence that *I* go with him while he told his parents. This darting suspicion was unacceptable and so it did not emerge but kept swimming furtively back and forth, from my awareness of Greg's nervous restlessness to his many trips, from his "the diamond doesn't really matter" to his "I'm going to rescue the family." Finally the rogue fish of my deep doubts hit on Lockhart's emergency surgery into my subconscious: *You are not guilty*, and next against the fact of the combination's use: irresistibly, in the wake of these two shocks, the subconscious suspicion spurted upward into the conscious fact.

Proof? I had no proof. It was worse than that, in view of such betrayal of two such parents: I had knowledge.

"Merry? Hello, it's Allan Prieston calling. No, I'm not at Edgewater, I'm in New Haven. . . . No, Greg didn't ask me to call you, he doesn't know I'm calling you. . . . Sounds suspicious, does it? Well, I um have to talk to somebody about something involving Greg, and I guess you just seemed like the logical person. After all, you're going to marry him—"

There was a slight intake of breath by her then, audible over the telephone line from Poughkeepsie to New Haven. I knew I was in a sense passing the buck to her; I was his roommate and close friend, to be sure, but she was engaged to marry him and he was or would be her responsibility more than anyone else's. But I sensed in the faint intake of breath that she was not one hundred percent ready to accept this responsibility, and that something in my tone had caused her to raise her guard.

"What's it all about?" she asked.

"Not something to talk about on the telephone. I'd like to see you, get together with you privately, not mentioning it to Greg or anybody else."

"You're not going to make a *pass* at me, are you?" she put in with a covering laugh.

"Nothing like that. It's ah—well, let's just say it's important, to me, more to you, and most to Greg."

"Goodness, this sounds dire. I'm getting ready to go to New York for the weekend. Greg's coming down at dinnertime tomorrow."

"I can be there at lunchtime."

"That urgent, is it?"

"I think so."

"I'm staying with my father's first wife's sister, you remember her, Connie Smith."

"Of course. Why are you so close to her?"

"I know it sounds complicated, but she taught me to swim."

"That explains everything."

"Don't be sarcastic. We western families are big and happy and together, and we don't let little things like divorces get in the way." She gave me the address: Gracie Square. I'd never heard of it.

Gracie Square turned out to be a single short block of very expensive-looking apartment buildings in the East Eighties, terminating at the East River. Merry's father's first wife's sister lived in the last building, overlooking Carl Schurz Park, Gracie Mansion, and the Triborough Bridge. It was both a secluded and spectacular corner of Manhattan, and in the pearl-gray living room, Merry, wearing a maroon dress and a hair ribbon, was waiting for me, looking serious.

She had sensed that the news I was bearing was not good. She went to the kitchen, returned with two glasses of beer; we sat down at the opposite ends of a very long couch with its back to the view of the river and the borough of Queens, and she asked me without preliminaries, "Well, what is it, what's Gregory done?"

When girls get engaged, I reflected with a kind of desperate irrelevance, they always substitute their fiancé's full name for the nickname.

In that instant I concluded that I could not possibly tell her what I knew. I did not in any rational sense really know it. I felt certain I was right, but I had not a scrap of evidence, and Merry was not a category labeled "fiancée" now, she was a very pretty and serious girl sitting looking anxiously at me.

"Merry," I swiftly improvised, "I'm worried about Greg. He's really keyed up and nervous and erratic, and to tell you the truth, I think he's drinking too much."

She frowned, a concurring frown. "I know. I feel better that someone else senses it, someone who sees even more of him than I do. What do you suppose it is, what's eating him? He—you know, he does have the most *erratic* impulses sometimes: that he and I will go to *Alaska*, start a cargo airline between the West Coast and Alaska, and then expand to include Russia! 'They discovered Alaska, you know,' he keeps telling me. 'It used to belong to them.' He says that that gives him a link with the place, and with my connections on the West Coast, we are 'in business' as he puts it. Then he says, 'What about Samoa?' He's really desperate to make a start in life leading to some spectacular results, and leading to them fast, and it's all so keyed up as you put it and so, I don't know, unrealistic and I don't understand his *urgency*! What's driving him? Sometimes he talks about his parents . . . and . . . I don't know. . . ."

Well, I thought slowly and calmly, I do know and I believe you should too.

She was on the brink of the same psychic discovery I had already made; it now seemed inevitable that I should tell her. "I think I have an explanation."

Her eyes looked with careful attention into mine. "Yes?"

But for all my determination I couldn't quite bring myself—not yet—to say what I knew I would have to say. Instead, I told her about the discovery that the safe at

Edgewater had not been broken into. Someone who knew the combination had opened it and made it look as though it had been forced.

"But what has that to do with Gregory?"

"The night of the party he got very drunk. I think in a reckless impulse he opened the safe and took the diamond."

"Oh no," she murmured, her right hand exploring her lowered forehead. "I can't believe it, I won't. . . ." She looked up defiantly, questioningly. "Have you any proof? You're just guessing, aren't you? Has he said anything when he was drunk, for instance, that would make you suspect him?"

"No."

"Oh God." There was a painful silence between us. Then, with an air of utter determination, she said, "Allan, I'm afraid you may be right. But how could he do such a thing? And what are *we* going to do? The horrible thing is, if he took the diamond, everything fits, what I've just said about the way he's been acting."

"I know."

"Why on earth would he do such a thing?"

"Desperate. He's like some banker who steals deposits so he can use the money to make more, and then put it back."

"He can't put back the diamond! And why should he feel so desperate?"

"I don't know."

"What are we going to do?" she asked. "We can't possibly tell his parents what we . . . what we suspect, can we?"

"Absolutely not."

"But we have got to do something."

"I've—we've got to find some way to get Greg to admit it. And then . . ."

"Then, patch it all together again, somehow," she finished forlornly.

"How was your weekend in New York?" I asked Greg over lunch in the Pierson College dining room on Monday.

"Swell," he replied with a grin.

But I sensed that it had not been. Greg was a good actor, but I knew him so well now that he would have had to be a great one to deceive me.

"What'd you-all do?"

He lowered his fork and frowned at me. "How many years have you been up here in New England at school?"

"Let's see: three years at Devon, and this is my third year here. Six."

"And you're still talking like a rebel. You-all!"

Boy are you irritable, I thought. "Well, then, what did you two do in New York?"

"We went ice skating at Rockefeller Center and then we had dinner at the Colony and—"

"The Colony! An arm and a leg."

"—and then we went to a place called the Versailles and heard Edith Piaf sing."

"Another arm and a leg. How was she?"

"Great."

If I know you, I reflected, you wouldn't allow Merry to pick up any of those checks.

"Merry and I are going to Bermuda for spring vacation. No, don't start to look knowing. There's nothing shady about it. We're staying at Connie Smith's house, you remember her. We'll be heavily chaperoned."

Guest or no guest, this trip would cost Greg money, one way or another. So the proceeds from stealing and selling the Militsa Diamond were being used to court Miss Merryfield Carr of Hillsborough, California, and Maui, Hawaii, heiress. She knows this, because I've interfered.

How had I let myself be caught up in this? What will happen if . . . when . . . he learns of my role?

"I've got a possible opportunity in," he went on, "you won't believe this, Alaska!"

"Oh I guess I can believe that somehow."

"I'm planning a quick trip up there too."

"I see," I said with a show of interest.

"Got to get cracking. In a couple of months I'll be out in the cold world."

"True."

"It's dog-eat-dog out there, they say," he added cheerfully. "I intend to be a Doberman myself."

"I would think that people like Merry . . . and even me . . . and your parents, of course, will be that much more important to you. As a backstop, or roots, or whatever."

"Yeah. What are you doing for spring vacation?"

"You're not inviting me to join you and Merry this time, I notice."

"What'd you say you were doing for spring vacation?" Greg asked.

"I'm going to spend the first few days here. I want to finish something I'm writing and show it to Mr. Lockhart and not lose the thread of it by going away. After that I'm going to Maryland to see the family. It'll be so peaceful around here. The White Shoe boys like you will be in Bermuda. The Brown Shoes will be in Florida. And even the Black Shoes will have gone someplace or other. Just me and my muse left here."

"You're sort of an oddball, you know that?"

There was a certain new, mean edge to this typically needling remark. "Am I? Maybe anybody who accomplishes anything in the arts is, although I don't really think so."

"Maybe. You could also fall between two stools, be an oddball and not accomplish anything."

"I'll try not to do that." I decided to go over to the offensive. "What sort of mood is Merry in these days?"

"Fine," he answered a shade aggressively. "Why do you ask?"

"Because I've got your best interests at heart."

"What's that got to do with her mood?"

"Well," I said in a sincere tone, "your best interests, your future life out there in the cold world, that's all tied up with Merryfield Carr, isn't it?"

"Maybe. I've got more than one iron in the fire. I don't mean another girl. I mean—well, for instance, Alaska. I've been very enterprising these days."

"Is that the word for it?"

He looked at me. "What's that supposed to mean?"

"You'd stop at nothing," I said with a pompous flourish, as though quoting a line of melodramatic dialogue, "to achieve your ends!"

At that, he really glared at me for a second, then looked away.

I was trying, bunglingly, amateurishly, to smoke him out.

In the middle of the afternoon, our telephone rang. It was Merry, whispering. "Is he there?"

"No, he's out."

"Did he tell you we were going to Bermuda together?"

"Yes."

"Are you surprised . . . or . . . shocked?"

"I don't think anything can shock me anymore." I was passing from naïve to world-weary in a matter of days, as Lockhart would later sardonically point out.

"I can't just break off with him suddenly, without having any reason that I can tell him."

"No."

"And I *can't* tell him the reason. It's after all just a hunch that you have, and I have."

"Right."

"And . . . there's one more thing. I think I . . . well, I adore Gregory Trouvenskoy," she finished with a kind of whispered passion.

"Well, good luck, anyway."

"We'll stay in touch. Have a nice vacation."

"Good-bye." I hung up, the front door opened, and Gregory walked in.

"That was a monosyllabic conversation," he said flatly. "I didn't want to walk in on it. Couldn't help hear. You sounded like a conspirator. Who was that?"

"That? Oh that was just—" and my brain treacherously locked and refused to release any name for my use. We stared at each other. A chill started up the side of my neck; ominousness filtered into the edges of the room. Then at last came a release: ". . . was just Miss Moncrieff"—What in God's name were the monosyllables he'd heard me say to "Miss Moncrieff"?—"telling me when to see Mr. Lockhart during the vacation."

He stood and looked at me some more. The best defense, I remembered from somewhere, was attack. "Well, what is it, Gregory?" I asked in a voice whose calmness surprised and relieved me. "Are you admiring my good looks today?"

The stare continued, the Romanoff stare, and then at last he said with an edge of scorn, "What could that lady say that was supposed to shock you?"

"Oh. That! Just that there—she saw a terrible review of those plays of Lockhart's they're doing in New York." Lockhart had always said my strongest gift was inventiveness.

What else had Greg heard: my words, "No, he's out"?

Apparently not, for he finally broke off staring at me and went into his bedroom.

This can't go on for very long, I warned myself. The ice is getting paper-thin. If it weren't for the holiday beginning the next day I would very likely have had to tell Greg then and there what I believed he had done, and even more provocatively and dangerously that I had convinced Merry of this too. I was being saved by spring vacation, or rather, reprieved.

Really to know an institution of learning it is essential to live in it, wander through it, take in a manner of speaking its slowed pulse rate when classes are suspended and virtually all the students and faculty have left. Then the stones themselves resume dominance, the lawns and trees, and the history: the long perspectives, those extended views of the campus from Elm Street to the Freshman Commons, and those longer vistas extending across the state and the country to the world and the past, to Yale-in-China for example, to archaeological digs in Crete, to libraries in Tokyo and laboratories in Glasgow. Temporarily freed from present imperatives, the university stretches itself, and settles back from the straining momentum of its current students and faculty to reoccupy its very slowly evolving place in the drama of the United States, a fragile linkage of tiny English colonies when Yale began, and in the unfolding story of scholarship around the world.

The library becomes a nearly soundless shrine to learning, its millions of volumes a monument to recorded knowledge and experience and folly and false starts; the gymnasium rears toward heaven like some well-preserved temple to the skillful and supple body; the courtyards and turrets of the colleges resemble a vast and rambling castle from which the king and court have been withdrawn, leaving a few servants and caretakers behind.

I appeared to be one of these. The Slave Quarters was very still indeed. I rarely met anyone, and never a student, on the courtyard walks as I made my solitary way out three times a day to meals in the banal-to-bad restaurants of Chapel Street.

Late on the third day of this solitude I completed the story, "Weekend on the Hudson," which was a fictional treatment of my visits to the Trouvenskoys; it was intended to be a story of character and atmosphere, with no mention of the Militsa Diamond and its loss.

I delivered it to Lockhart's house, and after another dinner on Chapel Street, went to a movie. The following morning at 7:45 the telephone rang. It was Millicent Moncrieff. "Will you come to lunch here at 12:30? By then both Reeves and I will have read it and be ready to give you our thoughts. I hope I haven't awakened you, calling at this hour."

Of course she had. "Oh no, I was just uh, doing my morning calisthenics." I was learning how to deal with these New Englanders.

After a dull breakfast I wandered over to the slumberous

Sterling Memorial Library and, sinking into an almost voluptuously comfortable armchair facing mullioned windows and an inner courtyard, reread Lockhart's latest novel, published two or three years earlier, *Not to Praise Him*.

It was an evocation of Julius Caesar, his wife, the poet Catullus, and other pivotal figures of the period told almost entirely through letters and diaries. All except one or two of these documents had been imagined and written by Reeves Lockhart. He knew how to speak for, be, Julius Caesar, just as he had confidently become Madame de Sévigné in his first novel, *The Road to Ste. Michèle*.

I read along through this interweaving of classical Roman life and vital human beings, legendary to us but coming alive on the page, and recognized that this was one of his virtuoso performances, erudition and imaginative creativity commingled. The technical control and the structuring alone dazzled me; for the moment I didn't even want to think about his minute knowledge of life in Italy two millennia earlier, nor the living reality infused into a Caesar, a Catullus, the wanton and destructive Clodia Pulcher.

And now he was bending his mind to "Weekend on the Hudson." Oh well, great oaks from little acorns grow, and also, come to think of it, neither Rome nor *Not to Praise Him* was built in a day, and not by a twenty-one-year-old undergraduate. I arrived at their door expectant but not intimidated.

"Come in, come in!" cried Millicent, a brisk little figure in a green knitted suit. We went through the hall into the long, low-ceilinged living room, brighter today from the spring sunshine outside. Lockhart got up to greet me cordially, and to murmur, with an encouraging nod, "Your story, it's um," and he smiled and gave another affirmative little nod of the head. I knew that he knew that I was in suspense as to his reaction, and he wanted to relieve that right away, and go into detail later.

Millicent brought three glasses of sherry, and now that I had them where I wanted them, so to speak, two literary experts who had read my story and were here, fully prepared to discuss it with me, I felt an impulse to stall, fend off their verdict for a while. I knew that it would be a joint, concurring verdict, and not a split decision. I felt an edgy impulse to put that off until later, and had a delaying tactic ready.

"Someone was discussing an essay of Edmund Wilson's the other day," I began. "It was interesting. He said that there are only a very few basic novel plots."

"Really?" exclaimed Lockhart with lively attention. "What are they?"

"First, there is a group of people caught in some special, often threatening situation."

"That's my *Road to Ste. Michèle*," he said with satisfaction.

"Then there is the young man setting out to make his way in the world, and what he encounters."

"In my oeuvre," he said with a wry chuckle at the pretentiousness of the French word, "that would be *Onward and Upward*."

"The re-creation of an historical period."

"That's my *Not to Praise Him*."

"And finally, there is the pursuit of a mythical beast—as in *Moby Dick*, I guess."

"Mm, yes," observed Reeves, stretching back a little in his chair, "I never wrote that one." I felt a faint twinge of disappointment or uneasiness at his reply: I would have preferred his saying, "I haven't written that one yet," reserving it as a possibility for the future.

His face had been alight with interest; he had thoroughly

181

enjoyed this game, enjoyed being told of this provocative boiling-down by the distinguished Mr. Wilson of all novels to few plots, and enjoyed laying his own work alongside it. This kind of analysis and comparison were after his own heart. Clarity, profundity, insight, constructiveness, those were his watchwords.

"Bunny," he began—I knew this was the nickname his friends had given Edmund Wilson—"has done a great deal of good. He and Malcolm Cowley have helped bring Fitzgerald back to public attention, and to procure Faulkner the audience he deserves. Bunny has followed my own work with the closest attention for twenty-five years. His reaction to what I've done has been mixed, intelligent and mixed. None of the savagery of some of my critics, of course. He's too grown up and sure of himself for that. He's not a novelist *manqué*, either, you know. He knows he's a man of letters, not a novelist. Failed novelists who turn into critics are of course savage towards those of us who have succeeded." He sipped his sherry calmly. "No one has been attacked more viciously than I have. Naturally I resent it when it is insulting and unfair. But then I just say to myself, Oh well, if that's what *you* think. I see myself as someone spreading presents of the best quality I can make around to those who want them. Nothing more, nothing less. Savage attacks—and you will get them—are fundamentally the attacker's problem, not yours."

I would get them? With inferences and passing remarks such as this I perceived Lockhart's estimate of my future.

"I myself am turning into such a cultural monument that to attack me now is almost irrelevant or impertinent. I represent the United States at UNESCO conferences. I tour South America for the State Department. I accept

awards. Sometimes I think I am ceasing to be an artist—
that is, one who at least aspires to the transcendent—and
becoming banal and useful and unremarkable. I hear myself
using the word 'artist' so often these days. When I was one
it hardly ever passed my lips."

"What nonsense!" cut in Millicent. "Of course there are
fallow periods at this stage in your career. Why, *Not to
Praise Him* is barely off your writing table."

"Finished four years ago."

"It's so fine," I put in.

"You'll hear the fire bell again one of these days," said
Millicent.

"And like an old horse," he chortled, "I'll lumber out of
the stable and try to help save the city, once again."

We laughed. There was a good deal of laughter around
the lives of Reeves and Millicent.

"And now you've written a good story," he said warmly.

"Oh yes." added Millicent.

I sat motionless.

"And do you know why?" he pursued.

"Not exactly."

"Because instead of dominating and overwhelming it
with your personality and, well, with unrealized parts of
yourself, you've infused these people with life, maintained
a balance between yourself as author and themselves as
characters. There is a certain objectivity present, at last, in
your writing. You have shed some sense of guilt. So selfish,
guilt. You have shed yours, some of it anyway, and it has
freed your imagination and enabled your maturity and a
certain objectivity about experience to emerge. Not that
you are uninterested in these people, these characters, their
story. Far from it." He hesitated, then went on with appar-

ent casualness, "And how *are* the Trouvenskoys? Anything happen about the diamond?"

Millicent focused expectantly; she was clearly fully conversant with the Edgewater situation.

"As a matter of fact, I think some progress has been made. We followed your advice, in a sense. I mean, we—well, I—looked at the young people who'd been at the party. There weren't many. And I knew—you made sure I knew—that I hadn't done it, no matter how drunk I was. And so that left, well—when Greg—" I was about to tell them everything.

"It's domestic drama," cut in Lockhart. "It should remain so. I believe it will all turn out with no grievous damage. At least, it can be and should be so."

He senses I am about to name Gregory as the thief, and he doesn't want me to. He does not wish to know. It is domestic drama, and should be confined to the Trouvenskoy family and the one or two non-Trouvenskoys—myself, Merry—involved. Don't tell us. Don't tell anyone else. Confine it.

His guess about Gregory was accurate, of course, and his belief that no grievous damage need be done to any of us ought to have been right too.

"Princess Zinaida," he ruminated aloud, leaning back, his gaze through the glasses roaming the ceiling. "What a psychic cost she has paid for being a Romanoff! Oh yes, a material cost too, a vast one. They were so endlessly rich. Before the revolution, her father, the grand duke Peter, simply took over Monte Carlo on a holiday. The family traveled with about a hundred retainers, I believe. In their private train. They preempted the Hôtel de Paris there. There were astronomical losses at roulette. If the grand duchess complained, he bought her another diamond. In Russia they were, well, demigods. When the tsar walked past, peasants fought to stand in his shadow. Even such an old aristocratic family as Alexei's, the Trouvenskoys, inhabited a world entirely separate and inferior. Tsarist Russia was the most immense estate the world has ever seen, run for the benefit of one family, the Romanoffs. They had no rivals for their exalted position in the world."

"The British royal family?" ventured Millicent.

"Not the same thing," said Lockhart firmly. "Quite apart from the severe—but by no means complete—limitations on the royal power there, the British monarch of that time reigned over a vast empire, true, but he did so from a reassuring familiar little island. Overpowering India was half a world away. The hugeness of their possessions was psychically manageable, because they were cut off by geography from all that vastness. They lived in London, at Windsor, in Norfolk. Familiar. Whereas the Romanoffs, it was all there confronting them, unthinkable reaches of land, unending hordes of people. It was as though a tidal wave had halted just on the outskirts of St. Petersburg, threatening constantly to overwhelm them. And at last of course it did. They existed in unbelievable wealth and privilege in an enormous sea of poverty and strangeness. It was terrifying. They were Germans, of course, the Romanoffs. Scarcely any Russian blood. Virtually all the heirs to the throne married German princesses, so *there they were*. Tall, willowy Germans, most of them, at the shaky pinnacle of an unknowable, Slavic, peasant world."

"Goodness," breathed Millicent.

"Yes, well," he went on with a sigh, "when the tidal wave broke over them, those who weren't drowned were thrown up like so much flotsam around the world, the source of their incomes wiped out. They didn't know how to do anything, anything people paid you for."

An inkling of why Gregory rejected this heritage so thoroughly occurred to me. There was something threatening about it. It had destroyed a lot of other people all around him.

"And Zinaida is carrying still another burden which may be the most onerous of all," Lockhart went on, as Millicent refilled our glasses. He was in his element: a rapt audience, a gripping theme, leading to an unforeseen revelation. "What I am referring to is the Anastasia case. I never knew," he said in a quizzical tone, "what she thought now about this woman, this 'Mrs. Anderson' who either was or was not the tsar's youngest daughter, saved by some miracle from the slaughter of the rest of the family. When I first met Naida and Alexei in Yugoslavia in the late 1920s, the case had just begun to attract wide attention. I remember one day on the beach at Dubrovnik the subject came up and Naida said very sadly, 'I'm afraid it's impossible. There was just no escape for them. She's just one more of all the imposters who've turned up.' And that seemed to be that. I forgot about it. But the case simply would not go away. What imposter has endured for thirty years without being completely unmasked? I never heard of one. At the time she said that, in Dubrovnik, Zinaida had not met Mrs. Anderson. Then, a couple of years later, Naida's cousin Princess Xenia Georgievna brought Mrs. Anderson to America. Princess Xenia, who had also known Anastasia intimately, was convinced of her authenticity. Naida and Alex had by then moved to this country. They met the lady in question, spent time with her. I knew that, but as it happens I did not run into Naida again, never saw her until"—he glanced my way—"the other weekend when I dropped in at their house on the Hudson. What a curious discussion we had! Didn't you think so?" he asked me.

"It was fascinating, but they did say she was an imposter"—I saw him frown slightly—"didn't they?"

"No," he said carefully, "they did not. Come now, Prieston, you must sharpen your perceptions a little more. Alexei as good as called her an imposter. But I would wager that Alex never met the real Anastasia in Russia. The tsar's daughters were virtually cloistered from any but relatives there.

"Zinaida, her cousin, playmate, intimate friend, Zinaida made few comments that day. Her whole demeanor was quite different from Alex's. He said, you remember that the lady 'couldn't' speak Russian. Naida said that she 'wouldn't.' Quite a difference. Officially, the family has rejected her. Alexei was simply sticking to the family's position. And he's not emotionally involved. He never knew that mischievous, devil-may-care little girl in Russia. Naida, you may have noticed, was very concerned about Mrs. Anderson's welfare and whereabouts. When I was leaving, she said in a facetious manner that I might clear up the mystery. She had to say something to me. She couldn't leave the subject alone." He held up his glass as though to close the subject. "Let's have just one more sherry and then we'll go in to lunch. Do you like omelettes?"

"Oh yes," I said.

"We're having a kind of brunch. What a terrible word. Milly is going to prepare an omelette Provençale, isn't that right, dear?"

"I learnt it in St.-Paul-de-Vence. It's delicious, we think. Then just French bread, a salad, some cheese and fruit. White wine. Does that sound adequate?"

"Scrumptious."

187

"Scrumptious! Now there's a good word. I never think to use it." He considered it to himself, murmuring once again, "Scrumptious."

"But you were saying," Millicent prompted, "that the princess hoped you would settle the Anastasia mystery."

"Hm? Oh yes. Well . . . yes. But you see, there is no mystery. She herself had resolved it during the course of that afternoon. It was I who brought up the fact that they had met Mrs. Anderson since I had last seen them, met her when she was brought to this country in 1930. And you remember Zinaida's reaction," he said to me.

"I—well she—"

"She began," he cut in, seeing that I didn't, "by muttering 'a ring, an embroidered handkerchief.' You understood what that meant?"

I had not, but under this pressure the answer popped into my head. "She was saying that if only the woman had preserved a ring or a handkerchief from those days which Naida could have recognized—"

"Correct. But the paradox is, if the lady was really Anastasia, such proofs of her identity were exactly what she would not dare have preserved. If her story is true, she had to cross half of Russia as a fugitive from the Bolsheviks, who were searching everywhere for her. The last thing she would have kept about her was any proof of her identity. It would have been a death warrant.

"But then there is, after all, the question of physical resemblance. It was you, Prieston, who asked them how the woman looked. You started to inquire whether there was any resemblance between Mrs. Anderson and Anastasia, and they both, nervously, I may say, interrupted you. Alexei simply said that too much time had passed since the revolution. His testimony, legally speaking, is anyway of no significance. He did not know Anastasia in Russia. Zinaida, a cousin and intimate friend, is of course a first-class witness. And what did she say?"

He looked at me levelly through his glasses. "Ah"—I struggled to remember, remember exactly, for only that would satisfy the almost demonic concentration of Lockhart—"she said, 'I couldn't tell,' I think that's what she said," I finished, my voice trailing off.

"Almost," he said decisively. "Those were almost her words. What she said was, 'We couldn't tell.' She was linking her reaction to her husband's, to lend herself moral support. But we already know that Alexei's opinion is worthless. Let us rephrase her statement as you unconsciously rephrased it: 'I couldn't tell.' "

There was a portentous silence in the still room. He took a sip of sherry. Nobody moved. A great actor could not have had a surer sense of timing. Then he went on: "The grand duchess Anastasia was born in 1901. When her cousin Zinaida last saw her, she was fifteen or sixteen, Zinaida a couple of years older. They had been close all their young lives. Fourteen years go by and Zinaida meets a woman purporting to be Anastasia. Asked by you if she could recognize her or not, Zinaida replies in effect, 'I couldn't tell.' " He paused. "I, frankly, was amazed at that reply. I had expected her to reject and denounce Mrs. Anderson out of hand, as she had done in Yugoslavia in 1927, before meeting her. She did not. She said, 'I couldn't tell.' But, I wanted to yell at her, you *could* tell! No one has suggested that Mrs. Anderson had been horribly burned, that her face had been reconstructed. We do know that she had been very ill. She was not ill at their meeting in

1930. And you will *always* recognize an intimate friend, whose every expression, tiny feature, glance, inflection, are familiar to you, after fourteen years. You," he said to me, "are perhaps not old enough to know that. I am old enough. It is not possible. When Zinaida said, 'I couldn't tell,' she was really saying, 'I *can't* tell,' I can't admit to you that she is indeed my cousin Anastasia because the Romanoff family won't let me!"

We sat in silence for a little. Then I ventured to say, "But she couldn't do that, could she? Be that callous? Not acknowledge her own cousin and intimate friend just because of family pressures? My God, if the woman's really Anastasia she's been through hell on earth. . . . Not recognize her! She couldn't do that."

That humane lady, Princess Zinaida, treacherously turned her face from a martyred cousin? It was a terrible and incomprehensible thought.

Lockhart was looking at me with understanding. "You are fond of Zinaida, even love her in a kind of way. You must remember that she is a human being who has also suffered a great deal. She has to survive, and she struggles for her immediate family—I mean Alexei and Gregory—to survive. Apparently she simply lacked the strength to go against all the dominant figures in the Romanoff family, and the dominant figures in the Hesse family—Anastasia's mother's people."

"But *why* were these people against Mrs. Anderson, if she was legitimate? Why wouldn't they have fallen all over her with joy?"

"The answer to that," replied Lockhart with a wave of his hand, "is complicated. Let me just say that she was a sick and disturbed young woman when she appeared, totally unexpectedly, out of the blue. She was a sick, disturbed, and above all uncontrollable young woman who knew some deeply embarrassing and compromising state secrets, German and Russian. That fact alone virtually proved her authenticity. It also made her dangerous, and forced them to reject her."

I stared at the wall across from me. Zinaida's humanity and sympathy had been so clear to me. I couldn't understand the apparent heartlessness of this rejection. Lockhart had said I was too young to know that Zinaida must have recognized an intimate friend after fourteen years. I was also too young to understand Zinaida's betrayal of her cousin.

Now I am fifty instead of twenty-one, and I am no longer too young to understand it.

13

The next morning was Sunday, and although the university was in recess, the bells of Yale and of New Haven were not. The city had been established for religious reasons originally and the school was brought into being by clerics; surviving all that religion most obtrusively in 1951 were the bells of town and gown: an authoritative doomsday tolling from some distant tower; a merry tinkle of joy from somewhere close by; a sober, solid come-to-church pealing in the middistance; the melodic, reverberant chimes of Harkness Tower; a small insistent tintinnabulation struggling to assert itself amid the paced and echoing cacophony of the many gongs of Sunday.

Suddenly, much closer, there was an insistent ring: the telephone in the living room. Millicent making another early morning summons? I struggled out of bed and into the other room. It was a person-to-person call for Gregory from New York. When I said that he was away, I could hear the voice of the calling party, an irritable, brusque male voice, making demands of the operator. "Find out where he is," it ordered.

"Do you—" she began.

"I don't have a phone number where he is," I interrupted; and if I did, I wouldn't tell that unpleasant voice, I added to myself.

"Tell him to find out," the voice demanded.

"You can call back tomorrow," I offered. "I'll probably know then." By tomorrow I would be gone.

I hung up and went into the bathroom to throw some cold water at my face. That ritual completed, I could think more clearly. Maybe I really should know how to get in touch with him, just on general principles.

I went out for breakfast, waded through the *New York Times* and the *New Haven Register*, and by the time I got back to the Slave Quarters it was ten o'clock. Naida and Alexei were not particularly early risers but I felt it was now safe, even on Sunday, to call Edgewater.

Naida answered in a low, almost muffled voice. She said that she had Gregory's Bermuda address and the telephone number somewhere in the house but couldn't remember where. Was it something important?

"I don't know. There was a call from New York."

"Oh well. I don't suppose it matters, does it? So many, you know . . . so little does, in the end. Telephone calls. Always interrupting us, and so rarely welcome. The things we let into our houses. Jewel thieves. Telephones. Anyone with a dime can call into our lives, our dreams."

She was rambling rather strangely this morning.

"Why are you still in New Haven? Why aren't you off on a holiday too somewhere, enjoying yourself?"

"I wanted to finish a story for Mr. Lockhart, and I did.

He likes it. At last I've written something he thinks is good, without any real qualifications."

"You do seem to be dedicated," she said vaguely. "That's what it seems to take. Alexei . . . well Alexei . . . " There was a sound and I thought to my amazement: I think she's beginning to weep.

"Zinaida? Zinaida! Is there something wrong? What is it, what's wrong? "

There was a silence, and finally she said in a low voice, "I had to put Alexei in the hospital two nights ago. He was having peculiar pains, in his chest. And I thought he couldn't breathe. He—they're giving him tests. . . . "

Oh no, I thought. Are you Job, and is God going to heap everything baleful upon you?

"You must call Gregory, get him to come home."

"No! No. What could he do here?"

"He could be here with you, be right there."

"He's having a marvelous holiday with that charming girl. I'm not going to break into it, not unless . . . I . . . unless . . . "

"Zinaida, let me come up there to Edgewater. I dry dishes so well. I've got nowhere really to go for this vacation. I'll come for a night or two anyway, until you hear about the tests."

"Oh no . . . you will? Do you really want to do that? On your holiday? This gloomy old house, you don't—"

"I'll drive up and be there I guess in the early afternoon. Can I bring you anything?"

"Yes," she said. "You can bring me something to cheer me up. You can bring me that story you wrote which Reeves Lockhart says is good."

It was a blowsy, blustery afternoon when I arrived at Edgewater. The old mansion looked weary, semiabandoned, as the wind sent tree branches flailing around it. Some of last year's leaves skittered on the driveway.

As I went up the few steps to the handsome white door, it opened and Princess Zinaida, wearing a black skirt, white blouse, and a gray overcoat, stood there to welcome me. "Not a nice day," she said. "The Hudson Valley is so moody."

Like you Slavs, I said to myself as I greeted her. But then you're not really a Slav, are you? I reflected. Lockhart has explained that. Greg, being half Trouvenskoy, is.

"I'm sorry to run as soon as you arrive," she said, "but I'm due at the hospital. I should be back around five. You're in your usual room at the top of the stairs." She paused and looked at me with her deep brown-black eyes. "Thank you for coming."

She went out and I was alone in Edgewater.

Just as universities reveal their essential natures when such semi-irrelevancies as the students and the faculty are absent, so houses, especially venerable and weathered ones like Edgewater, suggest their underlying reality when the family is away and a guest such as myself is alone in them.

This is an old and creaky house, it seemed to convey to me, as the wind moaned and gusted around it. There have been tragedies in any old house such as this in the past; this is not the first. Money needs to be spent here, on the roof, the basement, the pillars, the lawn, the plumbing, the floors, everything. Money was spent without stint when it was built in 1829, and a perfect small mansion rose on the banks of the Hudson. Now this is an old and creaky house after a hundred and twenty years. A lot of money needs to be spent again if it is to have a future. Gregory Trouvenskoy cares about that future. There have been tragedies here before; theirs is nothing new. This is a tired house. There are no surprises here: only that the house has never heard the Russian language before, that is the only novelty. It is not much of a novelty.

I wandered through the main living room, looking through the glass doors across the awakening lawn to the grayish currents of the Hudson, formidable and remote, bound for New York and the sea.

I moved on into the library. Even such a gloomy and overcast day as this one could not entirely extinguish its vibrance: the seven glass doors, the expansive skylight capturing every shred of natural illumination above, the white walls and vivid portraits, maintained its vitality.

It can't have been all tragedy here, I said to myself. There must have been a lot of happiness here too, in such a beautiful house.

That evening Zinaida and I had supper at the table in the pantry. In answer to my question, she said with subdued matter-of-factness, "As nearly as I can understand it, Alexei had something that verged on a heart attack, that's what the tests disclosed. To me, the only change is that he seems exhausted."

"What's the . . . well, the prognosis?"

"No one knows in heart cases apparently. With the right diet and so on, he could have years ahead of him. Or . . . no one knows. There has been such a strain. . ."

"The diamond."

She nodded. "It was too much," she murmured. "He feels that we—he and I—have had so much bad luck, ever since we were in our teens. And then when I bought Edgewater with my inheritance and we had the money for him to do what he'd always wanted to do, to devote himself to writing, and it hasn't really worked out, not financially, not at all really, that was a terrible blow to him and it made him almost frantic. I had gambled my inheritance on his talent, and I had lost. We had lost. That's not the way I saw it at all, not at all, but that's the way he saw it and nothing I could say or do would change his feeling of failure and despair. What *else* was I going to do with that money? He was my husband, we were together for life, he was the one who worked, who wished to change to other, more congenial work. Was I not going to use that money to make that possible? Of *course* that was the only thing to do with it and I did it and"—she looked at me—"I have never for an instant regretted it. What if I had not done it, had invested it and had a tiny income from it for the rest of our lives, in New York City, Alex toiling unhappily at his uncongenial work, never knowing whether taking that gamble might not have succeeded. We are *gamblers*, we Russians! Of course I did it and thank God I did. Imagine going through life with this possibility never tried and wondering whether or not it might have succeeded." She took a gulp of red wine.

I understood all that, knew she had done the only thing her character would allow her to do. It had been an experiment that they had had to attempt, and it had failed.

And then the diamond had disappeared, and that had been one loss too many for Alexei, body and spirit.

The next morning we found that the blustery weather had blown itself away and a fresh, blue, windy, sun-filled day spread over the Hudson Valley.

"It's time to do something about the gardens," observed Zinaida, standing at the kitchen window, sipping coffee, "time to turn over the soil in the flower beds and the vegetable patch. Are you any good at gardening?"

"I know how to turn over the soil with a shovel. Weed. Water."

"That'll do. I know everything else."

She gave me some old work clothes of Greg's to put on, donned an old pair of pants and a jacket herself, and, placing the telephone with its long cord on the entrance porch, we set to work with shovel and trowel.

Gregory had worn these clothes the day he repaired the roof of the boathouse. As I passed the hall mirror on my way out I caught a glimpse of myself and there was a startling and unsettling resemblance. I looked for an instant like a *Doppelgänger*, his other self; or else it was as though Greg's own *persona* flashed into existence within the mirror as I stood in the hallway, his replacement and his accuser.

We went outside. Although it was still windy and quite cool, the spring sunshine fixed its warmth and radiance on us. We began to work.

"One of the things I liked best when we acquired Edgewater was having our own earth around us, soil we could work."

We toiled away at the vegetable patch between the house and the wall separating it from the railroad tracks. "Why is it vegetables you grow yourself always taste so much better?" she asked rhetorically.

I shoved in the shovel, hauled up a wedge of earth, turned it over. I had something so dire to tell her, and also something so troubling to ask her, that I was more or less tongue-tied. *I can never tell her*, I said urgently to myself, *and I can never ask her.*

She broke the silence to observe with an edge of bitterness, "Alexei is in a ward. He looks terrible there. Terrible. I—well—he looks terrible. This afternoon I'm going to ask the doctor if I can't bring him home. It was just a very mild semiattack. I can't believe he wouldn't be better off here than there. What he had was more of a warning than anything else. I could make the green sitting room into a comfortable bedroom. Then he wouldn't have to be upstairs."

At noon we went in, sat at the pantry table to eat ham sandwiches and to say absolutely nothing to each other because it was the half-hour for listening to Naida's soap opera on the radio. That day Julia was announcing to Raoul that, much as she was attracted by his cosmopolitan charm and his glamorous life in Paris, she could never leave Stanley, it would hurt him too much, he had been too good to her in his own simple way. "I've been waiting four months for her to say that," growled Naida with a chuckle. The last line of the episode was Raoul's challenging: "I well nevaire geev yu op, nevaire. I weel tell Stanlee myself!"

"Wow," Zinaida breathed, switching off the radio. "Talk about 'tune in tomorrow.' What drama! It's wonderfully soothing at noon to escape to Julia and Stanley and Raoul. Such enjoyable *problems*! You can *wallow* in them." We got up from the table. "You know," she observed, "you do look like Gregory in those clothes. If I don't look directly at you, I could swear he was here."

"Greg's probably wearing gleaming white shorts and polo shirt right this minute, playing tennis with Merry at the Royal Bermuda Yacht and Tennis Club."

She said with a laugh: "Before going on to a champagne luncheon and a cruise on some yacht. He likes the so-called good things in life, Gregory. God knows he comes by that legitimately. When I think of my father. . . ."

Later I drove her to the hospital to see Alex, waiting for her outside in the car. After a half-hour she returned and got in, without speaking. I felt she was close to tears. "I can't stand that ward," she muttered intensely at last. "If he has a good night, they may let me take him home tomorrow. Thank God." There was another long silence as I drove slowly along. Then she said with some decisiveness, "Let's stop at the liquor store. We have hardly anything in the house."

"To welcome Alexei home with—?"

"Well, he'll never drink liquor again. Perhaps a little wine. This is for me, us. Some vodka."

"Let me buy it, my treat. They won't have the real, *gen-u-yne*"—giving it the Border State drawl—"Russian stuff, will they?"

"No, that has to be smuggled in, or something. There's an American brand"—she gave a single contralto chuckle—"called Romanoff! Buy that."

The wind fell toward evening and at first we thought we could sit out on the veranda among the pillars to drink our vodka and soda. But it was too chilly for that, so we settled for the library, amid the long glass doors, where Mary Maury and Harriet van Rensaaver joined us. They had brought the dinner.

After we had discussed Alexei's condition—and there was not much to discuss, he had had a "warning" and might live for years or, although no one would say so, die tomorrow—Zinaida's mind began to settle on the fact of human mortality.

"In Russia there always seemed to be a great many old people about. Every great house had at least a dozen or so elderly relatives or privileged family retainers who monopolized one end of the dinner table. They *never seemed to die*. They just gossiped, and made intrigues. They gave a kind of stability to the household, though, a continuity. I don't suppose that kind of keeping the old people about you exists anywhere in the world anymore. China must have been the last place, before *their* revolution. They're all put away in homes now, aren't they?"

She got up from the couch to close the French door facing the river. "Getting chillier by the moment," she murmured. "Do you know who was the hardest person in history to kill?" An unusual loquacity was coming over her; perhaps the whisper of life's end she had heard in Edgewater had released something, made her sense some urgency.

We all shook our heads.

"Rasputin! I remember how scandalized my mother was—not that Felix and Dimitri had killed him, that didn't bother her at all; it was about time somebody did, she seemed to think—no, she was scandalized at Rasputin's tasteless refusal to die! You know how it happened, or almost didn't happen?"

"No, I for one really don't," put in Harriet.

"Felix's wife, Irina, Princess Irina, the tsar's niece and my cousin, was—still is—one of the most beautiful creatures on God's earth. And as a matter of fact Felix at that time was hardly less beautiful. Some people insisted that Felix even turned Rasputin's head, and Rasputin was the womanizer to end all womanizers. Well, whatever that terrible man thought about Felix, he was eager to meet Irina. That's how Felix lured Rasputin to his palace on the

Moika Canal, to the cellar. Felix promised to bring Irina downstairs to meet him. Irina at the time was a thousand miles away, in the Crimea. Down there in the cellar, a very elaborate cellar with bearskin rugs and cushions and ikons, down there Felix poisoned him, he shot him, he and the others beat him over the head, and finally they dumped him into the Neva and only then did he finally die, by drowning. Mother thought that was the poorest taste imaginable. Any real gentleman would have dropped dead after the first bite of poisoned cake."

"Did you ever meet him?" inquired Mary eagerly. "Rasputin?"

"Oh good Lord no. You can't imagine what an ogre everyone thought him. I believe I was once at some reception in the Winter Palace when he was there—you know, along with about four thousand other people—but Mother would have put his eyes out with her hatpin if he'd come near me."

"Your father was such a distinguished-looking man," remarked Mary, looking at the photograph of him on the table.

"He had a lot more sense than people gave him credit for. He once said to my mother, 'These children have got to learn to earn their own livings. Who knows what kind of world they're going to face?' Unfortunately, neither he nor Mother acted on that, that very wise thought of his. We'd already had one terrible revolution in 1905, you see, and he sensed, a great many people sensed, that another revolution was coming and that this time it would sweep us away. Especially when the empress began to interfere so much, telling the tsar whom to appoint, whom to dismiss. And who advised *her*? Rasputin, the ogre. She thought his strange powers were keeping her son alive. Maybe they were. There were a lot of stories. . . ."

"What was she—well, what was the tsarina like?"

"We never called her that, 'tsarina.' That's a Frenchified form. It didn't exist in Russia. Her title was tsaritsa, or more usually, simply the empress."

"What was she like?"

"Beautiful," she said slowly, "and nervous, and sad. She liked me. She liked children. Adults made her shy, which everybody took for arrogance. Of course she could be arrogant, too. I remember her best on her chaise longue in her mauve dressing room, yellow roses from the Crimea all around her, beautiful, delicate features, reddish-gold hair. Of course in the last years she began to grow gray; she seemed to be sick, worn out. She had passed on hemophilia to her son and she knew it. He nearly died of it many times. Rasputin seemed to save him. And maybe he did. There were many stories. . . . The girls, Anastasia and the others"— the name came out very naturally—"were so happy and full of fun. But even they—they had a tinge of her . . . well, seriousness. I don't think . . . what happened to them in the end . . . was entirely a surprise. There was something tragic about the empress and it was in the air around her.

"My old nurse used to say, 'The empress came to Russia behind a coffin. She is bringing death.' Alexandra had arrived from Germany to marry Nicholas just as his father, Tsar Alexander III, died. The first the Russian public saw of her was in a funeral procession. They never forgot it. I don't believe she did either."

"Did the emperor like children too?" prompted Harriet van Rensaaver. I sensed that these reveries about Old Russia were very rare with Naida, and her friends were going to make the most of her present nostalgic, even fatalistic mood.

"Yes. I thought he was wonderful. I was just a girl growing up, I knew nothing of politics. He had the most beautiful blue eyes, and the kindest expression. Dreamy. Gentle. And I think I came to understand him, his predicament, on a visit to his study at Tsarskoe Selo once. I was about fourteen, and went there with my father. I have no recollection at all of what they talked about. What did make an overwhelming impression on me, and I can feel it to this day, was the unearthly stillness of that study. Silence. Isolation. Like the top of Mt. Everest if it were windless there, or the bottom of the sea. Removed from all the rest of life.

"I didn't understand what caused it then. Later of course I did. He was The Autocrat. He was the law for one-sixth the surface of the earth. That placed him in this terrible isolation; there was no argument, there didn't seem to be even any discussion. Everybody around him seemed to be afraid. Even *he* was afraid, afraid of his own power. And so a kind of vacuum was created around him, airless, soundless. Terrifying. A small, blue-eyed man sitting amid all this suspended animation."

"Waiting for the end," put in Mary.

Zinaida was gazing before her. After a pause she echoed, "Waiting for the end."

We had supper in the dining room. Harriet van Rensaaver had brought baked beans, I was not surprised to find, and Mary Maury had contributed sausages and some kind of dark fruit bread. We had apples for dessert. Harriet did not drink hard liquor, but the rest of us went on sipping vodka through the meal.

I had to say something, try to resolve at least one of the unspoken machinations at Edgewater. "When you said, Naida," I began, "that the tsar's daughters were basically serious, maybe because there was so much tragedy in the air around their mother, I read somewhere that one of them—Anastasia I think it was—was a regular little mischief-maker."

"Oh," exclaimed Naida immediately, "she was! What a mimic! She could make me laugh until I cried. There was an old countess at court who opened a door in Felix Yousoupov's palace unexpectedly one day and came face-to-face, face-to-muzzle, with Felix's pet bear! She fainted three times or something like that on the spot. When Anastasia imitated the old countess telling about it, she was so funny—'And my dear,' "—Zinaida herself imitated the countess in a thick Russian accent—" 'this huge wild beast came at me, to embrace me!' Well, we all laughed until we cried." Her eyes were bright now with the memory.

"And did you"—it was now or never, "when you met Mrs. An—" A rumbling I had been ignoring grew louder; a train was swiftly approaching. The great headlight of the engine flashed anarchically across the wall and the portrait, and the uproar of engine and cars hurtling past drowned out conversation. The train rattled and banged past for minutes on end; I distributed more vodka and soda to the three glasses, and waited.

At last the train sounds dwindled away northward. "You were—" I began.

"Trains," said Zinaida reflectively. "People today don't understand what a revolution they were when they came into existence, how they transformed countries, none more than Russia."

"You had your own private train, didn't you?" inquired Mary.

"Our family did, yes. We had so many people to take with us wherever we went."

"Was it very luxurious?" Mary persisted.

"Yes, yes it was. Very elegant. And practical. There were gutters around the tops of the bathtubs, to keep the water from spilling over when the track was rough. The train stations in the larger cities had special and very grand reception rooms, just to receive us! It was another world . . . . But what was I saying? Oh yes. Never mind about private trains. That wasn't the point of their impact on Russia. That was a frill. In a few decades Russia changed from a place where even the tsar could only move by horses or else by floating down a river, to railroad tracks, trains! You realize just how huge Russia was? Is? Hundreds, thousands of isolated districts, basically as they had been for a thousand years. Then suddenly, trains! Connections! Like blood beginning to flow through a mummy. Of course the blood carried the virus of revolution too. No one was more revolutionary, when the time came, than the railroad workers. How they turned on us.

"But, my God, trains certainly got into Russian life, the Russian imagination. Do you remember how Tolstoy has Anna Karenina die?"

"She"—I was beginning to see Zinaida's point—"threw herself in front of a train."

"After seeing her lover taken from her to the war, on a train," Zinaida added. "And where, in reality, did Tolstoy himself die?"

"I don't know," I said.

"He ran away from home. He was about eighty years

old. Still, he ran away from home, following the call of the train. He took a train to go off and away, and died in a railroad station. The Trans-Siberian Railroad was the greatest feat of its day. I *remember* trains, and how superb they seemed to all of us. Watching a huge steam engine coming into the Finland Station in St. Petersburg? There was no thrill like it." She began to carve up her dessert apple. "The first revolution, the one that didn't succeed, was in 1905. I was too young to realize much about it. Just that we stayed put that year, didn't make our usual trips from Petersburg to the Crimea to our country place south of Moscow. Ever after my mother referred to it, not as the Revolution of 1905, but as the time the Trains Stopped. That's how crucial they had become.

"We escaped, we got out of Russia in the middle of the revolution, the real one, because a White general commandeered a train for us, and soldiers to protect us, until we got across the frontier into Romania." She sipped a little of her vodka. "Otherwise I wouldn't even be here."

There was a rather taut silence, and then she stood up. "Excuse me! Such morbid thoughts. Let's just throw these dishes in the kitchen and forget about them. Allan, will you get a fire going in the Green Room? Let's finish off this vodka in there, and talk about cheerful things. Alexei coming home, for example."

And so we did, until about ten-thirty, when Harriet and Mary left. Zinaida showed no inclination to go up to her bedroom. After I had put the ladies in their cars, I found her still deep in her armchair to the right of the fireplace in the semidark room. The white face, black-hair-and-eyes aspect of her was more pronounced by the firelight than ever.

What could I tell this woman, and what could I ask her?

The shattering news, the outrageous question, could I, should I voice them? As I took the deep chair opposite her, feeling slightly like a usurper in Alexei's habitual chair, she emerged from reverie: "Yes, sit there. Alex wouldn't mind. He likes you. He also thinks you may have talent. I will read your story tomorrow. Obviously you do have talent, if Reeves thinks your work is good."

"I hope I do." For once in my life, this subject was not paramount with me.

I could not shake off the implications of the Anastasia case. Was Lockhart right? Had Zinaida really recognized Mrs. Anderson as her bedeviled cousin? And had she, to protect her own position in the family, viciously rejected her? Had this humane woman been capable of that brutal injustice?

"Tell me more about Russia," I said lamely.

"You are a curious one about all that's dead and gone, aren't you?"

I wouldn't be so curious, I answered inwardly, if it really were all dead and gone. Mrs. Anderson and the painful conundrum of her identity are very much alive. So is a young man starting out in life, my best-friend-in-spite-of-everything, who is entangled in the baleful toils of Old Russia. Curious? I was becoming obsessed with resolving the conflicts stemming from the banks of the Neva to the Valley of the Hudson.

"It's been so many years," she began in her low-pitched voice, "so many that what survives are scenes of nature more than anything else. Interiors, rooms, I can only recall an overpowering splendor, generalized vastness, pomp. It didn't seem any of those things to me at the time. Going to the Winter Palace for me was like a citizen of Rome going to St. Peter's. Splendid, yes, but a monument, apart. Even the tsar didn't live in it anymore. The empress couldn't bear anything so vast, and so close to the corrupt aristocracy of Petersburg. What she should have feared were the masses there, the mob. But she thought they loved her, poor woman. Luxury, Mary asked at dinner. Yes, luxury. But all that was external, jewels and ballrooms. Our lives, the children's lives, were very plain, plain food, camp beds, cold baths. It was the tradition, going back to Peter the Great—damn him. *Cold* baths first thing in the morning! It's a wonder they didn't kill me. Then we'd get all dolled up and parade through the court and it would look very sumptuous, and then our nurses would take all of it off and we'd go to sleep on a cot and get up very early for the cold bath and simple breakfast. And lots of studying, especially languages. My God, I had to study Russian, of course, and my governess was English and spoke that to me, and then we also learned French and German! A child toiling away at four languages at once. It was no picnic. But then there was of course the country, our place south of Moscow . . . I remember the long, straight, flat country roads leading to it . . . the peacefulness there, the endless peaceful summer days. . . . But then in the fall we would have to go back to Petersburg, and it soon became cold, a coldness you can't imagine. Someone once said that Russia was an amphitheater staring at the North Pole. That gives the sense of it. I can remember most vividly the Petersburg winter sky, during the few hours of daylight—it was the color of pearl, a terribly cold, beautiful, menacing color—I always think of those pearl skies as the color of revolution."

"And the empress and her children. Were—"

"Did Alexei ever tell you his naughty story about the empress? She so desperately wanted a son after bearing four daughters, and one day it was announced that she was pregnant, and she got bigger and bigger, and then it was the ninth month and, as he puts it so vulgarly, there was a loud whistling sound and her stomach shrank back to normal and the 'pregnancy' was over. Of course in the end she had the son and heir . . . tragic little boy. . . .

"Russia is an unhappy country; it was then, and it still is. I didn't know it then, although I sensed *something* . . . so many guards around us everywhere we went. There were always strikes of the workers going on. Can you imagine workers in Russia striking today? Old Russia, our Russia, was confined, fenced in; Russia today is in chains . . . How I loved the long, long perspectives, and then in the Crimea, all the cypresses and the sea and the gorgeous flowers. . . . It was so interesting, being part of such a big family . . .Felix and Irina . . . Grand Duchess Elizabeth, a saint . . . they found her body at the bottom of a mine shaft . . . and Grand Duke Alexei, head of the navy; someone said he was addicted to fast women and slow ships . . . the old empress, Alexander III's widow, who was so gay when she was young and so wise when she was old; she saw it all coming; Nicholas and Alexandra wouldn't listen to her . . . about half of the family died in the revolution . . . ."

"Which one was your favorite among your relatives?"

There was a silence, and then she murmured, "Anastasia."

There was another thundering silence and then I drove myself to ask, "Are you certain that Mrs. Anderson is not she?"

A long pause, and then, "We couldn't tell," she muttered, "so much time had passed."

"But"—I forced the words out of me—"Mr. Lockhart

says you *could* tell. It was impossible for you not to know, in 1930, whether or not this was your close friend and cousin of 1917."

"He did, did he?" she murmured. "I always sensed he was too—too—penetrating, always."

"He maintains," I forged on, "that since you didn't denounce her out of hand that you—recognized her, but didn't dare admit it."

"Oh," she said tiredly, "I met a woman in New Jersey. She spoke no Russian. It couldn't have been. Couldn't."

Sometime later I climbed the curving stairway to my bedroom, Zinaida saying she was going to stay downstairs a little longer.

About five the following morning it began to rain outside. At first it was just a gentle and steady early spring rain, but in an hour or so the wind rose and began to torment all the surrounding trees, in particular the tall, thin locusts. This obstreperous wind, hurling sheets of rain against the old walls of the house, seemed to emphasize its isolation. I had always loved rain, especially if I was snug in some pleasant place. I lay in bed listening to it beat against the house until sounds downstairs made me realize that Naida was up.

When I got down to the kitchen, she was standing at the sink with a cup of coffee, gazing through the window at the rain. "Good morning!" she cried cheerfully. "Isn't it exciting? My, but we have emphatic weather here on the Hudson. Such storms! Let me get you a cup of coffee. Then we'll sit down and have a proper breakfast. I love changes in the weather, don't you?" she asked.

"Yes." I took the cup of coffee she handed me. "I'll go to

the market today and get what's needed. Will you make out a list?"

"Yes." She went to the refrigerator, got out some eggs. "That winter we spent in Wyoming, it was unforgettable. The Grand Tetons! I never saw anything so majestic. Alex appreciated it all perhaps even more than I did. I don't know about this storm, though. We certainly can't bring him home today if it keeps up."

"We" can't bring him home: I had advanced another step into the circle of the family.

"Perhaps it will let up by the afternoon."

But it did not. Around noon I drove up the steep hill through flailing sheets of rain and bought all kinds of groceries and other supplies, not forgetting the Romanoff Vodka, purchasing much more than she had on her list. What else could I do to help? Be there, I decided, stay until Thursday. On Thursday Greg and Merry were due back from Bermuda. Then I could make a quick trip to Maryland and be back in New Haven on Monday for the resumption of classes.

I didn't know exactly when that day Zinaida began to consult the vodka again, but by mid-afternoon she was in a relaxed and confiding mood. We were trapped indoors by the weather. Zinaida did not spend time in idleness and she established herself in the library where the light was best to do some sewing. In the middle of this she suddenly remembered my short story. "Do go get it," she said. "I'll read it now."

After bringing her the pages I left the room—no sane author stays in the presence of someone reading his work—and wandered across the main living room to the Green Room. A tiny, glass-enclosed alcove, like a miniature

212

greenhouse, looked out at the lawn and trees. The wind and rain whirled and lashed; the locusts bowed, recoiled; beyond them the gray Hudson was all ruffles and whitecaps. The timbers in the house creaked like an old ship in a tempest, but an old ship that has weathered worse than this many a time.

Finally I heard Zinaida's voice calling me from the library. I went in to her. She was seated on the couch beneath the skylight, where a certain grayish lightness played down on her even on a day such as this; the room had its own quiet and unquenchable radiance.

Her sewing materials were around her as she sat, wearing black slacks and a white blouse; her reading glasses on her nose, the vodka and soda next to her on the table.

"This story *is* good," she said forthrightly. "I see why Reeves is pleased. Do you know how I know it's good? Because it's about us, about Edgewater, the Hudson, Gregory, and yet I was able to read it as though these were fictional characters and places. You made it happen on the page. As a picture of us, though, there's one thing you missed."

"I'm sure there is. What is it?"

"Well, you see, in the story the Russian couple look like us and talk like us and so on, but she's a lady and he's such a gentleman."

"Well, aren't you and—"

"No, not really, no, we aren't. I'm not a lady, not really, and Alexei is not really a gentleman. We know how, with an effort, to behave like that, but we're not. We don't have the feel of it, for genteel behavior. We're sort of aging bohemians. I knew how to be a princess; Alexei knew how to be a Russian landowner. It was simpler after all that ended to slip right through the genteel world and settle in bohemia. We're comfortable there—here. I'm afraid we disappointed quite a few proper people around here. When we first moved to the Hudson Valley they wanted to get to know us. But it didn't work. My politics were too liberal, for one thing. My clothes were wrong but not wrong *enough*. Once when we first moved here, we were invited to a very correct party in a very proper home and I was being introduced around as 'Her Highness' and I just turned to my hostess and said, 'I really need to pee right away.' " She laughed, her face almost contorted with mischievous glee. I saw why she and prankish Anastasia had been so close. "I don't know why I did that. I had to, somehow. It was all so phony and unreal at that party. The people were trying to be nice to us but we just couldn't fit in. You've met the friends we do have here, off-beat and eccentric and a little mad around the edges. They're the right people for the likes of us. We're poor exiles, we can't do the right thing."

There was something in what she was saying that applied to me, applied to me if I was going to be a writer. Last night I had encouraged her in her vodka-induced reverie, and tried to pry about Anastasia. That was probably an abuse of hospitality, and not the act of a gentleman. Sitting there in the library, I began to feel that artists were not gentlemen and responded to different promptings, maintained other standards, violated convention in the interests of truth. I was not then and am not now a gentleman; I was and am, to whatever degree, an artist.

"We're just a couple of aging bohemians," she repeated without pride or rancor. "I do feel a sense of family pride, family honor. That's quite a different thing from being a lady. We ruled Russia for three centuries, and now there is nothing left except that sense of family pride, or honor, or whatever you want to call it." She picked up her sewing, "I've tried to maintain the family honor."

The room was still then. I glanced across at the portrait of the Trouvenskoy lady that concealed the safe. Was it conceivable that I would ever say to Naida that I believed Gregory to be the thief? Was it my duty, or was I insane to consider it? "I think it's possible," I said, hedging, "that we may recover the diamond."

She looked up, gazed at me opaquely through her glasses. "Yes?" she said in a level voice.

"We may . . . we may be able to locate the person who took it. Reeves Lockhart again—he pointed us in the right direction."

"Did he?"

"He told me," I pressed on, "that the person who stole it was almost certainly young, young and impulsive and, that night, probably very drunk."

She made a gesture of impatience, almost of anger. "Reeves Lockhart! That man and his insights."

"So," I persisted, "we—well, I followed that line of thinking and—it's possible that we will recover the diamond."

"That would be wonderful," she said, "for many reasons. Keep me posted." She began to wipe the lenses of her glasses. "Getting blinder every day. What are you going to write about next? That story is so full of promise."

And the door was closed on who the drunk, impulsive young person might be who took the jewel. I thought it very odd of her, not to want me to tell her every detail. Not that I could have.

The following morning—glowing with spring sunshine and brisk with a fresh spring wind—Zinaida and I helped Alexei out of the hospital to my car. His face was grayish, and he moved slowly and painfully. But his spirits were up, effortfully up.

"Being out in the open, what a relief! What horrendous places, hospitals. The odors alone can take years off your life."

We got into the car, and I drove slowly off. "Alex," said Naida in an optimistic tone, "Allan and I have put that extra bed—the one that's been down in the cellar?—we've set it up in the Green Room."

"*Have* you?"

"So much easier, no stairs."

"Sounds rather spectacular, sleeping there, looking out at the river through the glass doors. I'm pleased," he said, perhaps more emotionally than he intended, "really *pleased*. Just a simple change like that, sleeping on the ground floor instead of upstairs, it'll be, well, a novelty. And," he finished half to himself, "I could use a novelty."

"There's the little bathroom adjoining—"

"Yes. What a relief. Home to Edgewater. Zinaida, thank you, my darling, for buying the house. Have I ever thanked you, really thanked you?"

"Of course you have and there's nothing to thank me for. I didn't buy it for you; I bought it for us."

After a silence I remarked, "It's a great house."

"Allan has written an excellent story about it, and us."

"*Have* you! I look forward to reading it."

"Reeves Lockhart," added Zinaida, "thought it was very good."

"I've never doubted," observed Alex in a more remote voice, coming now from afar, from his memories, distant hopes, "that you had talent and that you would succeed."

216

At the house I took Alexei's hat and overcoat, and Zinaida slowly led him to the bed in the Green Room, where she arranged him sitting up on the bed, his back propped on cushions heaped up against the headboard. She prepared some broth for him, and then drove off to the pharmacy in town to have some prescriptions filled.

Alexei asked to see my story. I brought the manuscript to him, and left him alone in the Green Room to read it. The telephone rang as I was crossing the entrance hall and I went to answer it. It was a reverse-charges call from Bermuda, for anyone at the number from Gregory Trouvenskoy.

With a creeping sense of foreboding I accepted the charges. "Who's that?" Greg's voice asked a little irritably. "Allan, is that you?"

"Yes, yes it is. How are you? How has your holiday been?"

"Fine," he answered brusquely, as though I had no business even to ask the question. "What're *you* doing at Edgewater?"

"Well, I . . . your father," I began. "He's had—"

"Something's wrong with Dad?" he interrupted. "What's happened?"

"It's not serious."

"Just tell me, for God's sake."

"He's had what they call a warning. The doctors say it's not a real heart attack. We brought him home from the hospital this morning. You don't have to worry."

"Is he in any shape to come to the phone?"

"He's in bed. We set up a bed in the Green Room. There's no phone in there, of course, and I don't know if he ought—"

"Never mind. We'll be on the first plane we can get out of here. Where's Mother?"

"She went into town to the drugstore to get some medicine."

"All right," he said decisively, in his most imperious manner. "We're flying home. We should get there sometime tomorrow."

"Don't you want me to meet the plane?"

But he had already hung up. Gregory was never one for excessive affability, frilly overpoliteness was unknown to him; yet even for him, his telephone manner this time had been spare to the point of starkness, even before he knew of Alexei's illness. What had happened between him and Merry down there?

I went to the door of the Green Room and looked in. Alexei, wearing gray trousers and a red plaid shirt, was leaning back against the cushions, my pages in his hand on the bedspread, eyes closed. Then he opened his eyes, raised his head, and slowly lifted the pages. I came into the room and told him that Greg and Merry were on their way home.

"Cutting short his holiday," he commented a little fretfully. "He needn't have done that. I'm not dying, yet. And"—the first sign of color rose in his face; he looked at me in a jocular and surmising way—"what if I am? What could he do about it?" He adjusted his reading glasses. "Sit down, I'm almost finished."

He read the last two pages and then said he shared Zinaida's favorable opinion.

"Yes, fine," I said, "thank you." I was now wishing that little story of mine would go away. First of all, it had missed a central point about them, their bohemianism, and secondly, too much of far greater import hung in the air at Edgewater.

"You see," he said, his head lolling back, gazing thoughtfully at the high ceiling, "you have the English language in

218

your blood, and a feel for this country. That's what I lacked. One of the things. I also started late. How old are you?"

"Twenty-one."

"As young as that? I didn't realize there was such a difference in your age and Greg's."

"The war—he was in it for three years, and I was a little too young for it."

"You write well. And then you have *Reeves Lockhart* in your corner. I never knew anybody who could help me when I was starting out. You know, on top of everything else, you have to have luck in this world, *especially* if you're trying to make a career in the arts. Lockhart, on top of his brilliance, had luck. I have an odd feeling you're going to have it, I don't know why. But then—I have had my marriage, and my son. I think of it now as inevitable, Zinaida and me marrying, but it wasn't, you know, not by a long shot. In the first years out of Russia, Zinaida was still very much a royal princess. Staying at Windsor with King George and Queen Mary. And she used to visit old Dowager Queen Alexandra at Sandringham. She met a number of very eligible and rich Englishmen, and even one or two Americans. There were proposals. A life of ease stretched out in front of her, like the one she had been born to. She was beautiful, you can still see that?"

"Yes."

"But they were not *Russian*. Oh, I know what people say, that the Romanoffs had virtually no Russian blood and all that, but most of them, whatever their ancestry, *felt* very Russian. Getting kicked out only intensified that. She just in the end couldn't bring herself to marry anyone not Russian. And then, well"—he turned to gaze out at the river and finished quietly—"we love each other."

"Maybe your next book will bring you luck, if that's one

219

of the things it takes to succeed. And I'll bet—I'm sure Mr. Lockhart would read it, you know, in manuscript, and help you, give you suggestions."

He did not seem to be following what I was saying with a great deal of attention or enthusiasm. He rubbed his hand exploratorily and wearily over his face. Then he murmured, "You're young. You don't know about energy yet. It's limited, you'll come to know that someday. Write another book? Months, a year, two years of grueling concentration, summoning up tremendous extra energy for the book? At the moment I haven't enough energy to pick up a pen, punch a typewriter key, let alone face slogging through another book." Then he looked at me, sensing the melancholy atmosphere he was creating. The expression on his face changed: "But I'm depressing you! Our guest! Don't let me. I think you're right about Reeves. He would—he will help me. You're right about that. That could make all the difference," and he checked my face rather furtively to see whether he'd succeeded in cheering me up again. Oh you're a gentleman all right, I reflected, a gentleman where it really counts.

"Can I get you anything?" I asked.

"Nothing at the moment."

"I think I probably should leave you, let you get some rest."

He seemed to consider that suggestion and to file it. "Tell me about Greg. Is he going to marry this girl?"

The idea that it was Greg's decision to make, and not hers, was such a novelty to me that I was momentarily stumped. Turning everything touching on this question around a hundred and eighty degrees in my mind, I then said tentatively, "They're—they've been very fond of each other. I guess maybe—well, I don't really know."

"Someone rich would help Greg, of course. He's too proud and too sincere to marry money, just money. He would have to love her. *Then*, if she has money, wonderful. He couldn't do the other. Too much like his mother for that. *Deep* feelings."

"I'm sure he cares for Merry," I said hurriedly.

"He's a complete old-fashioned Russian nobleman by nature. Likes horses, drinking, guns, gambling. In Petersburg, living on the rent-rolls from his estates of two hundred thousand rubles a year, he would have been in his element, a wild nobleman right out of Tolstoy. Instead, he's turned into an American guy with not a nickel behind him." He passed his hand wearily over his face again. "That diamond! If only that last piece of rotten luck hadn't hit us—"

Oh God.

"—we might have managed something. Helped him out in some practical dollars-and-cents way. This is the time in life when young men *need that extra cash*. They're making their bid, their supreme bid, to be whatever they feel they have to be. My life has been out of kilter because when that extra money came, I was already forty-four years old. When Grand Duchess Anna left those jewels to Naida. Too late, as it happens," he finished in a declining tone of voice. He could not overmaster his own melancholy for long, try as he might for my sake.

Alex fell silent; his eyelids began to droop. "Whatever it was they gave me in the hospital," he murmured, "it's making me drowsy."

"I'll be in the next room if you need anything," I said, getting up.

I went into the big living room and sat in a wooden chair beside one of the glass doors. A fruit tree on the front lawn near the river had, apparently overnight, sent forth hundreds of pink buds; a weeping willow across from it had acquired a fresh green sheen; a clump of forsythia sent forth a vivid patch of yellow next to the boathouse. The great river as it flowed by was green and gleaming in the spring sunshine.

The afternoon passed very quietly and then at five o'clock Alex asked if Zinaida and I would have afternoon tea with him in the Green Room. Afternoon tea was not a custom at Edgewater.

Zinaida recalled, and by rummaging around, found and brought out a sleek, if tarnished, kind of Art Deco silver tea service. "I'd really forgotten we had this. It was a wedding present from the Mountbattens. I'm sure it's valuable, although the style is pretty dated, isn't it. We can sell it one day. Or . . . I wonder, if Greg and Merry . . . well, do you think she would like this as a present?"

"I'm sure she'd love it," I said. Why had I ever spoken to Merry about my suspicion, or my certainty? Had I been crazy? Today at Edgewater I felt myself to be the very soul of treachery. Both Zinaida and Alexei were more and more banking on this marriage, and I couldn't see that it was any longer possible. Merryfield Carr marry a parent-robber? I thought I understood this trip to Bermuda: it was her kind, considerate, and definitive way of saying good-bye to him.

When the tea tray was ready, I carried it in and put it on a small table at the foot of Alexei's bed. Zinaida, sitting next to it, began preparing the tea. "I like seeing you do that," murmured Alex.

"What a ritual afternoon tea used to be," said Zinaida.

"It makes me think of my mother," Alex went on, "and of your mother too, afterward, in London." Afterward: there was Old Russia, and then there was Afterward. "It was a nice custom, a pleasant pause in the day, don't you think?"

"Yes," she said warmly, arranging the cups and saucers. "Maybe we should revive it now, and"—she gave her alto chuckle—"keep away from the vodka more."

"Yes," he said, "I think so."

She passed his cup to him, and mine to me. "And we could have crumpets, too," she said, "if only I could remember what they are."

"Weren't they a kind of cupcake?" he offered.

"Maybe."

"There were a lot of civilized customs in those days," he said quietly. "We dropped so many of them, didn't we? You see, Allan, back in the 1920s, we young people, well we had to be very modern. The older generation had brought on a world war, hadn't they, and for us a revolution. So we had to reject everything they stood for, thought we did. Everything with us had to be new and different, didn't it, Zinaida?"

"Bobbed hair. Dresses that showed the knee. I will *never* forget having dinner one night at Windsor, and I came to the table with what used to be called 'spit curls' on my forehead. King George had a fit! 'What's that gel got on her forehead!' he roared at my mother. 'Get 'em off!' I had to go to my room and change my hair."

Alexei was smiling nostalgically. "Civilization ended," he murmured, "in 1914. We didn't know it in the twenties. We thought we were so modern, changing the world."

Zinaida was looking at him. "I never heard you say that before," she said in a subdued tone. "You're beginning to sound a little like my mother."

"I never thought of it before."

223

"Do you believe it?" she asked.

"I don't know. Maybe. In some ways."

She dropped a cube of sugar into her tea. "Maybe I do too. You," she said, turning to me, "you, Gregory, Merry, people of your age, you're a very satisfactory generation. We were so awful. You do your duty, win your war, and then come back and go on with your education."

"Yes," said Alex, "Gregory's been on the whole a good boy."

"Yes," she said.

"We'll find *some* way of helping him," continued Alex.

"Just try to take a little nap now," said Zinaida, getting up. "We'll have supper around seven-thirty or eight."

The rest of the day passed tranquilly. We presumed Greg and Merry would arrive sometime the following day. I went up to bed around ten o'clock. Zinaida said she was going to stay downstairs, sleeping on a big couch in the living room. Winter's chill was off the house by now, and by throwing an occasional log on the fire in the living-room fireplace, she said she would be comfortable.

Stillness settled over Edgewater. I picked up a book I had started in the afternoon, *The Life and Tragedy of Alexandra Feodorovna Empress of Russia* by one Baroness Sophie Buxhoeveden, and read on. What a life, I thought as I read about the world coming down around her benighted head, and what a tragedy. A train approached from the distance, rumbled nearer, broke with a roar past the house, flashing its menacing light hurriedly over the bedroom wall, and faded, deeply muttering, into the distance.

Much, much later I was on a train, going along a track stretching into the far distance, endlessly. It seemed that Tolstoy, the great novelist, was aboard: a huge man with a huge beard. We were crossing Siberia, which was mostly swamp. Brackish water spread on both sides of the track. There was a ferocious bear, Yousoupov's pet bear, in a special railroad car, special but fragile. Was the bear going to break loose? The train was fragile too, and so were the tracks suspended precariously over the brackish water. Wouldn't the great Tolstoy somehow intervene, make the track safe, cage the bear securely? Rattle-rattle-rattle we continued shakily over the trestle over the brackish water, and was the bear going to escape or—

The pumping, gathering roar of an early morning train that had been approaching along the tracks finally broke in upon my dream and I was flung into wakefulness.

The reading light was still on. *The Life and Tragedy of Alexandra Feodorovna* lay open on the blanket. The thin light of early morning shone wanly through the window shade.

I lay for some time dozing there as this thin light gradually strengthened—an hour? three hours?—until I heard Naida come out of her bedroom across the landing, and then, putting on robe and slippers, I went downstairs to join her and Alex for breakfast in the Green Room.

"I had a good night," said Alex unconvincingly, a grayish figure propped up on pillows, holding a cup of tea. "I'm going to miss morning coffee," he said a little wistfully. "I wonder when Gregory will get here—and Merry, I'd like to see her too."

To give them, the two of them, your blessing, went through my mind.

"Sometime today, surely," said Zinaida.

"I'll bet they've had a wonderful time," he exclaimed with a rush of warmth.

The rest of the morning passed in the atmosphere of subdued, almost churchly quietness suited to sickness in the house. Zinaida and I crouched near the radio at noon to catch the latest developments in her soap opera—Raoul had not yet told Stanley about his passion for Julia—and after Alex awoke from his afternoon nap Naida was just going into his room to read from the afternoon paper to him when the main door flew open and Greg and Merry burst in.

Deeply tanned, in bright clothes, they looked completely out of place in somber Edgewater. "We came as fast as we could," said Greg in a rush as Naida went across to hug him.

"How is he?" Merry asked, taking my hand, her face incongruously glowing from recent pleasures and the sun.

"The same, I guess. He wants to see you. He wants to see Greg, too, of course, and also you."

I studied her eyes; she studied mine. Had she accused Greg, broken with him? I could not read that in her eyes.

"Hi, sport." Greg gave me an extra-firm handshake and one eagle glare in the eye.

Something had happened in Bermuda about the diamond theft, and whatever the outcome, the two of them were now here, together.

We all moved in a talkative, welcoming group into the big living room. Gregory turned toward the door of the Green Room to go in, and there, bravely dressed in pants and blazer, stood Alex, steadying hand against the door-jamb, smiling a little crookedly.

Greg went swiftly over and embraced his father. "Well, Dad, you gave us a scare." He drew back a little. "But you look—you look all right," he added very unconvincingly, clearly taken aback by his father's grayish appearance. "Should you be out of bed, though?"

"Tired of being in bed, and I want to say hello and welcome to Merry here."

She went over, smiling brightly, and gave him a kiss on the cheek.

"And now we're all going to have tea in the library," said Zinaida optimistically. "You'll help me in the kitchen, won't you, Allan? The rest will go and sit at the round table under the skylight. We're going to have a welcome-home tea."

"Tea?" queried Greg with an amused frown.

"Yes," she said firmly, "tea. We're getting formal here at Edgewater. My mother would be pleased with me, at last."

I went to the kitchen with her, and we got out the Mountbatten tea service again. "I'm sure I can sell this," she mused again, "unless Merry would want it, if. . ."

We made some small sandwiches, and soon tea, to the accompaniment of Moussorgsky on the phonograph, began in the octagonal library. Greg and Merry had changed into more subdued clothes.

". . . nothing at all," Alex was saying confidently. "It was just a little warning . . ."

". . . so much water everywhere," Merry said. "You're never out of sight of it. And for me, a California girl and a Hawaiian, that's happiness!"

". . . so everyone agreed I can't dance," Greg was saying, "but I *can* water-ski!"

". . . don't know what I'd have done without Allan," Zinaida put in. "The dear boy just volunteered. . . ."

". . . and Mr. Lockhart says it's the first good story I've written, so it was worth staying in New Haven. . ."

After a while I had to go to the downstairs bathroom and as I was coming out of it, Gregory was there foresquare in front of me. "So you had to tell her," he said in a monotone, more alarming because it was expressionless.

"Greg, I—"

"Get out of the way."

I moved aside, he went in, and, after standing there in a quandary for several moments—leave the house now? never see any of this baffling family and their guilts again?—I saw nothing to gain by running away.

After a while he came out and shot that blistering glare at me. "I wonder why you're out to wreck my life," he said in that strange monotone.

"Of course I'm not. I stumbled on the truth. I told Merry because—"

"Are you trying to take her away from me?"

"Greg, please. Of course not."

"She's ditching me. You knew she would."

"Did she say that?"

"She didn't have to."

"I wonder if she really—"

"Dad's dying. My relationship with her is wrecked. You fixed that. Plus I love her."

"She *had* to know. You can't *lie* all your life!"

"Takes money to court a girl like that. Where was I supposed to get it? Off trees?"

"Gregory! Allan!" called Zinaida from the library. "Stop muttering out there and come back in here."

We went back in and sat down in the glow of late afternoon light.

The conversation moved erratically forward. At one point Alexei suddenly said, the rich Russianness momentarily returning to his voice, "I'm so glad to have you children around me." Everyone paused to look at him as he raised his right hand vertically to in front of his chin, then lowered it, then moved it in front of his right shoulder, then his left: the Orthodox blessing. It was done simply and naturally; it seemed proper and appropriate, everyone looked pleased for a moment, and then the conversation went back to Bermuda's sunshine and the unpredictable moods of weather in the Hudson Valley.

The tautness in the air was nevertheless palpable. Greg continually glared into the space in front of him; Merry fiddled endlessly with her charm bracelet and smiled too quickly and too nervously; Zinaida spilled a cup of tea; I couldn't really look anybody in the eye, as though I and not Greg were guilty, the primal guilt Lockhart had exposed in me not yet entirely expunged.

Only Alex, in some state of ultimate warmth, of latent enthusiasm, of patriarchal serenity, sat quietly beneath the skylight and the sky, content, unaware and content. The loss of the diamond having literally broken his heart, he had no more to give to that loss, seemingly had ceased to be aware of it. All of his thoughts were now centered on "his children" and on the good, happy aspects of life, illusory though these might be.

"You look so good together, so right, suitable," he said at one point, beaming hopefully at Greg and Merry, who gazed, the picture of discomfort, back at him with forced smiles.

We had an early, light supper there in the library, and then Greg began helping his father to go to bed.

Zinaida and Merry had gone to the kitchen. As Greg was assisting his father out of the library, the old man—that was what he had suddenly become in my mind—turned his head toward him.

"I wish we could have helped you more," he murmured.

"Dad, you and Mother have done all you could. You've been great."

"But now—starting out—this is when you need that extra push. If only—if only—the *jewel*—"

"Dad!" Greg's voice was anguished. "It doesn't matter!"

"If only"—I heard Alex muttering as he shuffled, Greg's arm around him, across the big living room—"if only that *jewel*—"

I sat alone under the failing light from above. From the Green Room I could heard the rumble of Alex's voice and occasionally the sharp tone of Greg's. The modulations did not sound like an argument, they did sound like a very serious discussion.

After a while Greg came out, slowly crossed the big intervening living room, and came into the octagonal library.

He was wearing a pair of gray slacks and a dark blue sweater. His deeply tanned face was serious and I was very unnerved to notice that he apparently had been crying.

Apprehensively, I looked up at him. He drew a deep, slightly shaky breath. "Well, I don't think he's going to be with us long." He stared in the general direction of the family portraits. "It's the *diamond*," he said with final ruefulness. "He just can't take it, the loss. It's been too much for him." He slumped down in a chair. "How do you like that? It's the diamond."

"Give it back, for Christ's sake!" I hissed.

"I don't know where it *is* now," he groaned. "It's been sold, resold—I don't know. And just what would I use to buy it back with?" His left leg was thrown over the arm of the chair and he banged away at it with his fist. "Besides, that's not the point. The point is: if he found out I robbed them—yes," he emphasized defiantly, *"robbed* them—"

I wasn't going to contradict you, I remarked to myself.

"—that really would kill him, on the spot. So—well—that's the way it winds up—I killed him—I'm responsible—either way—I did it—that's it—" A truly Russian fatalism had invaded his face and voice, accepting and suicidal and ultimate.

"You didn't—there's no way—he—it might not—"

Greg got to his feet. "Going to take a walk. Don't come with me. No, I'm not going to throw myself into the Hudson. If I decide to knock myself off, you'll be the first to know."

Later, Merry, wearing a gray woolen skirt and a white blouse, wandered into the library. "I'm not due back at Vassar until tomorrow. I don't know if I could get into my room there tonight, and anyway I'd be scared to stay in that big dormitory without the other girls. Zinaida of course said I could stay here. I feel kind of—odd about it, in the circumstances, but. . ."

She sank down on the old couch. I started abstractedly pacing.

"We had a good time in Bermuda, can you believe that? I think Greg knew what was coming, what I was going to accuse him of. But he's such a fatalist. We sailed, I taught him the rhumba. We had a lot of rum. We really were having a very good time. Then we had it out. He took it," she said, "with a quiet matter-of-factness. You were right. He stole the diamond. He got drunk one night in Bermuda. I accused him of it—we were sitting on a pier, moonlight on the sea, beautiful; peaceful, and he just said, 'Yeah, I took it, for you. To be able to take you to the Colony Restaurant where you like to go.' He sat there without saying anything for a while, and I couldn't think of a single thing to say, not a word, and then he just murmured, 'So

231

now you ditch me and it's over. That's the way it had to turn out. I've known that all along, that you'd find out, that you'd ditch me, that I couldn't win.' I just sat there stunned in the moonlight, stunned even though I already knew he'd taken it. But his admitting it that way, so bluntly, so directly, so, I don't know, touchingly. I just sat there stunned in the moonlight."

There was a long pause, so weighted with her having something more to say and hardly daring think of it that finally I burst out, "Well, what is it, Merry? Are you going to tell me or aren't you? Say it or forget about it."

She gazed up at me with a kind of lip-biting doubtfulness that made her seem like a little girl for just a second. Then she said in a quiet, firm voice, "Then he made love to me. With few preliminaries. He began to—well, he began, and I was so pulled up, pulled into, so *engulfed* in what he was doing, in what I had to do in response, in everything, my body, his—we had never done this before—and now he used it, sex, his body, mine, he seemed to know everything, all I could feel, how to make me feel it." She paused again, and then went on in a low voice, "I have to say that it was the most—*rapturous* experience of my life. And the most . . . frightening."

I stared down at her and then I had to ask, "Are you going to ditch him?"

She looked up at me. "Is that what he thinks?"

"Yes."

"Oh," she said, in turmoil, "I don't *know*, I don't *know* . . . a *thief* . . . from his parents . . ."

Gregory had procured more Russian vodka during the trip, and sometime in the next hour the vodka, inevitably in this house with these people on this night, began to flow.

The four of us drifted through the old darkening rooms for a while, doing pointless little tasks, talking disjointedly with one another from time to time. No one could settle on anything. Zinaida, a radio addict, did not possess a television set.

She looked in on Alex from time to time. Finally she came to sit in the library, glass of vodka in hand. Merry and I were already there. Greg, doubtless also with a glass of vodka, was still out on the grounds somewhere.

A light sprinkle of rain began to fall. A few minutes later Gregory could be heard coming through one of the doorways in the big living room. He appeared in the door of the octagonal library.

"Well, just one big happy family!" he burst out, falsely jovial.

"Yes, come join us," said Zinaida companionably.

"Dad asleep?"

"Dead to the world," she said automatically, and then, hearing her own words, her eyes widened in shock.

"Mm," he growled, slumping down on the other end of the long couch from her.

We struggled against the odds to hold a casual conversation for a short time, and then Greg abruptly faced his mother. "The engagement's off. Merry wants out."

Merry, looking particularly pretty in her tautness, put in, "I haven't—we haven't really decided anything."

"Oh," he said with fake cheerfulness, "you have, you have." He leaned forward, elbows on knees, and looked over his shoulder at Zinaida. "You see, Mother, I stole the Militsa Diamond."

A look of horror slowly coming into her face, she turned to look with her opaque black eyes into his. "You," she began, in a hollow voice, almost to herself. "You couldn't have, couldn't have. How could you? Have you no sense of honor? Of who you are, who we are? You *robbed* us! Who are you then? Where did you come from? How *could* you!"

"I just did it," he said with ultimate flatness.

"How could you possibly do that to your father! Look at him!"

Greg, his face misery itself, took a deep breath, and was silent.

Zinaida, a formidable seated figure, black and white, in her low-pitched voice, demanded, "Why didn't you ask us to sell it and give you part of the money, if you needed money so badly?"

"Because I don't trust you!" he said, hurling the words at her.

She pulled back, stupefied. "Don't *trust* us?" she echoed, her face grimacing over this total conundrum. "Why, why not? How could you possibly not trust us? When have we ever proved untrustworthy?"

"I think," replied Greg with a kind of suaveness, covering deep rage or hurt, "I only need to mention the name of Her Imperial Highness the grand duchess Anastasia Nikolaevna, better known today as Mrs. Anderson!"

Zinaida's mouth fell slightly open. Her eyes stared at her son as though he were some menacing ghost. "Who?" she intoned.

"Your *cousin!*" he shot back. "The cousin you betrayed!"

"What could you know about that!" The words were torn from her.

"You betrayed her," went on Greg implacably. "She was your dear cousin and friend, but it just wasn't convenient to acknowledge her in 1930. Grand Duke Alexander and Dickie Mountbatten and Uncle Ernie wouldn't like it. So you betrayed her!" He frowned contemptuously at her. "Trust *you*! After that?"

Zinaida rose slowly to her feet. She was wearing a long black dress. She stood upright; all her habitual unpretentiousness had fallen away; she was a Romanoff. But she looked pale, haggard in the thin lamplight. "I did what I had to do," she said softly. "I did what I thought I had to do, for us all."

"But she *is* Anastasia, isn't she?" Greg pressed on.

Zinaida turned slowly to face him. "Yes," she said, drawing a shuddering breath, "I think she is. But I couldn't help her, in 1930 or anytime since."

Greg looked at her. "You could have loved her," he said.

She stood silent and motionless for several endless moments. Then she slowly nodded her head. "Yes," she murmured, "perhaps . . . yes."

"Sit down, Zinaida," I cut in, getting up from my chair. I was afraid she was going to faint. "I'll get you a glass of water." I moved to the door of the library, and across the dim living room I saw, thought I saw, was almost sure I saw a spectral shape move from the doorway of the Green Room back into its shadows.

Behind me Greg made a final thrust. "Family honor? *I've* betrayed the family honor?"

Alexei died quietly in the early hours of the next morning.

By the time I came downstairs and learned this, confusion had begun to come into the house in the form of friends and neighbors, and the barbaric transformation of mourning into something resembling a party began to take form.

235

The telephone rang; the front door banged; cars and a hearse came; food appeared; drinks.

I went into the Green Room before the undertakers took over. Prince Alexei's body, arranged by the doctor and Zinaida, was lying beneath the covers, his face with its strong bones waxen but peaceful on the pillow. There was an air of inevitability about his body in death and about the room itself, a certain stateliness, the strong-boned face, the high-ceilinged room, the long glass doors giving on the peacefulness and brightness of a spring morning.

Greg drove Merry back to Vassar around noon. "Come with us," she ordered me curtly.

So I went with them in the car, acting as a kind of buffer zone. Very little was said during the drive.

After leaving her at her dormitory Greg began to drive back, slowly. I tried to make conversation but he ignored me. As we were descending the hill to Edgewater, he broke his silence.

"Well, that's it," he said laconically. "Merry and I are finished. Edgewater's mortgaged. I haven't got any prospects, for a job that amounts to anything anyway. It's an old Russian story, you know that. Hopelessness. Despair. Suicide."

"Greg, for God's—"

"Why not?" he shrugged. "I had my run and botched it. Responsible for the death of my father. What else do you expect me to do?"

236

14

My lecture to the Yale students surprised me by how well it went. These students of 1980, it seemed, were quite unlike what we had been thirty years earlier. They apparently really wanted to learn something. So many of us, so much of the time, hadn't, not really. After all, we had just won World War II. We were now supposed to relax and have a good time, weren't we? To these students I was someone who had accomplished something in the three decades separating myself in 1980 from myself when I'd been in their shoes; perhaps I could impart some useful advice to them, a key or at least a clue, to a fulfilling future. They trooped into the Law School auditorium, and gave me a small ovation at the end.

Lecturing from the same podium where I had last heard Lockhart speak publicly—*Destiny aids and helps along those who recognize her, the blind she drags*—I was more conscious than I had been for a long time of his continuing and pervasive influence on me. I told them about counting on the second wind in writing a book; I told them to stop a day's work when they were going good and knew what was going to happen next; practical working advice I had learned from him, sometimes originating with Gertrude Stein. And implicit in what I said were broader observations of his: life is fighting; in life it's the look ahead that counts; we are all born equally far from the sun; there's a land of the living and a land of the dead, and the bridge is love.

Millicent Moncrieff sat at the end of a row of seats on the far left. I thought that I could feel her concentrated attention on me, on every word I was saying.

When I had answered the last question and autographed the last book, she was there, hesitating in the background. "Was it all right?" I asked with genuine uneasiness.

"Of course it was. How well you did that. You know how to speak to them. And they know who you are, not just what you wrote, but who you are beneath the writing. And now I suppose you have to appear at some reception they're giving for you."

"Yes, and you're coming with me, for moral support and all kinds of other support."

The reception, in the glowing, jewel-box interior of the Beinicke Library, was cordial and subdued. The university had far more important things on its mind than Allan Prieston but was prepared to give me my due, in passing.

Eventually the gathering dwindled to a handful of people finishing their glasses of wine in one corner of the building. Millicent was seated beside me on an ottoman. The wide graceful space around us, the luminous marble walls, the illuminated glass-enclosed pillar of books made a trivial conversation pointless, if not impossible.

"You know that as much as one act can change a life," I said to her, "one letter from Reeves Lockhart to me changed mine."

"Well, he could do things like that, I know. But no, I didn't. What did the letter say?"

"When I knew I was coming to New Haven I took it out to show you. Here it is."

A couple of years after graduating from Yale I wrote a novel, never published, and of course sent the manuscript to Lockhart. After telling me directly and kindly why it was a bad novel, there followed these deeply illuminating paragraphs:

> Now you have many a qualification for writing, and perhaps for writing a novel—But the qualifications rest in you really unactivated until you find a subject which you are deeply moved about, very much absorbed in. Then every fragment of conversation, every bit of description, all the characters, primary and secondary, will come into acute focus.
>
> This problem is a character problem before it is a literary and artistic problem. Keep a journal: note in it all the things of your daily life that do present themselves to you with sharpness, with passion, with temperament.
>
> Become increasingly aware of what does and what does not truly stir you—and select your next subject from the compelling elements in your life.

"Well," she said with satisfaction, handing the letter back to me, "that's Reeves at his most pungent."

"I threw away that first failure and I tried to follow the guidance of this letter in my next book, which was *Crossing the Frontier*. And *Crossing the Frontier* made the kind of life I wanted to live—had to live—possible."

"You know what Reeves said should be his epitaph: Here lies a man who tried to be obliging."

"*There's* an understatement."

"I remember the first thing you wrote that really impressed us. It was about your Russian friends. But I forgot," she said just a shade slyly, "you don't want to talk about them."

"Well, I didn't—haven't wanted to, for a long time. They all seemed to be so guilty, half guilty, which was worse. I couldn't admire them or stop feeling so much affection for them. I was afraid of them, of their story, in a certain way. It was so ambiguous, good and bad. I didn't want to deal with them or it. But I guess we have to."

"What finally happened to them?"

"Things turned out better than anyone could have expected. It wasn't such a tragedy after all. The father's death, well, that was the loss, the tragedy. But for the rest, they patched it back together. Everyone in the end more or less forgave everyone else for the crimes and betrayals."

"People have a way of doing that after a disaster, don't they? Good—and—bad people," she finished thoughtfully, "almost everybody."

"There's the princess, charming, touching, kind, denying her own cousin's identity."

"The Anastasia case?"

"And there's the prince. A failure. At the time I thought that was practically a crime too. Then Greg, the son, my friend Gregory, well, he robbed them," I finished a little grimly.

"Reeves led me to understand something of the sort at the time, now that you mention it. Whatever happened to him?"

"Oh, he got married. To the girl he stole the jewel for, Merryfield Carr."

"And the—ah—diamond?"

"Merryfield wormed the information out of Greg as to

where he sold it, and then her father's lawyers or detectives or somebody traced it and got it back."

"And returned it of course to the princess."

"Mme. Zinaida eventually sold it, and sold the house on the Hudson too. The last I heard she was living in the guest cottage on an old estate up there on the Hudson. It belongs to a friend of hers called Harriet van Rensaaver. She's a local character and people up there think she stole the diamond, returned it, and so laid the basis for a lifelong friendship with the princess."

"I gather she knew," said Millicent quietly, "that really her son had stolen it?"

After a silence I murmured, "Yes." I reflected on this old affair and then added, "There was a lot of deception and self-deception going on."

"And a lot of forgiveness," she said concurringly, "and self-forgiveness. But then tell me, how did the marriage of the Trouvenskoy son turn out?"

"Happy! Three children. He worked for her father for a while and then branched out. The father must be quite a card, speaking of forgiveness. He accepted him as a son-in-law and hired him for his company, knowing all about the diamond. Greg's been successful on his own. He hasn't committed the American crime of failure, and it meant everything to Greg, to succeed on American terms. His wife drinks. Has to go away every few years to dry out and then she comes back and everything's fine for quite a while."

Millicent sighed. "Weaknesses . . . flaws . . ." Then she turned brightly to look at me. "A flaw, a weakness: what's yours? You don't mind my asking, do you? This building, it evokes major questions, doesn't it? Don't answer: I was just teasing."

But she wasn't and I did try to answer. "You told me the

other day that Reeves said I would 'make it' as a writer and wondered what I would lose on the way."

"Yes," she agreed leadingly.

I reflected. "I'm coarser, tougher, more impatient. I think I could even be described in my student days as full of kindness and compassion. Now I'm much more brusque, not so kind. I'm not a gentleman. I'm dedicated. I'm a mischievous, conniving rascal and a cheat: a writer."

"Well, *that's* a direct answer. I think you're too harsh on yourself. But in any case, what you admit to is no real disgrace."

"I don't love my neighbor."

"That's *your* flaw," she said interestedly.

"And yours?"

"Ah, that's the privilege of age. I concede nothing."

As I drove away from Pierson College the next morning, leaving behind the moats and towers and turrets, I sensed that my past and my memories of it there held after all no threats to me. Reeves Lockhart did not have feet of clay, as I had perhaps subconsciously anticipated he might. Far from it: his firmly planted stance as man and artist had given strength to my whole now rather long life and career. The Trouvenskoys were not threats to my grasp of good and bad; they were life's intermingling.

And I had, to one degree and form or another, loved all of these people. If I could not love my neighbor, I loved them, my flawed surrogates for all the unknowable, unlovable neighbors of the world.